HANNA STORM: INTERGALACTIC

C.J. STARBRIGHT AND THE STARGAZERS

Redwood Mountain Publishing

HANNA STORM: INTERGALACTIC

First Printing, 2024

ISBN: 979-8-9906216-0-2
eBook EISBN: 979-8-9906216-1-9

Redwood Mountain Publishing
1034 W RSI Dr
Suite 120 E
Logan, UT 84321

Visit the Redwood Mountain Publishing website at www.redwoodmountainpublishing.com or use the QR code below to join the Nova Newsflash for exclusive Hanna Storm content.

**Redwood
Mountain
Publishing**

CONTENTS

To all the stargazers of the world!

PROLOGUE

"Exiting the corridor in three, two, one...We are now in normal space, Master Slythe," reported the helmsman. The entire bridge crew grew silent, awestruck at the sight of the blue planet below.

"Move!" shouted Slythe from his captain's chair. He slowly clenched his clawed hand into a fist and his green scales shimmered as they shook. His thick tail swished back and forth. Crewmembers jumped into nervous action, each of them glad not to be singled out individually. Catching Slythe's attention for dereliction of duty was a career-ending—and sometimes life-ending—mistake. "Control, how much time do we have?"

"We can hold the window for 23.6 cycles, Master," came the response.

"Tell me what you see!" demanded Slythe. "Anybody! I want information. Now!"

"The planet below has an oxygen–nitrogen atmosphere and is approximately seventy-one percent water. Teeming with life, Master," shouted one of the officers.

"We are definitely in another galaxy, Master. Waiting on our exact coordinates," said another.

"Master Slythe! We have a craft in orbit," a junior officer announced excitedly.

"Manned or unmanned?" shouted Slythe.

"Uh, indications are…that it's manned, Master," he muttered, his brow furrowed in uncertainty.

"Indications?" inquired Slythe. He leaped from his chair and confronted the crewman, putting his jaws as close as he could to that of the young officer. He repeated the question in a menacing whisper, "Manned or unmanned?"

"Manned, Master Slythe," responded the greenhorn, feigning an air of confidence while his thick tail quivered involuntarily.

"Set an intercept course. We can collect a few samples before our time is up." The young officer heaved a sigh of relief. Master Slythe returned to his seat and rubbed a manicured claw across his scaly, green forehead. Smirking, he slowly extracted a pistol-shaped hand cannon holstered at the side of his chair and aimed it at the young officer whom he had just challenged. All the bridge officers fell silent except for the target, whose back was turned.

"Point two cycles to intercept," the oblivious victim said confidently.

Master Slythe motioned to his Chief of Security, who also sported a sly grin, exposing sharp, gleaming, yellow teeth. He admired Master Slythe. He had the luxury of admiration; his competence had always kept him from the wrong end of the Master's hand cannon. The Chief of Security was by far the tallest and largest member of the crew. His bare arms were covered in scars where his scales would not regrow. The patch he wore over one eye did not fully cover a deformed wound that disappeared up into his helmet and extended beyond the bottom of the patch, parting the scales down his cheek.

"Boran," Slythe whispered out the side of his mouth. "How quickly can you get a replacement for that sorry excuse of a navigator?"

Boran's grin widened. "Less than two cycles, Master Slythe."

"Excellent."

CHAPTER 1

A Birthday Surprise

Hanna Storm could have had a normal childhood had her parents been normal. It just so happens, however, that they were not. Mr. and Mrs. Storm first met in the jungles of South America. Mr. Storm was an American serving in the Peace Corps. He was trying to help impoverished and remote villages by providing them with basic necessities such as water and shelter during a time of civil war. He dug wells, built houses, and taught English to the local children in addition to other noble endeavors. Mrs. Storm was a doctor from England who was also doing charity work in the same war-ravaged region. She bandaged up cuts and bruises and put back arms and legs that had come off. One day, when Mr. Storm was visiting the hospital, a group of rebel soldiers captured the international workers and carried them off, hoping to get a ransom for all the rich American and European doctors. Mr. Storm evaded capture, tracked the rebel army, and attempted to free the hostages. He was only able to free Mrs. Storm before getting himself nabbed. Mrs. Storm then returned the favor a few days later with a flawless rescue in the dead of night. Before their escape, they managed to execute Mr. Storm's original plan to free the other captives and even found time to destroy the rebels' ammunition stores just for good measure. They made their way out of the jungle and had been together ever since. That event remained one of their fondest memories.

Most parents had jobs to which they went in the morning and from which they returned in the evenings. Hanna's parents did things differently. They owned their own company, called Extreme Adventures, and guided the world's wealthy elite through various global excursions: mountain climbing in the Himalayas, deep-sea diving off the Great Barrier Reef in Australia, sky diving in the Sahara—they had done it all. Mr. and Mrs. Storm always made sure to include their daughter on their adventures, even when it required her to miss school. In fact, Hanna rarely spent a whole semester at school. "Experience is the best education," her father would always say. Hanna was never quite sure how a person could "experience" algebra, yet she managed not only to learn it but to master it. Indeed, thanks to her intense curiosity about everything, she was proficient in most academic areas. Her favorite subject by far was astronomy. The fact that astronomy was not part of the ninth-grade curriculum wasn't a problem for Hanna Storm. Flying to places like the Himalayas and Australia took several hours, providing the inquisitive mind with ample time to slake its curiosity, and that's exactly what Hanna did. She was apprised of most current theories regarding different astronomical phenomena and could easily locate multiple planets and stars in the night sky. If tour buses traveled in space, Hanna would be the perfect guide.

On the day of her fourteenth birthday, Hanna arose early, the signs of dawn still far off. She had scarcely been able to fall asleep the previous night due to her excitement at the prospect of the huge surprise her parents had promised her. It was a gift "never to be forgotten" they had said. The only other thing her parents had told her was that she needed to "pack her gear." They always said that before an "Extreme Adventure." Smiling, Hanna threw off her covers.

She knew exactly what to pack. Hanna Storm always carried a few key items in her trusty satchel, which accompanied her on all her adventures. This morning, she looked through the contents of the leather bag she had carefully packed the night before. She had her towel, a pocketknife, a tube of Vaseline, a headlamp, duct tape, a water bottle, one change of clothes, a mirror, some chocolate candy bars, and something to read (in this case, her current astronomy book). Most of these items had proven useful on adventure after adventure. Hanna Storm never climbed a volcano or trekked the desert without her gear. She tapped her foot; something was missing, but she could not figure out what it was. She stared blankly at her bag for a moment, before grinning as she recalled her most important piece of gear. She walked over to her nightstand, picked up a pair of drumsticks, and placed them neatly in her bag. She could not pack her entire drum kit of course, but that didn't matter; she could beat out a rhythm on any surface with her sticks.

Having checked her pack, Hanna carefully tied her auburn red hair into a long braid. Her hair and freckles were inherited from her mother's side of the family, she was certain. Her dark olive skin came from her father's side. She glanced in the mirror, pleased with what she saw, both for the excellent job she had done in taming her wild hair and because she saw a perfect mix of her parents in her own reflection.

Hanna went downstairs in search of breakfast and was surprised to see her father bent over the stove, wearing an apron stretched tight across his muscular bulk. The aroma of pancakes, bacon, and eggs filled her nostrils. Her mother sat at the counter drinking her morning cup of coffee.

"Good morning, Hanna," she said in a gentle voice. "Happy Birthday!"

Hanna loved her mom. Mrs. Storm was of average height with shoulder-length dark brown hair. She had a lithe feminine figure and carried herself with grace. Her eyes sparkled with intelligence and wit. Hanna occasionally noticed other men involuntarily staring at her mother wherever they went, be it the mall, the gas station, or the grocery store. Even Principal Jorgensen had once winked at Hanna's mother. Gross. It was so inappropriate, and Hanna wanted to smack each and every one of them, but her mother would simply smile and say, "It is certainly impolite to stare!" whenever Hanna raised it with her.

"Thanks, Mom," Hanna said as she bent slightly to put her arms around her loving mother. Her mother may have been of average height, but Hanna had been taller than her for at least six months.

"Happy Birthday, Squinks!," came her father's booming voice. "Breakfast is served." Mr. Storm stood at a height of six feet and seven inches. He had the broadest shoulders of any man Hanna had ever seen. His arms were thick and his legs resembled tree trunks. Hanna had once seen him lift up the back end of their car on a bet with her mother. Mom washed the dishes for an entire week, not just because he won the bet, but because he also strained a muscle or two.

"I'm fourteen, Dad," Hanna said with a tone of mock annoyance. "Legit teenager you're talking to here. Enough with the Squinks, okay?" she implored as she stood on her chair, throwing her arms as far around his thick neck as she could.

Smiling, he tapped his cheek and Hanna lovingly gave him a kiss. He smiled with absolute contentment.

"Hanna," Mr. Storm said in his deep voice, "We need to get going within the next half hour or we'll miss our flight." Mr. Storm's grin was more than a little mischievous. She glanced at her mother, who was trying hard to conceal a grin and a look of excitement herself. Hanna wondered what destination on Earth could have her parents so enthused. Could it be sledding with penguins in Antarctica or searching for shipwrecks in the Bermuda Triangle? Both were on her bucket list of must-have adventures.

"Well," Hanna answered, "I'm all packed and ready to go."

After a hurried breakfast, the Storm family loaded into their sport utility vehicle and began a long drive. Hanna knew the way to the airport by heart, having been there many times. Her suspicions were aroused when her father missed the usual turn. Still, she said nothing. Hanna's mind wandered to the time she had been on an Extreme Adventure with her parents in Jordan. The memory coalesced in her mind.

"Mom! What are we going to do?" Hanna yelled above her thudding heartbeat. "We'll never make it back to the camp!"

Mrs. Storm responded calmly. "Hanna, remember, what do we do in an urgent situation?"

Hanna took a deep breath. "Observe, assess, act," Hanna recited.

"What do you notice? What options do we have now, at this moment?"

"We can sit here and breathe," Hanna mumbled.

"That's good! That's very good. Let's breathe deeply," Mrs. Storm encouraged. Hanna sucked in the hot desert air. "Good," her mother hushed. "What else?"

"We can search our surroundings, look for anything that might be an asset." Hanna's breathing steadied and her heartbeat slowed.

"Right," agreed her mother. "We may not have the camel but what do we have?" Mrs. Storm sounded like a teacher in a classroom lecturing an attentive bunch of students. She didn't act the least bit ruffled, though Hanna knew that her mother had earned such composure through a lifetime of experience.

"We only have half a canteen of water," Hanna worried. "But," she enthused, "we have food in your pack. We have good walking shoes and a compass." Hanna paused and added, "we have you!"

Mrs. Storm laughed. "Yes, all accurate. And we know how to use the compass. I happen to know that we are only about 10 miles from the camp and can probably make it before nightfall.

"We are going to be just fine, aren't we mom," Hanna stated, rather than asked.

"Yes, Hanna," her mother agreed. "Besides, I've been this way before," she winked. Hanna and her mother shared a long, hearty laugh.

"Mom, I'm sorry I didn't tie the camel correctly. I never thought it would run."

Hanna blinked back to the present. They were headed west. She wanted to be surprised, but after they had been in the desert for a few hours, curiosity got the better of her.

"Dad, exactly which airport are you taking us to?"

"Oh, we're not going to the airport. It's more of a…eh…research facility…with a runway," he paused, "and launchpads." Mr. Storm looked desperately to his wife for help.

"Well, now that your father has blown the gaff, we might as well lay bare our little plan," Mrs. Storm said, rolling her eyes.

"I have not blown anything. No gaffs have been blown," Mr. Storm said defensively. "She doesn't know where we're going. Besides, she'll have it all figured out after we round that hill," Mr. Storm gestured out the front window.

Hanna looked at the hill in the far distance. Had her father just said the word "launchpads?"

"Are we going to see a rocket launch? Majestic!" Hanna said enthusiastically.

"Hmmm," her mother said thoughtfully, "I suppose you will see it launch," her mother admitted, failing to conceal her amused expression.

"What do you mean, 'suppose'?" Hanna asked. She frowned a little over her smirk and spoke again. "I think it's time you two just told me what my present is."

"Okay, Squin...Okay, Hanna," her father said, looking to his wife for approval. Mrs. Storm gave the nod and Mr. Storm continued. "Do you remember when we went on the Siberian hunting trip with Donovan Watts?"

"Yeah," answered Hanna. "Of course. He was a nice guy. I really liked him."

"And he really liked you. He said that you reminded him of his granddaughter," Mr. Storm reminded her.

"Right, the one who disappeared. Eloise, I think. That was a really sad story," Hanna said, remembering the nice old man's tears as he told them about his unfortunate granddaughter.

"Do you remember what Mr. Watts does for a living? What business he owns?" Mr. Storm continued asking.

"Yeah," Hanna replied. "It had something to do with building rockets. Are we going to see him?" she asked excitedly.

"Yes, Mr. Watts will be there," Mrs. Storm said. "And you are correct; he does build rockets. But he was especially concerned with a particular project. Do you recall? He talked about it quite extensively."

"I remember he talked a lot about a reusable rocket and about how spaceships will fly like airplanes and carry passengers in space and stuff," Hanna said, recalling her doubts about his ideas.

"You sound skeptical," Mr. Storm rejoined with a harrumph.

"Well, he never really explained the physics of it. I think it's going to be another twenty years at least before anyone figures that one out," Hanna stated confidently.

At that very moment, Mr. Storm emerged from a long turn that wound around the hill previously glimpsed in the distance. The Storms fell silent as they stared out the front window. Hanna saw what looked like a small airport with giant hangars and an office building. There was even a control tower. Near one of the hangars, not too far from the building, was a shape that Hanna recognized well. It was similar to the old NASA space shuttles, but this one wasn't standing vertically, nor was it attached to a giant orange rocket like she had seen in her school history videos. This shuttle was horizontal on the runway, parked just as an airplane would be. It even had windows lining the fuselage like an airplane. As they drew closer, Hanna saw the name "Eloise" scrawled across the fuselage in an elegant, cursive font.

Hanna's jaw dropped. She had seen many things in her travels and was rarely surprised, but this was most unexpected. She came to her senses as the Storm family's SUV stopped at a security checkpoint. The guard asked Mr. Storm for his name and some identification and directed him to a parking spot by the main complex. The clock on the dashboard indicated that it was nearly 5:00 in the evening. The drive had taken all day. Hanna became very excited as she realized that she was going to witness a piece of history. She would be there when the first commercial flight was launched into space.

Media trucks dotted the landscape, each with its own newscaster and camera crew. Intermingled with the white trucks and vans were very expensive-looking limousines. Hanna saw chauffeurs unloading expensive-looking handbags for people dressed in expensive-looking clothes. This was a gathering of some very swanky people. As Mr. Storm pulled up to the main complex, Hanna saw an older man with a cane walking toward their car. He looked familiar.

"Sebastian Storm! I'm so glad you made it," the old man coughed into his handkerchief. "Is she with you?" The gentleman could scarcely contain his excitement as he questioned Mr. Storm, who was just getting out of the car.

"You bet she is. Right on the other side of the car," he replied.

Hanna gathered up her bag, and before she could reach the handle, the door opened and the man with the cane stood before her, beaming like sunshine. As soon as Hanna saw that smile, she leaped from the car and embraced Mr. Watts with a squeeze so vigorous that he dropped his cane. He squeezed her back as they both fondly remembered the adventure they had shared.

"So good to see you Hanna, child," he said as he released her. "I'm so pleased you could come." He turned to the third passenger. "Sara Storm, as beautiful as I remember."

"And you're as charming as I remember, Donovan," Mrs. Storm said with a smile that caused Mr. Watts's knees to tremble.

"I suppose you've figured out what your present is by now, then, Hanna?" Mr. Watts fished.

"Oh yes, Mr. Watts!" came her enthusiastic reply.

"Please, call me Donovan," requested Mr. Watts.

Hanna smiled. She was beginning to like this man even more.

"Well, Donovan," she continued awkwardly, "I guess you did it. I mean, wow, a commercial space flight."

"We like to call it a space cruise," Mr. Watts corrected her.

"Then I am very excited that I get to watch the very first launch of a space cruise. I couldn't have asked for a better present." Hanna said with a nod and satisfied smile.

"Watch?" Mr. Watts exclaimed. "Gadzooks!" He turned to Mr. and Mrs. Storm who were standing by the Jeep. "Did she say watch?"

"We wanted you to be the one to tell her," explained Mrs. Storm, touching Mr. Watts gently on the arm. The old knees shook a bit more.

"Well, I shan't delay it any longer," he said, satisfied with Mr. and Mrs. Storm's decision. "Hanna dear, you are not going to *watch* the launch. You are going to participate in it. It is my gift to you."

"What?" Hanna asked in disbelief, shaken by what she had just heard.

"Marvelous!" he chuckled at Mr. and Mrs. Storm. He turned back to Hanna. "I'll repeat it more clearly for you child so there won't be any confusion. In precisely twenty-four minutes, you and I and all of these passengers are going to board *that* space cruiser." Mr. Watts gestured at the shuttle and guests quite dramatically as he spoke. "And," checking his watch, "in precisely 52 minutes we will be leaving this planet for a leisurely cruise around the earth. Now, does that answer your question?"

Hanna could scarcely believe her ears. She remained expressionless while Mr. Watts and her parents stared at her, awaiting some sort of reaction. Nothing came except a prolonged, stunned silence from her gaping mouth.

Mr. and Mrs. Storm were pleased as punch, grinning as they looked at their perplexed daughter. As they gazed happily at Hanna, Mr. Watts gazed at them with a similar expression. A series of beeps rang from Mr. Watt's watch.

"Excuse me. I have a few last-minute preparations to make. Just grab the young man over there in the blue cap and he'll help you get settled," he instructed Mr. and Mrs. Storm. "I may not have mentioned it before, but you two will be joining your daughter." He stayed just long enough to see the same discombobulated look descend on their faces before turning to Hanna with a giddy grin. "And you, Ms. Hanna Storm, I'll see you on board." With a quick wink, he twirled off to attend to some important preflight task.

Hanna's jaw dropped again, the first sign of expression after her lengthy blank stare. One word escaped Hanna's flabbergasted mouth.

"How?" she whispered. Hanna couldn't understand why this man felt the need to bestow such a gift on her and her family.

Hanna's father, who never failed to teach his daughter some eternal truth or moral principle, seized the opportunity to do so now.

"You had no idea how much of an impact you had on his life, did you?" Mr. Storm asked.

Hanna, staring at the ground with her mouth now closed, simply shook her head in answer. Her giant father knelt down on one knee squarely in front of his daughter and put his hands on her shoulders.

"Hanna, always treat everyone with kindness and respect, for the people who need it most might be the ones you least expect. Now, I'm not sure which gift is greater, a flight into space, or the feeling you get when you know you've made a friend in Donovan Watts."

Hanna looked up from the ground and smiled at her father. She loved his wisdom and insight.

"Dad," she said softly. "I know which gift is greater." A look of excitement slowly crept into her face. "I also know which gift leaves in twenty-five minutes!" she finished with a squeal. "We're going into space! Outer space!" She threw an arm in the air and waved at the boy in the blue cap. "Excuse me sir. I'm Hanna Storm."

"Yes miss Storm. Right this way." The boy in the blue cap ushered them toward the shuttle. As he guided them to the front of the line, affluent passengers threw disapproving looks in their direction, but the Storms had no choice but to follow their guide. As they reached the front of the line, the older couple behind them who had been demoted to second place introduced themselves.

"Pardon me," said the man, who was dressed in tan khakis and wore a navy suit jacket over an unbuttoned, white, collared shirt. "I'm Rory King, CEO of King Enterprises. Perhaps you've heard of me?"

Mrs. Storm extended a hand. "A pleasure to make your acquaintance. I am Sara Storm, and this is my husband Sebastian and daughter Hanna." Rory looked a little disappointed that Mrs. Storm did not appear to have heard of him. Turning to Rory's companion, Mrs. Storm extended her hand. "And you are?"

The woman hesitantly extended her hand with a disinterested look. "I'm Genevieve King."

"Ah yes. The Storms of Extreme Adventures," said Rory. "I've heard good things about your vacations."

"Adventures," Hanna corrected him.

"Yes, adventures," he repeated awkwardly.

Mrs. Storm knew the question was coming, but nonetheless winced a little when Genevieve opened her mouth to speak.

"So, how did you manage to be first in line? You must have paid quite a sum. We offered a small fortune to Mr. Watts so we could be first, but he refused it," Mrs. King said smugly. "He said it was reserved for someone important. I didn't realize your company was so profitable. Congratulations." Her sarcasm was not lost on the Storms.

Extreme Adventures catered to the rich. While most of the wealthy clients who availed themselves of Extreme Adventures' packages were perfectly lovely, occasionally the Storms encountered those who were a little self-absorbed. How he enjoyed talking with them!

"We didn't even pay for the tickets, let alone for a place in line," Mr. Storm said cheerfully. "It's our daughter's birthday today and this was a gift from Donovan."

Rory and Genevieve looked at each other in disbelief. "Happy birthday Hanna," they both said in turn with a somewhat questionable sincerity. That ended the conversation, much to Mr. Storm's satisfaction.

As the time for boarding finally arrived, Hanna could barely contain her excitement. She ascended the staircase while a nearby orchestra played a jaunty symphony by Mozart. At the shuttle's entrance, she was greeted by a flight attendant—or, rather, a space flight attendant.

"Welcome aboard, Ms. Storm. My name is Marie and I'm happy to be at your service. Let me show you and your parents to your seats."

Hanna entered an elegant cabin with oversized leather recliners opened in pairs on either side of a single aisle. Hanna was more excited than nervous, but still, she found Marie's warm and friendly manner reassuring. Marie motioned to a seat in the very first row next to a small window. She then directed Mr. and Mrs. Storm to seats across the aisle. Hanna handed her pack to Marie and took her seat. It was so comfortable! It struck her that such a comfortable seat might cause a person to fall asleep, and who wanted to sleep during a space flight?! She made a mental note to recommend less comfortable seating to Donovan.

Hanna looked across the aisle at her parents who were also comfortably seated with excited looks on their faces. Mr. Storm usually did not fit in airplane seats and often had to buy two seats to accommodate his size, but Hanna could tell from his satisfied grin that this chair suited him perfectly.

Hanna wondered who would occupy the empty seat next to her. Other passengers began to board, and she studied each one as they entered. Rory and Genevieve came first and took their seats directly behind Mr. and Mrs. Storm. They were followed by two men who looked as though they were brothers. Hanna noted they were about the same age as her parents. She watched as other passengers filed past while the seat next to her own remained empty.

A young boy about Hanna's age entered through the doorway followed by a woman who must have been his mother or aunt, or perhaps she was his au pair. He noticed Hanna and paused. Their eyes met and he smiled, offering a courteous hello that she returned. He was about to introduce himself when they both heard the woman behind him say, "Move along now, Henry." Coming out of the moment, he started down the aisle. Hanna couldn't help but turn her head as he walked away and found him looking back over his shoulder. Their eyes met again, and she quickly returned to a forward-facing position. She could tell her cheeks were flushed, and she felt a little embarrassed. He was handsome for sure, but Hanna had never paid much attention to boys. She turned toward her parents, who were both staring at her with large grins—they didn't miss anything! She rolled her eyes and resumed watching the final passengers board the shuttle.

After the last passenger to board had settled into their re-cliner, Mr. Watts made a grand entrance. Everybody began to clap and whistle loudly. Hanna leaped from her chair and very nearly knocked the old man over as she threw her arms around his neck and kissed his cheek.

"Oh ho! So, you like my gift, do you?" Mr. Watts said in a some-what labored voice, hugging back with all his strength so as not to be crushed embarrassingly by a fourteen-year-old girl.

"Your gift? Oh, the space flight. Sorry. Space cruise." Hanna corrected herself. "The hug wasn't for the trip to space," she taunted. She did not need to say anything else. Mr. Watts smiled warmly and gave her a much gentler hug than he had received. Mr. and Mrs. Storm beamed as they watched their daughter hug her newfound friend.

"Thank you, child," Mr. Watts whispered. "Now," he stumbled, hesitant to release Hanna, "let's get you properly fastened into your seat." Turning to the cabin he boomed, "We'll be on our way shortly," to which everyone responded with cheers. Hanna was sur-prised when Mr. Watts plopped down next to her. Marie took his cane and placed it in the same compartment where she had stowed Hanna's pack.

Hanna took a few moments to observe the environment in which she found herself. Her father had taught her to always be aware of her surroundings. She looked for the exits. She tried to observe who might be able to help and who might need help in an emergency. "It doesn't matter how old you are; when someone takes charge in an emergency, others follow, and it could mean the difference between life and death," her father had always taught. She noticed her dad taking stock of the shuttle and passengers as well and smiled to herself.

The chattering voices of the crowd began to stand out as she paid attention to them. The excited hum of the other passengers stirred up new feelings of excitement in Hanna.

"It's almost time," an older woman said, checking her watch.

"I know. I can't believe we're doing this!" replied the young woman with whom she was speaking.

She had barely enough time to assess her environment before a voice came over the intercom. "Ladies and gentlemen." The conversations all ceased simultaneously. "On behalf of Mr. Donovan Watts, I would like to welcome you all to this first of many space cruises." The crowd of passengers cheered in response. Hanna let out a shout and clapped while Mr. Watts grinned with pride. The voice continued.

"I am your captain, Jack De La Vega. Before we begin this monumental adventure, we need to share with you a few items concerning your safety. Our chief attendant will explain those to you now." A new voice came over the intercom.

"Good evening, everyone, and welcome. My name is Marie, and I am the chief attendant. Welcome to this historic event. As you know, the *Eloise* was fashioned from old NASA space shuttle designs, but what allows us to travel into space is the innovative WXV Wolverine rocket, developed right here at Watts Industries. The *Eloise* will take off like a normal airplane using our extended runway. After we reach approximately 20,000 feet, Captain Jack will direct the shuttle's nose straight up in the air and ignite the Wolverine rocket. You may experience some discomfort as we accelerate, but this should be mild. For your convenience, there are plastic-lined bags in the pockets located at the side of your seats. Once we reach space and establish an orbit around the earth, you will be able to leave your seats and enjoy the view. A meal and drinks will be served shortly after orbit is established."

Marie entered the main cabin and showed the passengers how to use their life vests in case of an emergency water landing, where the exits were, and how to use the five-point safety harness. Although this was a space flight, Hanna knew that most airplane accidents occurred during takeoff or landing.

"Captain Jack, we're ready," said Marie with an enthusiastic smile at the end of her presentation.

Unnoticed by Hanna, the shuttle had taxied into position on the runway. Without much warning, the shuttle began to barrel down the long, straight path. A shiver of exhilaration ran up Hanna's spine as the big engines roared to life. She felt the familiar sinking feeling in her stomach as the *Eloise* took flight. Hanna looked out her small window and watched as the ground below fell away. This was it. She was on her way to outer space!

CHAPTER 2

The Eloise Takes Flight

Hanna felt the shuttle level off from the upward course it had been taking. She pried her eyes away from the window for the first time since they had taken off and looked over at her mother and father. Curiously, they were staring at each other rather than out of the window. They spoke softly to each other, making it impossible for Hanna to hear what they were saying. This was good, because Hanna did not want to hear what her parents were saying to each other when they were all goo-goo-eyed.

She noticed Marie coming toward her. The slim space attendant bent down and whispered something in Mr. Watts' ear. He unbuckled his belt and raised himself carefully to his feet. Marie handed him his cane and Mr. Watts worked his way down the aisle and back through several handshakes and congratulations. When he sat down again beside Hanna, he looked at her and smiled as he extracted several gadgets from his jacket pocket.

"An official countdown is required for a proper launch, wouldn't you say?" Mr. Watts said to Hanna. She nodded her concurrence.

"As owner of the vessel, I would be honored if you would lead the effort." Mr. and Mrs. Storm watched proudly as Mr. Watts handed her a stopwatch and a small microphone that clipped onto her shirt. When Hanna was ready, he turned to the front of the cabin and nodded to Chief Attendant Marie.

"Be sure and say BLASTOFF!" Mr. Watts whispered enthusiastically to her.

"Ladies and gentlemen," came Marie's voice, clear and crisp through the intercom. "We are about to ignite the Wolverine rocket and begin our air launch into space. Ms. Hanna Storm has agreed to lead us in the countdown." Chief Attendant Marie spoke in such a cheerful manner that everyone on the plane beamed and nodded in agreement.

Marie walked down the aisle one more time and made sure everyone was properly buckled into their five-point harness. Hanna had always been a little uncomfortable around crowds, but she thoroughly enjoyed this moment of small fame.

"Ms. Storm," Marie said with a smile, "a mic check if you please?"

"Oh," Hanna said so loudly that some passengers covered their ears. "Sorry," she said more softly, accustomed now to the intensity of the microphone. "Testing, testing, one, two, three...I think it works."

"So it does, Ms. Storm," replied Marie. "If you would please check your watch and begin the countdown when ten seconds remain." Hanna looked down and saw that one minute remained on the stopwatch.

"And don't forget to say BLASTOFF!" Marie added as an afterthought. The passengers all gave a unified chuckle. After a few moments, the *Eloise* started to climb and was pointing nearly straight up as the stopwatch hit 15 seconds remaining. Hanna felt her stomach begin to make its way down into her feet. She stared at the stopwatch.

"Ten, nine, eight..." Hanna felt the butterflies in her stomach, or rather, she felt butterflies where her stomach had been a few moments earlier. She stared at the numbers on the stopwatch. The other passengers had joined in. "Seven, six, five, four," she continued in a tone that grew more excited as each second passed. She moved her eyes from the watch and looked out the window. She felt the powerful Wolverine rocket begin to fire up. "Three! Two! One! BLASTOFF!"

Hanna felt the rest of her insides join her stomach down at her feet. It was as if all her guts wanted to take a vacation to her toes. She was certain that her pancreas, liver, and spleen were all invited. She heard multiple people gasp as the rocket hurled at a tremendous speed toward the upper atmosphere.

Looking out the window, Hanna saw the landscape below begin to curve. Stars began to appear in the sky as though twilight were approaching, followed by night. Soon there was only the black expanse of the universe before Hanna's eyes, dotted with bright stars and galaxies.

Hanna felt the velocity of the shuttle subside. Her innards returned home from their vacation. The shuttle settled into a stable position. It seemed to be simply floating in space, but Hanna knew better. She knew that they had moved into orbit around the earth and were still traveling with great speed. The earth, however, was not visible from her window. She couldn't see it now that they were in orbit.

The quiet buzzing of moving machinery filled the cabin. It was a low sort of hum. Hanna looked around to see if she could identify what was causing it. She heard several people gasping in awe and followed their eyes upward. The roof of the shuttle was splitting apart. The outer hull opened to reveal a giant, clear ceiling that allowed for a breathtaking view of her home planet below. Hanna tapped her parents and motioned for them to look up. Silent awe gripped the entire shuttle. Not a single word was uttered for several minutes. Everyone just stared, amazed at the scene that lay before them. The earth was beautiful and serene. Hanna could make out the shape of Africa as they glided smoothly in their orbit. Blue seas and white clouds commanded the passengers' attention.

"Of all my adventures, this is the most amazing," breathed Mr. Storm, his whisper scarcely breaking the prolonged silence. Someone toward the rear of the cabin began to clap. Mrs. Storm joined in, and the other passengers soon followed. The clapping grew louder and faster with the addition of shouts and calls of "Bravo," as though a Russian ballet corps were taking their final bows. Hanna joined in, clapping and whistling.

"Ladies and gentlemen!" Marie's cheerful voice once again sounded over the intercom. "The captain and crew are pleased that you are enjoying the show." She paused as the passengers all laughed. Another familiar voice came over the intercom.

"This is Captain Jack. Welcome to space! We've reached our cruising altitude of 400 miles above sea level and are safely orbiting the earth at a speed of 6,800 miles per hour."

Hanna tapped Mr. Watts on the shoulder.

"That can't be right," she insisted. "The formula for determining orbital velocity is the square root of the mass of the earth divided by the distance from the center of the earth to the object's cruising altitude. If we are at an altitude of 400 miles…" Hanna looked up and absentmindedly counted on her fingers, as she often did when performing calculations, "then we should be traveling at 16,800 miles per hour." Mr. Watts was astonished.

Just then, Captain Jack's authoritative voice came on over the intercom. "My apologies folks. We are traveling at a speed of 16,800 miles per hour, not 6,800. You are now free to unfasten your safety belts and float about the cabin. Note the handholds throughout the cabin to help you maneuver." Several small, stick-like protrusions automatically appeared from the recesses in the cabin walls.

Hanna felt a giddiness like none that she had ever experienced before. She unlatched her belt and with a gentle push of her legs, she floated toward the transparent roof. It was magical to be floating there in space with the earth, shiny and blue, below her. She looked over at her parents and laughed.

"Hey, Mom. How does it feel to weigh the same as dad?" Hanna was well aware that the respective mass of each person did not change, but mass and weight aren't the same thing. Weight is determined by gravitational forces, and up here, there were no such forces, so technically her parents weighed the same as one another.

Mrs. Storm chuckled. She grabbed her husband's enormous arm and kissed him on the shoulder.

Hanna turned her attention back to the earth and stared in serenity. She could hear the hushed voices of other passengers commenting to each other. It was spectacular.

"It's beautiful, isn't it?" came an unknown voice.

Hanna startled out of her reverie. She hadn't noticed the handsome young man who had caught her eye earlier approaching. He floated a little closer.

"I didn't mean to startle you. I'm Henry."

Hanna smiled. "It's nice to meet you Henry. I'm Hanna, Hanna Storm."

For a moment, Henry just smiled. "It's amazing that we're moving so fast. It feels like we're standing still."

"As Einstein would say, everything is relative." Hanna laughed a little at her own joke. Both resumed their silent gaze toward the earth above, or was it below?

Hanna noticed some movement to her right and saw Mr. Watts floating toward her, still holding his cane. "Ironic," she thought to herself.

"Hanna, child. I have a surprise for you. Please follow me." With that, Mr. Watts turned and headed toward the cockpit. Hanna shrugged and, with a parting look at Henry, pulled herself gently along on a protruding handle and floated after him.

Marie was waiting for them near the door of the cockpit. "Captain Jack says now is a perfect time, Donovan," she said.

"Excellent!" replied Mr. Watts. "Hanna, how would you like to see the cockpit?"

Hanna's eyes grew big with excitement. "Technically it's a bridge, right? I mean, we're on a space cruise, which means we're on a cruiser, which means there's a bridge, not a cockpit."

"Yes, of course," grinned Mr. Watts. He pushed an intercom button on the wall and said "Captain Jack, this is Donovan Watts and Ms. Hanna Storm. Permission to enter *the bridge*."

"Granted!" came the reply over the intercom. The door to the bridge slid open, and Hanna floated in behind three occupied seats in a curved row. The two seats on the left faced an identical set of controls, consisting of a desk-like structure with a flat-panel display, keyboard, several raised buttons and switches, and small joystick. The seat on the right had a different setup entirely, facing a wall of different screens and monitors.

The middle seat was occupied by a rather short and muscular man with a military-style haircut and a beret leaning smartly to the side of his large head. Hanna had met U.S. Marines before, and everything from his polished boots to the crisp lines in his pressed blue tactical pants screamed Marine. His white zippered jacket sported a plethora of pockets and several patches, most prominent among them an embroidered picture of the *Eloise*. A pin bearing his title of "Captain" shone brightly above the breast pocket of his jacket. To the Marine's left was a woman with blonde hair tucked up under her beret and sporting the same blue pants, though not as neatly pressed as her colleague's, and a zippered white jacket. She had fewer patches on her uniform, but she had a polished "Captain" pin of her own. She sat half a head taller than her counterpart and Hanna wondered just how tall she might be if she stood up. The chair on the right was occupied by a petite woman with short dark hair wearing the same blue and white uniform as the other two.

"I'm Captain Jack De La Vega," proclaimed the man as he turned his captain's chair toward the new guests, "but I go by Captain Jack when I'm working." The two women seated on either side turned and smiled at Hanna. "This is my copilot, Captain Carlie Bask," Captain Jack said with a tilt of his head toward her. "We take turns in the captain and copilot seats."

The blonde woman let out a hearty laugh. "He won the coin toss for the first flight, but I'm a better pilot. Nice to meet you, Hanna," she smiled. "You can call me Captain Bask," she smirked while throwing a side glance to Captain Jack, "because I'm a professional."

Captain De La Vega gave his own laugh. "It's true," he said. "She very professionally lost the coin toss." He motioned to the woman on the right. "This is our navigator, Haruka Moriyama."

Haruka smiled and bowed slightly in her chair. "Konnichiwa! So nice to meet you!"

Hanna bowed in return. "Konnichiwa. Hajimemashite!" Hanna returned the greeting. Everyone looked surprised, but Hanna had been to Japan more than once with her parents on their Extreme Adventures.

"Would you like to take the copilot seat?" asked Captain Bask, rising.

"Yes! Definitely yes! I have so many questions." Hanna moved toward the chair, passing Captain Bask on the way.

"Will you do me the pleasure of joining us in the main cabin, Captain Bask?" Mr. Watts requested. "I'd like to introduce you to some of our guests."

"Of course, Mr. Watts. That sounds delightful." She took Mr. Watts' arm, and they floated off the bridge with the door sliding closed behind them.

Hanna lightly touched the joystick in front of her and stared in awe at all the lights, buttons, and screens.

"It's really not as complicated as you might think," said Captain Jack. "This joystick controls your thrust, drag, and yaw. You push it forward for thrust to go forward and pull back to slow down and engage the forward thrusters that push you backward. Turn it right and the nose will turn right. Turn it left and the nose will turn left. Simple. Don't try it now though, we're in a pretty solid orbit and I'd hate to lose it."

Hanna gave him a reprimanding look. She knew they were in orbit and to engage thrusters now would be ill-advised. "So, the main engine is tied into the directional controls. Brilliant! That takes care of the x and y axes. How do you control roll and pitch?" Hanna had actually flown a plane before. On a previous birthday, her father gave her a flying lesson at the local airport. Captain Jack was impressed.

"That's the four-direction arrow pad to the left of the joystick. Right arrow rolls right. Left arrow rolls left. Top arrow pitches down. Bottom arrow pitches up."

"Bottom arrow pitches up? That doesn't make sense," Hanna replied.

"Maybe not at first, but it makes sense when you get used to it. I think of it as the bottom arrow pushing the tail down and the top arrow pushing the nose down."

Hanna noticed that the fuel gauge was still nearly full. "What about the Wolverine rocket? Is there still fuel in it? Do we need to use it for reentry?"

"We won't need it for reentry, but we have enough fuel to get us to the moon and back if we wanted. Right now, we're on autopilot, and the computer is keeping us cruising with main engine thrusters adjusting automatically as needed."

Hanna was absolutely impressed. She was just getting settled when Captain Bask returned with Mr. Watts. "Alright, young lady," she said. "I need my chair back."

Hanna rose with a grin and a nod and moved toward Haruka, who gave her a quick rundown of the navigational computer and how she made her calculations.

"This is the most sophisticated navigational computer in the world," Haruka boasted in her accented English. "It uses the latest mapping of the global night sky and is updated automatically with data gathered from our external cameras and sensors."

"Does it factor in the expansion of the universe and anomalous gravitational forces?" Hanna asked. Captains Jack and Bask exchanged looks of disbelief.

"It does!" exclaimed Haruka. "In fact, it uses an algorithm I developed to calculate a changing Hubble constant based on the new data we gather."

"Wow!" said Hanna. "A dynamic algorithm to account for the Hubble tension!" She was almost squealing.

"Exactly!" said Haruka, matching Hanna's energy.

"You are outstanding, Ms. Storm" said Captain Jack. "We don't want you to miss dinner service though, and we have some protocols to run, so let's get you back to your seat."

"Come back later though, okay?" added Captain Bask.

Hanna thanked them all and turned to the door. She paused mid-air and twirled around.

"Permission to leave the bridge, Captain?"

Both captains answered simultaneously. "Permission granted!"

#

Hanna and Henry were gazing at the earth below while engaged in a vibrant debate about how best to eradicate gender inequality in rural sub-Saharan Africa. Henry proposed that cultural norms were important and should be respected; Hanna disagreed entirely.

"Wrong is wrong," she said, repeating a phrase often used by her mother, "whether today or 2000 years ago," she argued. Henry was about to respond when Mr. Watts' voice came over the intercom.

"Ladies and gentlemen, I've been saving this announcement for you alone. Watts Industries has successfully developed an artificial gravity engine, something once thought impossible. We will be engaging the artificial gravity in a few moments and ask that you return to your seats and engage your safety harnesses. Once gravity has been restored, we'll be serving a seven-course gourmet meal. I intend to announce our discovery at the press conference scheduled upon our return and I hope some of you will be reliable witnesses to the effectiveness of this incredible invention."

Hanna gasped. She couldn't quite believe that someone had actually managed to generate an artificial localized gravitational field. She had so many questions, but for now she parted with Henry and returned to her seat next to Mr. Watts, who had already buckled himself in. Marie floated through the cabin to ensure everyone was situated and then buckled herself down.

Captain Jack came over the intercom. "Ladies and Gentlemen, I'm initiating artificial gravity in three, two, one…"

Hanna felt the weight of her body return, but something was not quite right. She still felt light.

As if reading her mind, Mr. Watts leaned over and explained, "We're producing just enough gravity to keep the food on the tables. If you were to step on a scale now, you would only weigh a fraction of what you would on Earth."

The aroma of the first course eased its way into the main cabin before the food arrived. Hanna pulled the tray out and Marie came by, handing out hot towels and small white tablecloths for the trays. She moved down the aisle with trays of salads. Hanna was about to take her first bite when a buzzing sound filled the cabin, like a bumble bee flying close to her ear. It grew louder. Then, pop! Hanna let out a squeak and jumped in her seat. Her brain immediately ran through possible sources of the noise. Someone uncorking a champagne bottle? A gunshot? Some malfunctioning part of the ship?

Hanna heard a commotion toward the rear of the cabin and turned around to see people screaming, desperately trying to unbuckle themselves and stand up. Hanna saw someone—or something—that appeared to be out of place among the frantic passengers. She felt the familiar rush of adrenaline that had come to her so often on adventures with her parents, but this time it was accompanied by a more rare emotion. Fear. This creature had scales instead of skin. Its eyes were large and occupied a much larger portion of its face than a human's eyes would. It had arms and legs but also a thick tail. It was armored, including a helmet, and brandished a weapon that reminded her of the guns she had used in laser tag competitions. It uttered unintelligible words in a slithering and slurred voice.

Hanna froze, watching the events unfold as if in slow motion. There was a second pop, a third, and then another. Each time, an alien creature appeared in the cabin. One of the creatures placed a small round disc on one of the passengers, followed by a buzzing sound, a loud pop, and the complete disappearance of the passenger.

Mrs. and Mr. Storm were out of their seats in a flash, their movements so smoothly coordinated that it was as though they were communicating telepathically. Mrs. Storm unbuckled Hanna and pulled her to her feet and then helped Mr. Watts with his harness. Hanna caught a glimpse of Henry toward the rear. She watched as one of the aliens slapped a small disc to his shoulder, then he was gone.

Mrs. Storm dragged Hanna to the small closet where her pack and Mr. Watts' cane were securely stashed and threw her in. "Stay here. Don't come out until your father or I come for you." Her mother shut the door and disappeared.

Hanna was stunned for a few seconds but quickly gathered her senses. She wanted to see what was happening and to help if she could, but her mother had used her serious voice—like the time she warned Hanna not to pet that porcupine—and Hanna did not dare to disobey. Still, she opened the latch just a crack and tried to peer out. The ship was mostly empty of passengers. She counted five alien creatures resembling lizards. She could not see her mother, but her father had his thick arm around one of the creature's necks. It crumpled to the ground. He delivered a huge right-handed blow to another but was unable to avoid the tiny disc slapped to his back by an unseen third. He disappeared with a pop. Hanna wanted to scream, but she had gained her composure and was able to maintain it. She closed the latch and waited.

CHAPTER 3

A Daughter Gives Chase

Hanna listened carefully as the popping sounds faded. It seemed like an eternity, but it was less than a minute after the last pop before she quietly opened the latch and peered out. There was nobody in her line of sight. She continued to inch the latch open, careful to observe the increasing view of her surroundings. Still, there was nobody in sight. Confident that the creatures had gone, she slowly emerged into an empty cabin. The only signs of struggle were the overturned dinner cart and random pieces of food strewn about the cabin as though there had been a giant food fight. Otherwise, there was no evidence that anyone had been in the cabin at all—no bodies and no blast marks.

Hanna made her way to the bridge. The door was open and the chairs empty. She stared out into the darkness. The *Eloise* was no longer in orbit but was floating in empty space like a spaceship-shaped cloud in the sky. She patrolled the cabin and found no one. She briefly thought that she should search other parts of the shuttle, but deep down, she knew that each pop had been another person disappearing. Hanna had kept her cool in her hiding place, but now that the tussle was over, she felt herself beginning to panic. Hanna instinctively took several deep breaths to calm her nerves. What was she going to do?

"Don't panic," she told herself. On her Extreme Adventures, she had encountered her fair share of frightening situations. Once, her father had fallen through a crevice while they were ice-climbing a glacier. Hanna recalled how her mother had sprung into action with such calm and control, shouting out instructions to the other climbers. Hanna had frozen (no pun intended), and her mother had to shout two or three times for Hanna to anchor herself. After the ordeal was over and her father safe, her mother counseled her that panic in an emergency can kill.

"Panic is evolution's way of telling us we need to act, move, but how you act matters," her mother taught her. "Act quickly, but with intention and purpose." Hanna took that lesson to heart and learned how to keep her composure in chaotic situations, but she had never faced anything quite like this.

Hanna took a deep breath and said aloud, "Observe, assess, act," just as her father had taught her. "Okay. I'm not done observing. Observe." Hanna looked up and saw that the viewing screen was still retracted. Her mouth reflexively dropped open in awe. She had not been expecting to see what she knew to be another spaceship.

The alien ship was considerably larger than the *Eloise* and shaped like a tube with an oversized orb at one end, which she assumed was the front. A green laser emanated from the orb to a position directly in front of the ship. Hanna couldn't reconcile what she was seeing with her knowledge of physics. At the point where the laser's beam appeared to end, a shimmer of wavy green light was growing, similar to the Northern Lights she had once seen in the Alaskan bush country but more concentrated and with a clearly outlined border that slowly expanded.

The rear of the alien ship began to glow red; its engines were powering up. Hanna skipped the "Assess" phase and ran for the bridge, buckling into Captain Jack's seat. She turned the shuttle's nose around to pursue the alien vessel. The control stick was well designed, intuitive, and comfortable in her hand. The thrusters engaged, and the *Eloise* lurched forward into the turn. Hanna saw the alien ship advance and the orb disappear into the shimmering green light, its long tube of a tail in its wake.

The edges of the energy field started to shrink. In a matter of moments, the alien ship was through and out of sight. Hanna jammed the joystick all the way forward, and though the *Eloise* was gaining momentum, she knew the field would close before she reached it.

"Come on, *Eloise*! We're losing them," Hanna cried, as though a verbal command would increase thrust. Thrust! Hanna looked frantically for the Wolverine rocket ignition switch and clicked it into the firing position without a second thought. Proceeding straight from "Observe" to "Act" while bypassing "Assess" had its dangers, but Hanna was filled with adrenaline. She thought only of her parents and the other passengers without a glimmer of thought for her own precarious position.

"Watch yourself," she whispered to the alien vessel. "A Storm's comin' for ya."

CHAPTER 4

The Eloise in Pursuit

The *Eloise* surged forward with a burst of new energy and blazed through the closing portal. Hanna could see greenish hues of light surrounding the ship. She had the sensation of forward momentum as the light glided past her window, but the alien ship was nowhere in sight.

The *Eloise* began to tremble. A small vibration built to a vigorous, earthquake-like shake. Hanna cut the Wolverine rocket and reversed thrust. The ship slowed, but the shaking persisted. It wouldn't be much longer before the shuttle shook itself apart. Hanna desperately searched the instrument panel for something—anything!—that might help.

She spotted the artificial gravity engine switch and turned it to its "off" position. The shaking ceased and the scene shifted. Green light floated past, serene and beautiful. As her speed decreased, the green light began to close in until it formed a wall directly in her path that seemed to extend around the entire ship. She instinctively cut the engines to reduce thrust, but there was no time. She was powerless to stop it. With only a few seconds to go before impact, she could do nothing but sit and watch.

When the *Eloise* encountered the wall of green light, it simply continued through, emerging into normal space on the other side and coming to a stop. Hanna exhaled slowly and scanned all of the windows on the bridge. No sign of the alien ship. She also checked the large observation window in the main cabin and every other window she could find. Nothing; just cold, dark space punctuated by the faint glimmers of distant stars.

#

Several hours passed. Hanna stared out of the window of the bridge and wondered how she could ever have been so intrigued by the absolute nothingness that was space. How could nothing at all be so captivating? She thought about her parents and their fate. She thought about what may have happened to Donovan Watts and Captain Jack and the cheerful Chief Attendant Marie. She wondered how Henry was faring. She thought of Captain Bask and Haruka Moriyama, the navigator.

Navigator! Hanna snapped out of her thoughts and floated to the observation window in the main cabin. She steadied herself using the handholds and tried to make sense of the stars that she could see. If she was anywhere close to Earth or even near her own solar system, she should be able to orient herself. She did not recognize a single constellation.

Hanna sat down in Haruka's chair and looked over the instruments. The navigational computer had the latest information on the mapping of the universe, and Hanna set to work on the computer interface to try and pinpoint her location. Using Earth as the origin, the computer was able to extrapolate an estimated position.

"This can't be right," Hanna said aloud. If the calculations were correct, the *Eloise* was approximately 780 kiloparsecs from Earth in a direction that would put her just inside the Andromeda Galaxy.

She knew from her studies that Andromeda was the closest major galaxy to the Milky Way, but traveling at the speed of light, it would take a spaceship two and a half million years to reach it. She had so many questions. How in the universe did she get here? How would she get back? But most importantly, where were her parents?

Realizing that she could not answer any of those questions right now, Hanna turned her thoughts toward her own situation. She was stranded. Rescue was impossible. There was nowhere to go. The reality that she was totally alone in the darkness of space in a galaxy that was not her own was overwhelming. She felt tears begin to rise and, once again, instinctively took several deep breaths to try and stop her hands from shaking. This time, however, each breath brought a surge of tears and she sobbed into her shaking hands, collapsing to her knees. She had never felt so alone. Even when she was by herself, on one of her own little adventures, it was always by choice, and she knew her mother and father would be there whenever she returned. Hanna took pride in always being honest, even with herself, and if she was being honest, the likelihood that she would see her parents again seemed extremely low. Meanwhile, the likelihood that she would be dead within a month seemed extremely high.

"No!" Hanna screamed, bounding to her feet. She tensed all the muscles in her body and let out a roar. "I do not give up, remember?" Hanna recalled her experience of flying with her father in a small two-seater airplane when the engine had stalled. She had been certain that they would die and panicked. Her dad had calmed her with his eyes and smiled, his voice coming into her headset in peaceful, soothing waves.

"Hanna, daughter, we're not dead yet. I need you to look around for a place to land." Hanna had responded and had identified a long stretch of golf course on which her father had been able to land the plane safely.

"I'm not dead yet," she asserted. "Back to the bridge to check the oxygen levels." Hanna made her way to the bridge and found that the tanks were nearly full. She could calculate how long the oxygen would last at a later time, but she reasoned that it would be enough to sustain one person for a few days, at least. She checked the main engines' fuel levels: three-quarters full. The internal temperature controls and lights were still on, confirming that there was a power supply. Finding no other fuel gauge, she assumed that they were powered by batteries or by the same fuel source as the main engines. The Wolverine rocket's fuel gauge was showing at half full. It had been used twice for about the same amount of time in each instance. Hanna figured she had two more burns if she needed to quickly build momentum. However, oxygen was required for fuel to burn. To what extent would a burn deplete the oxygen supplies? Did the Wolverine have its own oxygen source? There were too many questions with no answers.

Feeling discouraged, she thought back to her little adventure in the two-seater airplane. Even that Cessna 152 had its own thick operating manual in the plane itself. Hanna looked around the bridge, opening the latches on whatever compartments she could find. In one of the cubbies near Captain Bask's station lay a thick manual.

"*Shuttle Crew Operations Manual*," she read aloud. She plopped down on the floor behind the center captain's chair and opened the book to the Table of Contents. The manual was over 1100 pages long; she would have to prioritize.

"Section 1, General Description. Section 2, Systems...Perfect." She continued to glance through the subsections. "Section 2.1, Auxiliary Power Unit/Hydraulics. Section 2.2, Caution and Warning System. Section 2.3, Closed Circuit Television...Don't need that...Section 2.4 Communications...Not going to work out here...Section 2.5, Crew Systems...Maybe later...Section 2.6, Data Processing Systems." Hanna continued on down the list, prioritizing Section 2.9,

Environmental Control and Life Support Systems and Section 2.16, Main Propulsion Systems.

Hanna read aloud as she often did when studying, but on this occasion it also provided the reassurance of the sound of her own voice. "Oxygen from the power reactant storage and distribution system (cryogenic oxygen supply system) is routed to the pressure control oxygen system 1 and system 2 supply valves. These valves are controlled by the ATM PRESS CONTROL O2 SYS 1 SUPPLY and O2 SYS 2 SUPPLY switches on panel L2." Hanna looked around the console and found the L2 panel with the corresponding labeled switches. This small victory gave her the confidence to continue, and she soon learned the basics of how the life support and propulsion systems operated.

After several hours of reading, Hanna glanced back at the Table of Contents to see which section she should read next and noticed Section 2.12, Galley/Food. As if on cue, her tummy growled, and she realized just how hungry she was. She placed the manual back into its compartment and made for the main cabin. Unopened trays of food were still in the overturned cart, which was now floating up near the observation window. Was it still good? She decided to find out. She pulled out a tray and took in the aroma of beef wellington with mashed potatoes and string beans. As the food floated up off the tray, she leaned forward and started to take bites. It tasted so good! Despite knowing that she might regret it later, she finished the tray and then ate one more for good measure.

Hanna looked around and decided that she needed to clean up a bit. She didn't dare start the artificial gravity engine, as she did not yet know how much fuel it would use or how it functioned, not to mention how big a mess it might make if everything that was floating in the main cabin came crashing down. Kicking off walls and using the handholds, she moved about the cabin gathering up the unopened trays of food and placing them in the cart. She then moved the cart to its proper storage compartment in the galley. Looking through the compartments in the galley, she found a large plastic trash bag and floated into the main cabin. She couldn't help laughing as she played acrobat, bouncing off the walls and holding the large sack open, scooping up the floating food and empty trays. With the cabin mostly clean, she felt tired and decided to rest.

Hanna closed off the bridge, the galley, and the rear sections of the *Eloise* and routed the oxygen and nitrogen mix to the main cabin only. She found some very plush blankets and pillows in one of the compartments and turned down the temperature. Settling into her recliner, Hanna looked over to where her mom and dad had sat during the launch.

"Goodnight, Mom and Dad. I'll find you," she promised herself, "or die trying." She dozed off with determination in her heart.

CHAPTER 5

The Lost Earth Girl

Hanna awoke to a bright light radiating through the observation window. Had the ship that attacked them returned? She leaped to her feet and ran for the bridge, the air from the main cabin rushing behind her. She restored the oxygen levels and turned up the heat, but for now, the cold served to sharpen her senses.

Hanna ran through the checklist for starting the main engines and double-checked the fuel levels for the Wolverine rocket. If that ship was back, she wanted to be ready to pursue it. She ceased her flurry of activity when she traced the source of light back to the outline of an alien ship. Her heart sank. It was not the same one. The newly arrived vessel was much smaller than the alien ship that had taken her parents captive and far sleeker in its design. It was shaped with one end rounded and smooth and the other coming to a point, as though someone had put one end of a giant egg in an equally giant pencil sharpener.

Hanna wasn't quite sure what she should do. She ran through various possibilities in her mind. This could be a rescue, an attack, or something else entirely. The only way to find out was to wait. Hanna went through all of the sci-fi alien and space movies that she could recall, attempting to find a familiar scenario that would help her predict what might be coming. Pacing the bridge, she spied her trusted leather satchel. She threw it over her head and put one arm through, wanting it close by in case anything unexpected happened. She realized that the phrase "expect the unexpected" was not as useful as it appeared, as she was still uncertain as to what unexpected thing she was expecting to happen.

The buzzing noise started up once again, building to that familiar popping sound. Pop! Pop! She counted two, but they were not on the bridge. They must be in the main cabin. Hanna heard alien voices, but they differed from one another. One was high-pitched and sharp while the other was more of a series of grumbles and groans. Neither of them sounded like the slithering, slurred speech of the aliens that had attacked the *Eloise*. Hanna waited nervously as the voices grew louder. There was a pause, then a knock at the bridge door. Hanna jumped. The knock came again.

Hanna's curiosity got the better of her. How could she not open it? They were polite enough to knock! She gathered her courage, trusted her instincts, and opened the bridge door. Before her stood two beings in similar uniforms. One of the aliens had a flat head with two large eyes and long skinny arms and legs. Its skin was lightly tanned, and it stood almost as tall as her father. The other was shorter, with fat arms and no legs that Hanna could see. The frame of its orange body and head were of equal width up until the very top, which was rounded. It had two large eyes and a mouth that was vertically rather than horizontally arranged on its face, and its head was covered in flexible, tubular protrusions that were colored a dark red. It reminded Hanna of a short and stocky trick-or-treating child covered in a sheet with holes cut out for the eyes.

The taller alien emitted high-pitched sharp noises that Hanna was certain she could not replicate, while the shorter, bumpy-headed creature made more of a low humming noise that resembled a groan and constantly changed pitch. They conversed for around a minute, each occasionally looking over at Hanna, the taller one with a curious expression. Hanna noticed that the bumps on the shorter alien's head changed colors while he conversed with his taller companion, but his facial expression remained blank. The taller alien, on the other hand, waved his arms and blinked wildly while talking to his partner.

"Hey! Who are you?" Hanna interrupted, finally deciding to speak.

The two looked over at her, looked at each other, and took a step toward her. Well, the tall one stepped; the shorter one appeared to glide along on the bottom of its body, as though it were walking on its waist. The tall one looked at her and began to speak, waving its arms and blinking its eyes.

"I don't understand what you are saying," Hanna explained, shaking her head. "I don't speak your language."

The tall one made an expression that Hanna interpreted as surprise. The short one made no expression, but the tips of the many bumps on his head turned a light color of orange. They looked briefly at each other before the short, plump alien began to speak.

"Hmmm ooh hmmm," it began.

"Look, I don't understand what you are saying. I'm sorry. Do you speak English?" Hanna asked hopefully, "or French or Japanese?"

The two aliens exchanged a few words with one another. The tall one dipped its long finger into a tiny compartment on its belt. Removing his finger, he raised it to Hanna's ear as though he was holding something delicate on his fingertip. Hanna instinctively jumped back, startling both aliens and causing the taller one to almost drop whatever it was carrying on its fingertip. The bumps on the short one's head turned red.

Hanna second-guessed her instinct. They had not been aggressive, but rather their discussion and mannerisms suggested inquisitive natures. "Sorry," she said, hoping that what she was about to accept wouldn't harm her.

The stick-like alien slowly took Hanna's wrist and turned her palm up, placing a small metal ball in her hand. It was about the size of the head of a pin. She looked at it for a moment and then stared inquisitively at the aliens. Both of them motioned for her to place it in her ear. Unsure of what would happen, Hanna followed their direction and carefully placed the tiny ball in her right ear. She felt it moving deep into her ear canal, tickling her terribly.

"Can you understand me now?" came the high voice of the stick-like alien. Hanna was amazed. This was certainly a shock. She knew they had been trying to communicate with her, but whatever device they had put in her ear allowed her to hear them in English. She became excited as she imagined the technology that must be involved in such a device.

"Yes! Yes! I can understand you," she exclaimed. "What an amazing device! An absolutely universal translator!"

"You've never zzzeen a tranzzzlator?" asked the short, stubby alien in his low, humming voice, the translator seemingly unable to pronounce the "s."

"No, I've never had one. It's amazing. I must inform you that this is the first time I've ever met someone from a different species," Hanna confided, hoping that honesty was also the best policy way out here in space.

"Curious," said the skinny stick-like alien in his sharp, high-pitched voice. "We don't have your ship design or your genetic mapping in our database."

"That'zzz right young girl. We don't hold your recordzzz."

"Are you the police?" Hanna asked, almost certain what the answer would be before she had finished asking the question.

"Yes. We are part of the Corridor Patrol, a section of the Galactic Peace Force. We patrol the corridors. We saw your ship emerge from an unauthorized corridor in a remote region of space. It took us nearly three galactic standard days from the closest hub to get to you," the tall alien said.

Hanna was bursting with questions. Her curiosity was brimming. She didn't much care that she might be in trouble. She still could not believe that there was a Galactic Police Force.

"My name is Hanna Storm. What's your name? What planet are you from? What do you call this galaxy?" Hanna asked without pausing.

"Zzztop the questionzzz," demanded the stubby alien, the bumps on his head turning dark.

"How can you speak perfect English?" Hanna asked the stick figure. "And why does he speak, um, less-than-perfect English?"

"Some languages are more compatible with each other," answered the tall one, who did not appear to mind Hanna's barrage of questions at all. "Your Mung is the best I have heard from any species. I can hardly understand Boother here, even with the translator."

"Mung. Is that your language?" Hanna inquired.

"It is my language and the name of my planet and species," answered the alien. Both Hanna and the Mung noticed that Boother's bumps were turning darker, almost black. "Right," acknowledged the Mung. "Where do you come from?"

"Oh, I'm from Earth," Hanna answered, matter-of-factly. The bumps on Boother's head turned bright orange. The Mung gasped loudly, his eyes widening.

"Impossible," he said. "It is a deception."

"So, you've heard of it!" Hanna was so excited at the prospect of her planet being known, as thoughts of hitching a ride back to Earth flitted through her mind.

"Earth izzz juzzzt a myth," Boother said in an annoyed tone.

"Let's hear her out," answered the Mung. "She's not in our database after all. Hanna, was it? Tell us what happened to you and how this ship came to be here."

Hanna recounted her birthday surprise of the first commercial space cruise, the alien attack, her pursuit, and her attempt to learn how to survive on the *Eloise*. She described the alien creatures in detail with their scales and tails and armor and weapons. The Mung looked astonished and gasped several more times as she relayed her tale. Boother remained expressionless, but his bumps turned from orange to dark orange, to almost purple, then black, then back to orange again. When she had finished recounting the events that led her here, she paused, awaiting their response. The officers did not speak for a few moments and were clearly processing what they had just heard.

"First, we wish you a happy name day and hope that you have many more to come," said the Mung.

"Thanks!" Hanna said with sincerity. How unexpected!

"If your description is accurate, it appears that the Dorians attacked your ship and took your parents and other passengers as prisoners. This is not uncommon with systems outside the Galactic Treaty. The Dorians are not part of the treaty and sometimes attack other non-treaty systems to gather laborers for their mining operations."

"Can you take me to them?" she interrupted.

"Impozzzible" said Boother. "The Dorianzzz mine on hundredzzz of planetzzz and the Galactic Counzzzil hazzz no diplomatic relationzzz with them."

"Boother is quite right. Members of the Galactic Treaty don't cross the border into Dorian space, and even if we did, we have no way of finding your parents."

Hanna was not discouraged. Every piece of information helped, and she now knew where to look. The Mung noted the resolve in her expression and decided the best course of action was to resume questioning.

"A few elements of your story do not add up. First, we have heard of Earth, but it is merely a myth, albeit a well-known myth. Earth lies in the Sister Galaxy, and no species in our galaxy, Galaxy Prime, has any known means of intergalactic travel. Second, you are clearly describing a corridor, but a corridor is unidirectional. If there is no corridor engine near Earth, there can be no way for a ship to return."

"What's a corridor? Can you explain it to me?" inquired Hanna.

"Certainly. A corridor engine essentially bends the space–time continuum to produce a direct path between two points in space."

"Wormholes! At least, that's what we call them," Hanna added sheepishly.

"An interesting and perhaps appropriate analogy," mused the Mung. "They can occur naturally, but this is rare, and I have never heard of an intergalactic 'wormhole' from any reputable source. The corridor engines mimic the conditions required to open a 'wormhole' but one has to maintain a certain velocity to reach the destination one desires. As I said, if there is no corridor engine on the other side, there can be no return."

"Could they have brought their own corridor engine?" Hanna speculated.

"Not likely. Corridor engines have a limited range. It requires thousands of jumps just to get from one side of Galaxy Prime to the other. If you really are from Sister Galaxy, it would have taken you over one hundred thousand galactic standard years to get here."

"I'm telling you they had a green laser pointed right at it and I barely made it through before it collapsed," Hanna said, repeating what she had told them earlier.

"Corridor enginezzz don't uzzze lazzzerzzz. If the Dorianzzz have developed an alternative technology, the Galactic Treaty planetzzz may be in danger. We have to report thizzz to Command." Boother's bumps were turning dark again.

"Agreed. Hanna, you are considered a youth in your species, are you not?"

"That is correct," Hanna replied hesitantly.

"Excellent! Boother, when we get back to the ship, transmit this information to Command and then get us to the nearest corridor engine and plot a course for Sendori. We will drop Hanna there and take her ship back to Command for analysis.

"Take me where?" she asked incredulously.

"To Sendori. There is a place for youth there and you will be safe."

Hanna was uncertain how to respond. She did not want to be at the mercy of these two and if she was ever going to see her parents again, she needed a ship, *her* ship she reckoned—the *Eloise*. She weighed her options carefully. She could not find her parents if she was dead and at this Sendori she would at least find food and shelter and perhaps more answers.

"Where there is food and shelter, there is opportunity," she thought to herself, another lesson learned from her adventurous parents. She also knew the *Eloise* would be at Command, wherever that was.

"All right. I'll play ball on this one."

"Excuzzze me?"

"I believe she means that she will be cooperative," said the Mung. "That is an excellent choice because you have no other. We'll bring you aboard our ship and engage the tractor beam."

"What should I call you?" Hanna asked, suddenly realizing that she knew only his species and thought it polite—and fair—to inquire.

"My species is oriented toward the collective and not the individual. We are all called Mung."

"Then," she paused, "I will call you Mung," came her inevitable reply.

Boother reached down to his belt and took out three tiny discs, similar to those Hanna had seen the Dorians use on the *Eloise*. Hanna jumped back again and Boother's bumps turned red.

"What are those?" Hanna asked with a tinge of fear in her voice.

"Those are transport discs. They are like mini corridor engines that transfer a person or small objects from one space to another within a short distance. It's how we arrived here and how we'll get back to our ship. Boother, please demonstrate." Mung was very courteous in his explanation, perceiving Hanna's concern.

Boother passed around the discs and then slapped one on his shoulder and disappeared with a pop.

"Now it is your turn, Hanna."

She hesitated while Mung waited patiently. She adjusted her satchel and slapped the disc to her shoulder. She never heard the pop, but found herself standing before Boother in a sparse, clean room. The whole experience was strange to her. There had been no perceptible departure, travel time, or landing. One minute, she was standing in front of Mung, and the next, she was standing in front of Boother. She patted her arms and legs to make sure that everything was where it should be. Her pack was still slung over her shoulder.

Mung appeared with a buzz and a pop, and Boother exited the room, presumably to send a transmission and get them on their way.

"Please remain in these quarters. Let me show you how to operate the room."

Hanna paid close attention as Mung walked her through the room, stopping at different panels and explaining their use.

"This is where you may rest if you require sleep." Mung pressed a small metallic button and a flat panel about the size of a twin mattress emerged slowly out of the wall. It was hard and made out of some kind of metal, but it had controls along one edge for vibration, temperature, and rigidity. Hanna marveled at how the metal softened when she lowered the rigidity. What kind of metal was this? What kind of technology?

"This is where you can bathe. You are carbon-based, so I presume two parts hydrogen and one part oxygen will work best. You may program it here."

He pressed a similar small metallic button situated near the first and a compartment the size of a small shower on Earth came out of the wall. It had a nozzle for spraying and trays that contained a variety of scented gelatinous liquids.

"Huh. Even has soap," Hanna said.

"Indeed. This is your matter synthesizer. You can select from various designs to create objects you may require. There are safety limitations, of course, but you can make a brush or a comb, robes, or other necessities.

"Like a 3-D printer." Hanna was in awe.

"That is accurate. It 'prints' three-dimensional objects. What a curious language!" Mung's response led Hanna to believe that this universal translator sometimes translated ideas and sometimes translated literal words.

"What about food?"

"Ah, yes. Sustenance. This is your food matter synthesizer. Our ingredient list is limited to proteins, fats, and various carbohydrates, all of which come from non-sentient vegetation. Simply select the combination that you desire, and it will produce a rather bland porridge that should sustain you."

"Sounds delicious," Hanna said sarcastically. Maybe she could program it to make chocolate chip cookies—plenty of carbohydrates and fat in those.

"And this is where you can place any waste you produce." Mung pulled down the latch to a chute. It would take some doing, but Hanna had survived worse toilet options on her many adventures.

"Is there anything else you require?" asked Mung.

"I think I'm all set. Thank you."

"Of course," he said and headed for the exit. He paused at the doorway and turned back to Hanna. "I am sorry about your parents. I hope you can accept that they are lost." With that he exited, and the door slid closed behind him. Hanna went straight to the bed, selected a comfortable rigidity and temperature, and fell asleep, her determination to find her parents greater than ever.

CHAPTER 6

How Fare the Captives?

Captain Jack De La Vega woke up strapped to a cold, metallic table. His head was immobilized, as were his arms and legs. He could barely move his wrists and ankles. His mind was foggy, and he had trouble making sense of his surroundings. It was the same feeling he had had waking up from the colonoscopy that his doctor had insisted on last year. He remembered being on the bridge of the *Eloise* and hearing a buzzing sound and a loud pop. He remembered seeing...what was it that he saw? Not anything human. It had reached out for him, and then he had suddenly found himself standing in a room with other passengers. Yes. He remembered being in that room with some of the passengers. He was starting to think more clearly. One of the passengers in the room appeared right before his eyes with a buzz and a pop, just as the aliens had.

"Aliens," he whispered. They *must* be aliens! Captain Jack groaned as he regained the physical sense of his body. His muscles ached. By his estimate, all of the passengers must have been in the room. Before anybody could make sense of it, Captain Jack had witnessed multiple people blacking out, and he soon followed. After that, nothing, until now.

Captain Jack grew increasingly lucid as each minute passed. His bodily aches were no worse than those that he had occasionally felt after a good run. He tried to assess his surroundings, but it was dark, and he had difficulty seeing. He suddenly saw a square of light appear to his side. A door opened and he caught a glimpse of the room he was in. It was filled with all manner of machinery and equipment that he could not identify.

Two aliens with green scales and thick tails entered the room. One of them was particularly large and wore a patch over one eye to hide what must have been a serious injury. The other, who walked in front, had the manner of a leader, of someone in charge. When Captain Jack was a Marine, he had seen a few colonels who walked that way and many who had tried to but failed. This one was definitely in charge. If there was any doubt, the weapon holstered at his side indicated that he was not to be trifled with.

"Good, he's awake," said the alien leader.

"Where am I?" asked Captain Jack. The fact that he understood the alien crossed his mind as strange but largely irrelevant to his current predicament. The ability to communicate was a plus, and he wasn't at all interested in the why or how.

"Interesting," said the humanoid lizard leader. "Do you think you are in a position to make inquiries? Do you believe you can make me answer your questions?"

"I'm awake. My voice works. I seem able to make inquiries. As for making you answer, I'm not sure yet. Why don't you let me out of here and we can find out." Captain Jack was testing his captors' boundaries, which was not in strict accordance with his training as a Marine. He knew it was risky, but his instincts told him that a little push back might earn him some respect. While it was a dangerous tactic, it was also consistent with Captain Jack's defiant nature.

The larger subordinate burst forward, his hand raised as if to strike. Captain Jack did not even flinch but waited for the blow, which landed squarely across his face.

"Show respect!" growled the enforcer.

"Interesting," mused the master. "You are technically correct that you are physically able to voice questions. Perhaps I should make myself clear by removing that as an option." He clicked a button on a panel attached to the table. Intense pain shot through Captain Jack's entire body. His teeth clenched shut and he writhed in agony, unable to make any noises except the groans that escaped through his nasal passage.

"I ask again. Do you now think that you are in a position to make inquiries?" The alien leader smirked. He moved in close to the sweaty face of his tortured captive and whispered. "Do you believe you can make me answer your question?"

Captain Jack struggled as he tried to breathe through the pain. Difficult though it was, he maintained eye contact with his captor. Mustering all of his mental will and effort, he formed the word carefully:

"Nope."

"Excellent," responded the leader, impressed that his captive had managed even a single word. The irony that his captive could still speak and, therefore, still ask questions seemed lost on the alien, which made Captain Jack just a little disappointed. Master Slythe pressed another button and the pain stopped. Maybe it was a blessing that he hadn't caught the irony.

"Now that we've established who is in charge, I have a few questions for you. I've demonstrated that I am in a position to ask you questions and that I am capable of eliciting a response. Where are you from?"

"Let's see. I was born in Juarez, Mexico, but moved to Phoenix when I was young, so I guess I would call Arizona home. At least, that's where I pay my taxes." Pain shot through his body. This time it lasted for over a minute.

"My apologies. Let me be more precise. What planet are you from?" Master Slythehissed.

"Planet? We call it Earth." A look of satisfaction crossed the leader's face and he turned triumphantly to his larger companion.

"I knew the legends were true." He placed a hand on his enforcer's shoulder, who returned the gesture, his own visage breaking into a triumphant smile.

"And what is the population of your Earth?" the leader inquired, returning his attention to Captain Jack. This was a disconcerting question for a captive Marine. He recognized that this was an enemy. He also knew that his answers could potentially endanger his passengers and crew—if they were still alive—as well as all everyone back on Earth. He had to play this carefully.

"Approximately eight billion," he answered honestly. The pain shot through his body once again. The larger alien gasped.

"Did he say eight billion? That's almost half the Dorian Empire Master Slythe, including the lesser species," he said. "Our translators must be faulty."

Captain Jack breathed through the pain and took note of everything the aliens said: Master Slythe...Dorian Empire...Population, sixteen billion...Multiple species.

"He's obviously lying, Boran" retorted Master Slythe. "No single planet could sustain those numbers." He pressed a button and the pain stopped.

"Let's try that again. What is the population of Earth?" inquired Master Slythe. "To be clear, I am talking about humanoid inhabitants such as yourself."

"There is nobody like me," he joked, but quickly answered when he saw his captor about to press the pain button. "But including myself and the twenty-four other people you kidnapped, Earth's population is, I'd say, about eight billion and twenty-five. You heard me right, and it is the truth, so stop with your pain button."

The two aliens turned their attention away from Captain Jack to converse with one another. Captain Jack listened intently to their conversation.

"If this is true," Boran began, "we would have enough resources within a galactic standard year to overpower the Galactic Peace Force and claim the worlds that rightfully belong under Dorian rule."

"Yes. I agree. We know how to locate and navigate the corridor, but finding a natural rift to facilitate our return was a statistical impossibility we won't be able to repeat."

"I'll put the engineers on notice to develop a means of identifying natural rifts," said Boran.

"That line of research could take years. This corridor requires the same time as any other corridor in Galaxy Prime, but the distance it traverses is inexplicable. No. We need a more immediate and permanent solution, especially if the resources of Earth can sustain eight billion lives." The greedy look in Master Slythe's eye curdled Captain Jack's blood.

"We need to construct a corridor engine on both sides, engines large enough to sustain an armada of transports," instructed Slythe. "It will allow the engineering team to more quickly calculate the necessary size of the corridor engines needed to gain access to a corridor at our convenience."

"Their ship had no weapons. I don't think these Earth people can defend themselves," said Boran. "Master Slythe, this was your discovery, and you should be the one to lead us to victory against the Galactic Treaty planets."

"Thank you for your confidence, Boran. I agree. For now, we keep this to ourselves. Once Clan Slythe builds the corridor engines and we have the Earth people, the other clans will be unable to stand against us and will unite under my banner."

"Glorious Master! Glorious! Victory is surely yours," praised Boran.

They exited the room, and Captain Jack was left in the dark to contemplate what he had just heard. He repeated the details to himself. Corridor engines, distances, resources, Clan Slythe. He assumed that their reference to "enough resources" had meant people—Earth people. His people. Perhaps they would be used as unwilling soldiers or maybe laborers, or—in what he considered to be the worst-case scenario—as meal rations.

Captain Jack was surprised by the amount of intelligence they had allowed him to overhear. There were only three possible reasons for that: 1) they weren't particularly shrewd military tacticians, 2) they were confident in their ability to thwart any resistance, or 3) he wasn't going to be alive long enough to tell anyone. The first was *ideal*, the second something he could *deal with*, and the third? *No deal.*

\#

Mr. and Mrs. Storm sat huddled together. They were in a large holding cell with bars made of some unknown metal. Mr. Storm had not yet tested their strength, but they looked solid enough. The other passengers were all accounted for, except Hanna and Captain Jack De La Vega. They had been given some flavorless paste to eat and fresh water, but the conditions were cramped.

The alien guards seemed to understand what they were saying. When Chief Attendant Marie demurely asked one of the guards whether there was a bathroom, they pushed a button on the wall that opened a small rectangular room. Apparently Marie was expected to figure out the rest on her own, but at least the guards were responsive.

Mrs. Storm was in observation mode, noting when guards were coming and going and trying to distinguish them from one another. One of the guards had a huge bump on his face, his eye swollen shut and his scales missing and discolored. She was certain her husband was responsible for that. The guard glared continuously at Mr. Storm, who maintained a meek posture and did not return the stare. Eventually, the guard came forward and shouted at Mr. Storm. The other passengers parted, and he gestured for Mr. Storm to come forward. Mrs. Storm grabbed her husband's arm in protest.

"Don't," she said.

"I'll be alright. I can take it. Better that he take it out on me than on you or anyone else."

"Alright," she agreed, "but I'm going to watch."

"Are you sure? It's such a heroic act, you'll probably want to smooch afterward and that would be awkward, you know, given our circumstances."

"Not the time, Sebastian. This is serious." Mrs. Storm reprimanded.

Mr. Storm smiled and walked away. He approached the guard still smiling and knew instantly that this was a mistake. The guard took a baton from his side and, through the bars, delivered a jolt of electricity that tore through Mr. Storm's entire body. His eyes were down, but he kept his feet under him, which seemed to annoy the guard even more. He delivered another jolt, this time allowing it to last for several seconds before disengaging. Mr. Storm fell briefly to one knee, but quickly stood again, eyes still cast downward. The guard snarled and readied the baton for another blow, but it never came. He had collapsed and lay motionless on the floor.

An eye-patched alien, almost as big as Mr. Storm, had entered the room, pulled out his side arm, and dispatched the offending guard with a single shot. He said something stern to the other guard, who, with an intense look of fear on his face, dragged away his dead comrade. The big alien locked eyes with Mr. Storm. This time, Mr. Storm returned the intense gaze. The monstrous alien grinned, turned, and departed.

Mr. Storm buckled to the ground, holding his side where the electrocuting stick had made contact with his body. Mrs. Storm and Captain Bask rushed to his aid.

"Feeling macho are we, Sebastian?" Mrs. Storm inquired.

"No. No. Not really," he lied.

"Well, I do want to kiss you now, you brute," she laughed. He laughed too, which made him wince in pain.

"Well, get on with it" said Captain Bask with a smirk and her arms folded. Mr. and Mrs. Storm stared back at her with blank expressions.

"Come on. I'm joking! It helps me stay positive."

"And we do need to stay positive," said Mr. Watts, who had made his way over. "Are you all right, Sebastian?"

"I'll be fine. Second degree burns that could get infected if the blisters pop. It's painful, but I'll survive." He lifted his shirt to show the crowd.

"Do you have any idea at all where we are or where they are taking us?" asked Mr. Watts.

"It's obvious that they are from Mars," interrupted Rory King, his wife Genevieve at his arm. "I'm certain that is where they are taking us. If I could just communicate with them, I could offer to pay a ransom for our release. I may not be able to pay for everyone, but I can at least negotiate for some of us."

No response. Silence. Silence and blank stares.

Rory and Genevieve turned in a huff and went back to the corner from whence they came.

"We have no idea where they are taking us," continued Mrs. Storm. "The guards' treatment of us has been largely humane—except for you, of course, honey—and their senior officer murdered one of his guards when he was abusive. It seems clear they want us in good working order, not harmed. So, whatever we *are* facing, we are facing it alive. I recommend that we cooperate as best we can until we find out their intentions."

"Agreed," said Mr. Watts. "I feel responsible for all this, and I'm determined to keep us safe. We have to find out what they intend. I'm relying on you, Captain Bask, to lead us in our captivity."

"It's my duty," she said cheerfully. "I did teach seventh grade for a few years before I joined the Air Force. If I can handle those monsters, this will be a piece of cake."

"Do you think Hanna is alright? I can't stop thinking about her and I'm so worried." The adults turned to look at young Henry, who had made his way over to Mrs. and Mr. Storm.

Mrs. Storm gently placed a hand on his shoulder. "I have no doubt she is faring far better than we are," she said. "Hanna usually remains calm in an emergency. I'm sure she has figured out how to work the radio by now and has made contact with the control team. Without all of us, she has enough food and oxygen to hold out for a rescue."

"Hah!" chortled Mr. Storm. "I'd be surprised if she hasn't landed the *Eloise* herself by now." Relief broke over Henry's visage.
Just then, the large alien with the eye patch walked in, dragging Captain Jack behind him. Everyone except Captain Bask instinctively stepped back as he approached. The alien opened the door to the cage without concern and gave Captain Jack a shove. She reached out to catch him as he collapsed inside. The alien shut the cage, engaged the lock, and moved on.

Captain Jack lay on the floor groaning.

"What did they do to you?" asked Captain Bask. "You look awful."

"Thanks a lot, Carlie," came a groan, but this time with words. "You, on the other hand, are a sight for sore eyes." Captain Jack didn't move from his position, with his back to the floor and his feet flat on the ground, his knees raised. "What's the status of the passengers?"

"With you here, everyone is accounted for except Hanna Storm," answered Captain Bask dutifully.

Captain Jack looked at Hanna's parents with concern.

"Don't worry Captain," said Mr. Storm. "My wife hid her in a storage compartment near the front early on. I don't think they got to her. We're sure she's still on the *Eloise*."

A wave of relief washed over Captain Jack, but his expression quickly returned to one of concern.

"Hanna is very resourceful," said Mrs. Storm. "I'm sure she has already contacted mission control and is working on getting home," interpreting his concern correctly. "Our energy is better spent on resolving our own situation rather than speculating on hers."

"You're right," said Captain Jack. "I've learned a few things you all probably should know." He recounted all of the facts he could remember from Slythe's remarks. Astonished, the prisoners settled in to await their fate.

CHAPTER 7

The Sendori Sanitarium for Homeless, Lost, and Discarded Children

Hanna awoke to the most beautiful singing she had ever heard. She first became aware of the soft melody while she was still sleeping. It sounded as though it were coming from somewhere deep inside her. It entranced her, and she moved toward it, searched for it, until she awoke to a tall and slender alien standing next to her bedside, singing softly. Sleep had fled and she felt wide awake and refreshed.

Hanna sat up in her bed and looked around. She recalled the previous night when Boother and Mung had dropped her off. Her pleas to remain with them were rebuffed, but she was glad of the change of scenery. She needed more information about this galaxy, about the Dorians, about the Galactic Police Force, about wormholes, about everything! Maybe she could get some of those answers here.

All around her, she could see strange-looking creatures getting out of their beds and stretching their tentacles, arms, trunks, or whatever they had. The beautiful singing trailed to a soft echo, and

Hanna hardly knew that it had stopped until that same melodic voice asked her a question.

"How are you feeling this morning, Hanna?" she asked lovingly. The words trailed in echoes until they all caught up with one another to reach her ears simultaneously. Hanna looked up to see who was speaking to her, and her eyes met those of the alien, which were a deep, glossy blue and featured prominently on her feminine face. They looked so full of something—kindness or love or honesty or goodness. Hanna searched those eyes and knew that this alien could be trusted. This alien cared about her. She didn't understand how she could know that, but she did.

"I feel fine," Hanna answered. "I feel rested. That was beautiful singing."

"Thank you," trilled the alien..

"You know my name. What's yours?" Hanna inquired.

"Tsarana," answered the alien.

Tsarana stood taller than Hanna by about a foot. Everything about her exuded elegance and grace. Her skin was moon-gray, and her robe, which appeared to flow around her body, was a pale blue. She had two arms and two legs, like a human, but that is where the similarities stopped. Her body and appendages were thinner and longer than those of a human. She had silvery, flowing hair that cascaded lightly down her back. Hanna stared for a few moments, studying this new species. It, or she, was beautiful.

"Welcome to the Sendori Sanitarium for Homeless, Lost, and Discarded Children," said the alien, her words floating into Hanna's ears. She imagined that this must be what angels sounded like. "We were told that you are from the planet Earth. Is this true?"

"If I am, is that good or bad?" Hanna asked honestly. Tsarana looked thoughtful for a moment.

"Neither good nor bad, just interesting," she answered, quite sure of herself.

"Well then, yes. I'm from Earth. Why is that so interesting?" While Mung had given Hanna his explanation, that had merely revealed that Earth was considered to be a mythical planet from what they called the Sister Galaxy. She was curious to see whether Tsarana's story matched and to get more information about this myth.

"We can discuss that later; right now, it is time for breakfast." Tsarana motioned to a doorway near the furthest row of beds. The last of the aliens were filing out of the room. Hanna felt famished, but she wanted answers. She decided to aim for a compromise.

"Promise that we can talk about it later?" Hanna asked with hopeful eyes.

"We can discuss anything you wish, but later," Tsarana answered softly. "I've given you trousers and a tunic that I believe will fit you." Tsarana motioned to the end of Hanna's bed where a neat stack of white clothes lay carefully folded on a chest. Hanna picked them up and looked them over. They seemed quite plain, but the material was both light and sturdy at the same time. It felt like a crime to put such clean, white clothes on a body that had not been washed.

"Can I take a shower first?" Hanna asked.

"You mean bathe, correct? Yes, you may bathe. I believe Earth people use dihydrogen monoxide to bathe. Is that correct?"

Hanna thought for a quick moment. "Yes, that's correct. Two parts hydrogen, one part oxygen. And some soap would be nice, but I don't know what it's made of."

"Soap would be nice? I do not understand," Tsarana said, confused.

"I also require soap to bathe," Hanna tried again. She marveled at how the translator differed in its translations among the species she had encountered thus far.

"Yes, of course. It 'would be nice' to have soap. I understand," said Tsarana with a look of satisfaction. "Do you require privacy as well?"

"Yes, please," Hanna said gratefully. She had not thought about that.

The shower was similar to the one on Boother's and Mung's ship, but it was larger and more technologically advanced. A nozzle emerged from the wall, but there were no handles or knobs. Instead, there was a panel that Tsarana tapped with her long slender fingers. Hanna assumed that she must be programming the shower. After the shower began spraying water, Tsarana adjusted the temperature and provided Hanna with a square of soap, though Hanna didn't see where this had come from. It had a mild citrusy smell to it, which Hanna found refreshing.

"I also require a toothbrush," Hanna said politely, "oh, and toothpaste."

"Please explain, Hanna," requested Tsarana. Hanna explained their purpose and Tsarana walked over to a panel on the far wall. She touched the screen with her fingers, and lines began to appear. Hanna watched as they took shape, forming a toothbrush.

"Does this look correct?"

"Yes, it does," answered Hanna, impressed. Tsarana pushed a button, and a tray popped out containing a toothbrush.

"I need to learn how to program your 3-D printers," Hanna said aloud to herself.

"Our what?" asked Tsarana.

"Your matter synthesizer."

"Fascinating. It does indeed 'print' three-dimensional objects." Hanna felt a touch of deja vu. "It is quite simple to operate but can create a wide variety of useful things. Toothbrush is now stored in its memory."

Hanna grabbed her towel from her pack and headed into the shower. She managed to bathe comfortably and dressed in her new all-white outfit. Hanna had never been particularly interested in how clothes looked, being more concerned with how functional they were. However, she couldn't help but notice that these clothes looked exceptionally good on her. The pockets were in all the right places, with a few extra ones on the trouser legs. Hanna loved clothing with lots of pockets. She often lamented the lack of pockets in what was considered to be fashionable women's attire on Earth. If she had her way, even her shoes would have pockets! Hanna moved her hand away from one of the pockets and it sealed on its own. Only when Hanna put her hand by the seam did it reopen, as if by magic. She was impressed.

Now dressed, Hanna paused, uncertain of what she should do next. Her silent question was answered when Tsarana opened the door and motioned for Hanna to follow her. They walked down a long corridor before stepping into a large elevator with transparent walls. As the elevator descended into a large atrium, the stunning architecture took Hanna's breath away. The building comprised approximately twenty stories, and the space where the roof would have been was open to a pale green sky. Exotic vegetation of every color on the spectrum floated in hovering pots at different elevations. There was also an array of flying alien fauna with feathers and skin that were equally as vibrant as the plants. Hanna soaked in the wondrous spectacle. She had so many questions and wanted to document every plant and creature she saw. She reached for her satchel, but it was not there; she had left it in her room. No matter. Hanna had to focus on finding her parents.

The elevator came to a halt, and the doors opened up to a room lined with tables and benches that stretched from one side of the large dining hall to the other. The air was fresh and smelled of citrus, which fascinated Hanna's senses. Creatures of all shapes, sizes, and colors sat at these tables, gobbling down whatever it was on the trays in front of them. Several of them were taking empty trays over to a counter set beneath a clear tube. The tray and all of its contents floated up with a whoosh. Hanna's translator worked at full speed.

She managed to catch snippets of conversations, but mostly she just heard a cacophony of noise. Suddenly, the noise was replaced by whispers, and numerous aliens began to turn toward her and stare. She caught amazed whispers of "Earth" and "myth." Hanna looked around the room at the crowd of aliens and reminded herself to breathe.

"This is where you pick up your meal and there is where you put your tray when your meal is finished." Tsarana pointed as she spoke, and Hanna paid careful attention. "You may sit wherever you like."

A commotion at a nearby table distracted Tsarana. "I will find you after breakfast. You have orientation to attend today," and with that, she moved gracefully off to see what the ruckus was about.

Hanna's eyes followed Tsarana toward the scene. As Tsarana approached, a large and tentacled alien alerted his two coconspirators and the three of them scurried off, leaving the most beautiful being Hanna had ever seen standing alone. He was almost human in appearance. He had a slender build with slightly pointed ears and a soft blue color to his skin. He was covered in food and stared at the floor with a look not of embarrassment but of shame. Tsarana put a slender arm around him and helped wipe the food away. She motioned him over to the counter where food was being served, and he made his way over there, never taking his eyes off the floor.

Hanna would have stared at him for hours had her tummy not rumbled insistently. She had not eaten in some time and was ravenous. She walked over to the serving counter and stood next to the beautiful blue alien. She rehearsed in her mind the best way to start a conversation, but nothing seemed appropriate. Carrying his food on his tray, he began to walk away when Hanna blurted out "I'm new here, and, umm, I don't know anybody. I mean, I know Tsarana, but I don't know anyone else, but I'd like to...can I sit with you?" Hanna finished with an awkward smile.

The blue creature looked over his shoulder with a slightly bewildered look, as though this were a new experience for him. "I didn't understand a lot of that. Did you ask to sit next to me?" he asked in a less than confident tone.

"Yes, yes, I would like to sit next to you for breakfast," Hanna said, relieved that she had managed to say anything at all. "Is that okay?"

"Why?" he asked, seriously. Hanna hesitated, unsure how to answer his question. She wanted to say that he was gorgeous and that she wanted to spend eternity just staring at him, but she settled on a different, more respectable truth.

"Well, umm, I'm new here and I wanted to meet you, or anyone. Everyone else seems to be finishing up and we're just getting started, so I thought we could sit together." Hanna hoped that this would be enough to convince him.

"I guess so," he said, suspicious. He led the way to a large table that was now empty. The remaining occupants of the cafeteria stared at the couple. Hanna was unsure whether they were staring at him or at her. She looked around and saw that Tsarana had left the room. Perhaps she had gone in pursuit of the bullies.

For the first time, Hanna looked down at what she had been served for breakfast. On her tray was a pile of white, pasty stuff, resembling oatmeal, and some green smooth stuff, resembling pudding, and some brown-looking pellets, which resembled either raisins or rabbit poop; she wasn't sure which.

Hanna had eaten strange food before. In the wilderness, her father had taught her, "if you're too cautious, you'll die from starvation; too cavalier and you'll die from the Rocky Mountain Quick Step." Her stomach rumbled again, and Hanna decided that this was an occasion to be more cavalier than cautious. She took what resembled a flattened spoon and scraped some gray paste onto it. A quick sniff revealed that it was odorless. She put it in her mouth and discovered it was also flavorless. "Could be worse," she thought.

Hanna's dining companion had not uttered a word, nor had he begun to eat. He simply stared as Hanna ate. It was an awkward silence, and Hanna decided to initiate the dialogue.

"So, I'm Hanna, Hanna Storm. What's your name?" The blue alien studied her intently, as though assessing her sincerity. measured her sincerity with his eyes.

"I have not yet chosen my name," he said. Hanna was curious and wanted to know more, but she kept her questions simple for now.

"How long have you been here?" she asked, shoving a helping of white mush into her mouth.

"Only a few galactic standard days," he murmured.

"Oh. I just got here yesterday, but you probably noticed that. Where are you from?"

"You really don't know, do you?" he asked in surprise.

Hanna pondered this statement. Clearly, something about this alien caused him to feel ashamed, but she couldn't imagine why anyone so beautiful might be ashamed—not that ugly people needed to be ashamed of anything...Calm down, Hanna!

"Before yesterday, I had never met anyone who was from a different planet," Hanna stated casually. "Where I grew up, we're just beginning to imagine what kinds of life might be in the universe besides us. I don't know anything."

This seemed to satisfy the blue alien and he began to relax. "I am from a planet called Makara."

"What were those other three doing to you? Why were they so mean?" Hanna tried to make her voice sound sympathetic and understanding to reflect how she felt.

"We change our forms to join existing societies, but we are rarely accepted by them."

"Change your form? You mean, like shape-shifting?"

"I guess. We do 'shift' our shapes, so you're right in a way. Makarans evolved to mimic other species. When we find a species we like, we select one of them and begin a transformation process to mimic their DNA. We become them."

Hanna cringed a little, imagining herself being deflated like a balloon while an alien sucked up all of her DNA. Her expression was not lost on her blue companion. He started to rise, an expression of shame on his face. Hanna stood and pleaded with him to sit back down, which he did.

"We have to physically touch the person we want to become and then consciously enter the metamorphosis. Nothing happens to the other person, but many species feel as though their identity has been stolen. It's not in the Galactic Treaty or anything, but most systems have banned Makarans who have undergone the metamorphosis. We are difficult to find, but anytime two different people with the same genetic markers show up, there is a hunt to identify the Makaran and banish them, or worse."

Hanna was appalled, but more importantly, she had questions.

"If you completely change your DNA, how does your species perpetuate itself? Where do baby Makarans come from?"

"When we hatch from our shells, we are hatched with a small egg of our own. The egg is buried and draws nutrients from the ground until it grows large enough to breach the surface, where it hatches with an egg of its own, which it buries, and the cycle sustains itself."

"That is so fascinating. So, you could touch me and exit your metamorphosis as an exact copy of me? That's amazing! My mother always taught me that I get to choose who I am, but you take that to a whole other level!"

"You aren't disturbed by this?"

"Not at all. I'm amazed by it. Oh!" she said with a sudden realization. "That's why you haven't chosen a name yet. You haven't chosen what species you want to be."

"That is correct. I don't know who I want to be," he said forlornly.

"Well, for now, I think you should just be you. You seem really great, and I like you," Hanna said honestly.

"Just be me? I don't understand. I'm hated by everyone. Why would I want to be me?"

"Oh please. I like you. So, if you want to be honest, you need to say that you are hated by many and liked by some."

The blue alien stopped speaking and looked down, a mix of confusion and disbelief crossing his face. Perplexion. "I like you too," he finally said. "I've never had a friend before."

"Well, now you do, Blue. That's what I'm going to call you, by the way, until you choose your own name."

Blue began to weep a little, and Hanna reached out and grabbed his hand to comfort him. That's when they heard the laughing. The three bullies from earlier had returned and now snickered at the two new-found friends.

"I guess there are bullies in every galaxy," Hanna said, eyeballing the alien she had deduced was the ringleader. He had dark green skin with occasional yellow splotches. His face had eyes, ears, nose, and mouth, though his head was much larger than that of a human. He had no arms but had four tentacles, two on each side, and one thick tentacle for each leg.

"Why are you bothering with this Makaran. He's just going to steal your soul. I don't know why they let him stay here. On my planet, we just kill them when we find them. Maybe I'll kill him. Maybe I'll kill both of you!"

The other two aliens, both from the same planet as their dear leader, laughed uproariously. Hanna rose to her feet. The alien bully placed a tentacle on her shoulder and was sliding it up to her face. Tray in hand, she smashed it across the alien's face, and he fell to the floor.

"No unwanted touching! Ever!" Hanna warned.

An alarm suddenly sounded, and a large blob of an alien slithered into the room. It was wearing an official looking uniform and the cluster of aliens who had gathered to watch stood very, very still with their eyes downcast, but not Hanna. She maintained eye contact with...wait, no...yes, they were eyes, she was pretty sure. Was that a wig? It *was* a wig and a hideous one at that. Several sizes too small, the wig balanced precariously on top of a giant round head. The alien's width seemed immeasurable and it stood a good two feet taller than Hanna.

"Ah, the so-called Earth child," she said in a deep disdainful voice, looking down at Hanna over what would have been her nose if she'd had one. "My, my. Merciful stars! A filthy Makaran! Don't you touch me! I've no doubt you two are the cause of this mess. Striking another student? How vile! Both of you will report to the detention hall. Now!"

Hanna started to protest, but she was cut short by the beastly administrator.

"I said NOW!" she seethed. "Tsarana! Blast it to the stars! Tsarana!" she screeched into a small communication device. Headmistress Blurch's obnoxious, urgent shouting was juxtaposed with Tsarana's calm, melodic voice.

"Yes, Headmistress Blurch?" came the angelic voice.

"Come to the dining hall at once and escort the Earth child and this disgusting Makaran to the detention hall. And don't let it touch you. He'll steal your soul."

"Yes, Headmistress, I will be there soon," Tsarana said patiently.

Hanna was furious, but before she could protest, Headmistress Blurch twirled around, if the series of slow, short lurches could be called a twirl, and rolled away with her head upturned.

#

The detention hall was sparsely furnished with a few small benches and tables. Hanna and Blue sat still. Speaking was not permitted.

Hanna was incensed at the injustices she had witnessed. Those other three tentacle-wielding bullies should be in here, not her. She had always been a model student; this was a new experience for her that brought with it novel emotions.

No monitors or cameras were visible in the room, the sole occupant of which was a humanoid with bright red skin, as if it had a full-body sunburn, and a solitary arm that protruded from its chest. This alien was in charge of detention. Attached to the arm was an enormous red hand holding a book. This creature said nothing and completely ignored Hanna and Blue.

"Is it always this unfair?" Hanna whispered to Blue.

"I don't understand," Blue responded, perplexed. "Fairness is unattainable. I thought everybody knew that."

The one-handed red alien put his book on the desk, stood up, walked over to where they were sitting, and glared them into silence. Having accomplished his duty, he returned to his seat and continued to read.

Hanna had no idea how long they would be there. The monotony was broken when Tsarana glided into the room.

"I greet you, Mr. Gambrio. You are dismissed. I will oversee the remainder of their detention."

"I greet you, Tsarana," grumbled Gambrio. He eyed her. "Are you certain? Headmistress Blurch was highly specific in her instructions."

"I have alerted Headmistress Blurch. If you have objections, you can take them up with her. Or I could issue a formal citation to your file for failing to follow a direct order by a superior." This last sentence got his attention.

"That won't be necessary, Tsarana. I wish you well." Mr. Gambrio gave a curt nod, glared at Hanna and Blue, and departed. He turned to face the room once more so that he could close the door with his only appendage.

"I'm so sorry, children. I should have warned you about Headmistress Blurch," Tsarana said in a sincerely apologetic tone. "Children have been known to go missing on her watch, so it is best not to attract her attention, let alone her wrath."

Hanna and Blue remained silent, uncertain as to whether they could speak.

"I promised you a conversation about Earth, Hanna. I'm happy to answer any questions you might have." Hanna took this invitation to speak and began her inquisition.

"The Corridor Patrol did not believe me when I said I was from Earth. They said it was a myth. Where did the myth originate? What does it mean?"

"The story has been told for many generations. When the Dorian Empire first began to expand through the Galaxy, one system had the strength to oppose it: the Kamal-Etet system. The system itself was ultimately destroyed, but not until the Kal-Ets had rallied almost all of the remaining systems in Galaxy Prime, unifying them under the Galactic Treaty. Though Kamal-Etet was lost, the members of the Galactic Treaty were able to curb the progress of the Dorian Empire, and the border has been maintained for millennia now. Are you familiar with corridors?"

"A little. I know they are unidirectional and need corridor engines to function. They only work for limited distances too."

"That is the general understanding, but some scientists have theorized the existence of naturally occurring corridors that lead to other galaxies. The Kamal-Etet system supposedly boasted one such corridor that linked to a small system in the Sister Galaxy with a single habitable planet. It is said that the great Emperor Erthe of

Kamal-Etet escaped there before his system fell to the Dorians. The planet was dubbed Earth after the Emperor. The Kamal-Etet system now lies in Dorian territory. A few adventurers over the millennia claimed to have found the corridor, and some even claimed to have visited Earth, but these are largely dismissed as hoaxes, as are beings who claim to be *from* Earth."

"That makes sense!" Hanna said excitedly. "Boother and Mung, the Corridor Patrol officers that brought me here, were very concerned about the connection between the Dorians and me being from Earth. If the stories are true and there's a wormhole between Earth and Kamal-Etet, and the Dorians found it, it makes my claim to be from Earth more credible."

"Wait," said Blue. "You really are from Earth?"

"Yes! I mean, I don't know about any Emperor Erthe, but we call the planet 'Earth' in my native language. Some other cultures on my planet call it a variation of Terra, from the original Latin, like Tierra in Spanish or Terre in French." Hanna caught the somewhat confused looks of her audience and ended her linguistics lesson. It dawned on her that irrespective of whether she said "Earth" or "Terra," their universal translators may have interpreted both as the same word in their respective native languages, which would have made Hanna sound a little cuckoo.

"What about the Dorian Empire? Do you have any idea where they may have taken my parents?" inquired Hanna, hopeful.

"Very little is known about the Dorian Empire. Most of our information came from our direct confrontation millennia ago. Who knows how they might have evolved since then? All we know is that the borders hold. You would have to find a Dorian to gather any insight, and they are rare in the Galactic Treaty systems." Tsarana's little frown suggested a recognition that her answer must be discouraging for the poor Earth child. Hanna, however, was starting to plan how she might get hold of a Dorian.

"Just one more question," Hanna ventured. "Where is the Galactic Police Force Command? I may want to properly thank Boother and Mung someday."

Tsarana hesitated, perhaps uncertain of Hanna's motives.

"That is located in the Capital system," offered Blue, "along with all other galactic military and administrative institutions." He spoke as if repeating something he had memorized from a textbook. He flashed a victorious smile.

Hanna now had a purpose. She had to somehow find a Dorian, retrieve the *Eloise* from the Galactic Police Force Command, find her parents, and then find this Kamal-Etet system and the naturally occurring corridor that led to Earth!

"Piece of cake," Hanna thought to herself. "Piece of chocolate frosted cake." She tried to ignore the pit in her stomach that warned her of the odds of success.

#

Boother and Mung stood in front of thirteen aliens seated in a semicircle. Each alien represented a different species, but they were all wearing similar uniforms, each with numerous pins and buttons and patches that signified their rank, seniority, and many, many accomplishments. Boother's bumps were a nervous green. Mung stood tall and confident.

"That is our report," said Mung, officially.

"Most disconcerting," said the centermost seated alien. Her giant eyes flashed while her two long antennae vibrated wildly. "Most disconcerting indeed."

"I agree," stated another panelist with enormous, rock-like hands that thudded on the table. "If the Dorians have discovered how to open a corridor to another galaxy, we must take action to fortify our defenses."

"Colleagues, colleagues, please!" rumbled a third alien. "The Sister Galaxy corridor is just a myth, as we all well know. Let us not forget that it is just a myth."

"Concurrence," shrieked another. "The Hanna Storm cannot possibly be from Earth." The debate descended into chaos as the aliens began speaking over one another, many shouting animatedly. Mung and Boother listened to the arguing. They had made their full honest report and repeated all the details Hanna had shared.

The centermost alien picked up a long stick with her pincers and slammed it against a gong that stood by her side.

"Members, please," she admonished. "Her genetic structure was not in our database. Her spacecraft is not in our database, and none of you have seen the like of its design. Yet, her story is too fanciful to be entirely true. We must get to the bottom of this mystery, and she holds all the answers. Boother and Mung, you must bring this Hanna Storm before the Chamber. We would question her ourselves. You are to retrieve her from the Sendori Sanitarium for Homeless, Lost, and Discarded Children and bring her before us as soon as possible. Dock her spacecraft at the yard for further analysis."

"It will be done, Lady of the Chamber," stated Mung with an official air. He gave a curt nod, and he and Boother exited the chamber.

"Lady of the Chamber," said one of the seated aliens who had been silent during the entire debate. "Intelligence has a covert operative in the Dorian Empire. I will contact him and find out if he can corroborate any of this."

"Please do so," she agreed.

CHAPTER 8

Just Another School Day

After what must have been only a few hours in detention, Hanna and Blue rejoined the regular school day and ended up in Ms. Golgolax's Galactic History class. Students sat at their own individual desks, which were aligned in neat rows. Ms. Golgolax sat daydreaming at the front of the room while students searched through their tablet readers. Ms. Golgolax greeted the two newcomers and waved them to their assigned seating.

"You are to study the chapters on the post galactic war renaissance." Hanna and Blue nodded their understanding and took their seats. The tablet readers were about the size of a textbook and Hanna's curiosity was piqued. She didn't even know how to turn the machine on. She picked up the tablet and the screen lit up. The text on the screen was made up of a cacophony of lines, curves, circles, squares, and every geometric shape imaginable. Hanna could not read it, yet the words came to her mind in English. It was a strange sensation to look at alien writing and understand it in English. She imagined it must be similar to how blind people read braille, as little bumps on a page are transformed into words as they touch them.

"What language is this?" she whispered to Blue, who was seated next to her.

"It's Galactic Standard," Blue replied matter-of-factly.

Hanna pressed on the jumble of characters that she was sure said "Index." She looked through the various chapters and found Chapter 375, which was entitled, "Post Galactic War Renaissance," but that was not what Hanna cared to learn right now. She needed information that would help her accomplish her mission. She found a chapter on the Dorian Empire and began to read carefully.

The Dorian Empire's economy is based on acquired foreign labor. Rather than rely on innovative technological advances in robotics and machinery, the Dorians raid other systems to acquire laborers for their factories and mines.

It occurred to Hanna that the mines would be a good place to start looking for her parents. Perhaps there was some information in here about mine and factory locations. She searched through the entries and the index but found no maps or mention of worlds where factories or mines might be concentrated. In fact, the section on the Dorian Empire was very sparse.

The rest of the school day did not yield any more useful information for Hanna, but she did learn several interesting things about physics, math, alien biology, and the politics of the Galactic Treaty systems. She and Blue were in nearly every class together and had the good fortune that nobody wanted to sit next to either of them.

"What's next, Blue?" Hanna asked.

"The worst is next," said Blue. "The final class of the day is Physical Recreation."

Hanna followed Blue into a spacious hall. Numerous, diverse aliens were engaging in a variety of strange sports and exercise routines. All around, the students engaged in feats of strength, speed, and agility. A tiny pickle-shaped green alien blew hard on a whistle, and everyone stopped.

"All right, you dried leaves," he shouted into a voice-enhancing device, not unlike a megaphone. "It's time to play some target ball. Go put on a target vest. It does not matter if you are red or blue, there are enough target vests for everyone."

Everyone suddenly rushed to an open container and brutishly grabbed at the vests. Hanna saw Blue's bully and his cronies donning red vests, so she grabbed a blue vest for herself and one for Blue. He pushed the vest back at Hanna when she tried to hand it to him, eyes down and head shaking.

"Everybody plays!" said the coach, apparently quashing Blue's hopes of sitting out the game. "The rules are simple. Hit your opponent's target centered on their vest. It will light up and they will be eliminated. If you get hit, your vest will light up and you are out, so don't let your opponent hit your target. Ready? Go!"

A large box attached to the ceiling opened and it rained down hundreds of small rubber-like balls, each roughly the size of a tennis ball. Everyone made a mad dash for the ammunition. Hanna picked up as many as she could and ran back to face the opposing team. This game was a simple mix of dodgeball and laser tag, and she excelled at both.

Nearly everyone targeted Blue in their initial volley, and he was immediately eliminated. He didn't even bother to try dodging. He sulked over to the benches and sat down. Hanna was targeted to a lesser degree, but she had enough awareness and agility to avoid being hit by the initial onslaught.

"My turn," she said under her breath. She unleashed two quick throws and accurately hit the target vests of two opposing team members. She searched for the three youths who had bullied her and Blue earlier. Having identified her targets, she began to formulate her strategy. Each of them had four tentacle arms. They were throwing with two and defending with two. Hanna would have to get them to drop their tentacles to expose their target vests.

Her first victim never saw it coming. She threw a ball with all her might right into his face. He raised the tentacles covering his target vest and she let fly another ball that hit its mark. One down, two to go. The second victim was aware that his friend was out but failed to realize that Hanna was the cause. He turned his attention to a different target and met the same fate of one quick ball to the face and a second to the target vest.

The lead bully witnessed this and targeted Hanna. He unleashed four quick throws and Hanna managed, just barely, to dodge them all. She returned a volley of three throws to his target, and he blocked all three. He was now defending his face and his target vest. It was time for a new strategy. Hanna was unsure whether it would work; her understanding of this alien's biology was limited, to say the least. However, she observed many similarities among the species she had encountered. She wound up and let a ball fly right between his thick tentacle legs. It worked magnificently. He doubled over and exposed his target vest, which Hanna managed to hit easily. She hadn't noticed the others get tagged out, but she was the last one standing.

"Blue team has it," said the coach.

Hanna ran back to Blue, fists pumping in the air with a great deal of excitement. "Did you see that?" she squealed.

Blue's head was down, and he grumbled his response. "Congratulations." He stood up and sulked out of the gym. Hanna followed.

#

Hanna and Blue huddled together at their dining hall table while the noisy crowd bustled around them. They had an entire table to themselves, and Blue avoided making eye contact with anyone, even Hanna.

"I'm sorry people bully you, Blue," she said, pausing mid-bite.

"I just have to deal with it, and you are not doing yourself any favors by befriending me," he reasoned.

"Both of those statements are false," replied Hanna. "Do you come from a species of liars?"

"No," Blue said, a little upset at the insult. "Of course not."

"You shouldn't have to deal with it, and I benefit a great deal from being friends with you."

Moments after Hanna's insightful statement, the bullying resumed, with a few shouts and jeers and cautions to Hanna not to touch the demon boy, but it wasn't until someone threw a mess of gray paste at Blue that she exploded. She jumped onto the cafeteria table and let out a loud two-fingered whistle, like a football coach at practice. The crowd went silent.

"You should all be ashamed! How would you feel if someone made fun of your home planet, or called you names, or told lies about your species? You'd feel terrible. I'm not afraid to be friends with this guy because he is a being just like you or me and deserves the same respect!" She spoke with anger and authority.

Blue's face displayed a look of mortification mixed with respect, perhaps with a hint of gratitude. With the exception of Tsarana, he had probably never experienced someone standing up for him or even willing to interact with him. Everyone else remained silent, their eyes glued to the spectacle. Hanna looked down at Blue and extended her hand to him. He hesitated. She motioned again and he grabbed her hand, joining her up on the table. She raised their held hands into the air.

"If you can't respect someone different from you, I don't have time for you. The next person who insults my friend here or throws something at him will have to deal with me. I'm Hanna Storm and I'm from Earth, so watch yourselves!"

The room was silent. Blue was not the only one who had never seen someone stand up for his species. The dumbfounded student body stared blankly at both Hanna and Blue. A flash of gray slop flew through the air and landed on Hanna's face. The crowd erupted, hysterical with laughter. Hanna was incensed! She spotted the alien bully who had been on the receiving end of her breakfast tray earlier that morning exchanging high fives—or ones, or tentacles, or whatever—with his two partners in crime, having apparently recovered from his target ball injuries. Hanna started to get down from the table but felt the pressure of Blue's grip hold her back.

"Please don't," he requested. "You made your point and I feel gratitude. Let's just finish eating."

Hanna exhaled and calmed herself. They climbed down and resumed their meal. It wasn't long before she noticed a few aliens from a different table rise from where they were seated and make their way over to her and Blue. She prepared for a fight.

"May we sit with you?" asked a young Mung. "Your words had meaning, and we'd like to join you and the Makaran."

"His name is Blue," she said with a bit of anger still coating her words.

"I understood Makarans don't take names until they undergo metamorphosis," said Mung.

"She gave me the name. It's temporary until I choose one for myself," explained Blue.

"How pretentious!" argued the Mung, "taking it upon yourself to name someone you have no right to name and choosing a name based solely on the color of his skin. If you accept it though, Blue, I will cede to your wishes and refer to you as Blue. You deserve that respect. We ask that you respect us and our wishes by not touching us if we join you."

Hanna felt the anger mounting inside her but paused for a moment to assess the situation. The fact that they were at the table constituted a victory, and she decided that now wasn't the time to discourage their atrociously imperfect bravery.

Hanna noticed Blue smiling as he engaged in conversation with the others, and it warmed her heart. There was something about the Mung's words that nagged at her though. Was it wrong for her to give him a name? Was it wrong for her to call him by the color of his skin? She thought back to the lessons she had learned about race from her parents and her own family's history. How did enslaved people feel when they were forced to take new names? How did it feel to have a boss change your name because they found it difficult to pronounce? It was completely pretentious. She tried to imagine giving someone on Earth the name Black or Brown or Red or even White, and her hands drifted toward her nauseous tummy.

"Blue," she said. "The Mung was right. I had no right to name you and I shouldn't have used a name based solely on the color of your skin. I'm so sorry," she said. "Can you forgive me?"

Blue looked confused. "I'm thankful that my friend gave me a name," he said sincerely, looking at his skin color. "It's accurate and I like the name Blue. There's nothing to forgive." He grabbed Hanna's hand and smiled.

"Blue it is then," Hanna said.

"To admit one's mistakes is a rarity among the species of this galaxy," said the young Mung. "I'm impressed."

"It can be a rarity among us Earth people as well," admitted Hanna, "but we try to learn from our mistakes. Thank you for speaking up." The Mung looked up with confusion.

"Speaking *up*? As opposed to speaking down? Or perhaps as opposed to not speaking at all. What a strange language!" The Mung returned to his conversation with Blue.

#

That evening, as Hanna prepared for bed, she checked the contents of her pack: towel, pocketknife, Vaseline, headlamp, duct tape, water bottle, change of clothes, mirror, candy bars, astronomy book…wait, candy bars! She took one out and devoured the chocolatey goodness; it was enough to make her miss Earth. Rarely had she wished to be somewhere else while on an adventure. Now, she only had two bars left.

For comfort, she reviewed her strategy again—find a Dorian, retrieve the *Eloise* from the Corridor Patrol, find her parents, and find the naturally occurring corridor that leads to Earth in the Kamal-Etet system. She added a final step: Eat a huge candy bar when I get back to Earth.

Hanna yawned, stretched, and knelt down to say her prayers. Her father was very religious, like go-to-church-every-Sunday religious, and her mother was agnostic. Hanna wasn't sure what she believed, but she found comfort in prayer. At the very least, it offered her a means of meditating on and analyzing the events of the day. In asking for help, she was able to organize her thoughts around what she needed to accomplish; in articulating what she was thankful for, she was able to experience gratitude, which helped her have a positive state of mind and gave her hope. Plus, she sort of felt like there was someone listening.

Hanna believed in the power of gratitude. She recalled an experience from an Extreme Adventure when one of the local guides with whom her parents often worked had shown up to their next adventure without an arm. Hanna had been very upset.

"Hanna," he had said, "It was an unfortunate car accident. I can be upset that I lost my arm, or I can be grateful that I didn't lose my head. I suppose I can be both at the same time, but it's hard to be upset when I'm still feeling grateful just to be alive." Hanna had taken that lesson to heart and tried to meditate on what made her grateful. She thanked God, if She or He was out there, for her parents and her friend Blue. She prayed that the passengers would stay alive long enough for Hanna to find them. She climbed into bed, aware that all of the other alien kids were staring at her and her strange bedtime routine, and fell fast asleep.

#

Hanna awoke with a start, unable to breathe or make a sound. She frantically grabbed at whatever was covering her mouth and nose. It was somebody's hand! She tore at it wildly without success. Her eyes adjusted to the dark, and she saw a giant red outstretched arm. The body to which it was attached carried a head with a mustached face smirking joyously. Hanna lost consciousness.

CHAPTER 9

Into the Mines

The shackled humans wielded rudimentary mining tools in an effort to extract some vein of metallic ore from the mine wall. A single chain ran through the leg cuffs that were secured to each of the captives, who were evenly spaced every few yards. Mr. Storm lifted a giant sledgehammer and slammed it down on an unfortunate boulder that shattered into several pieces. Mrs. Storm and Henry shoveled up the pieces and placed them into a nearby cart. Mr. Watts hunched near the mine wall with a small pickaxe, delicately extricating a piece of metallic rock from an otherwise benign boulder. The cheerful Marie was close by his side performing a similar task.

Mr. Watts paused his labor and wiped the sweat from his brow with the spotted neckerchief he carried in his shirt pocket. He breathed heavily, gulping in the damp mine air.

"Are you okay, Mr. Watts?" asked Marie.

"I am fine, dear, thank you. I just need a little water."

"You should take a rest," she suggested.

An angry hiss from one of the guards interrupted their conversation.

Crack!

Mr. Watts winced as he grabbed his shoulder, a trickle of blood running down his arm. The guard smirked as he slowly coiled his whip and hung it back on his belt.

"Please, he just needs some water," Marie pleaded.

The guard motioned to another, who exited the cavern and returned with containers of water for everyone. He motioned to Captain Jack.

"Tell them it's time for a short break and to take water. Then back to work," the guard sneered. Captain Jack relayed the message to the other captives while the guard distributed the water. Mr. Watts raised his container to drink when the whip cracked again, and his water spilled to the floor.

The laughing guards departed and took the half-filled mining carts with them. They were there to ensure that the work was happening, not to keep laborers from escaping. That was the chain's job. Taking the mining carts was simply an additional precaution. When the laborers took a break, the guards could as well. The result was a lot of breaks, for which the humans were grateful.

Mr. and Mrs. Storm walked over to Mr. Watts and Marie to share some of their water. Captain Jack, Captain Bask, and Haruka followed suit.

"Thank you," said Mr. Watts sincerely. Despite the frequent breaks, he was pale and his breathing was labored.

"Does anyone have any extra water for Genevieve and me? We'd be happy to compensate you fairly for it," Rory solicited.

"What would you trade for it, Rory?" asked Captain Bask. "How about your pants?"

Mr. Watts blushed. Mrs. Storm snorted with laughter. Mr. Storm smiled.

"Give her your pants, darling," instructed Genevieve indifferently. "Do you want me to die of thirst?"

"No Bunny-Cakes. Of course not. It's just that...."

"I knew you didn't care about me. You don't even care if I die!" Genevieve stormed off and Rory followed.

Captain Jack glared disapprovingly at Captain Bask.

"Come on! That was funny," defended Captain Bask. "I've said it before, and I'll say it again. Humor keeps me going in tough situation....and that was funny," she argued.

"Definitely funny," agreed Mr. Storm, "but we have more important things to do while the guards are out. How is the escape plan going?" he asked Captain Jack.

"The guards don't give much intelligence, but I did figure out from their conversations that there is contact between the mines and 'the enemy.' Apparently, smugglers bring in needed supplies from what they call the Treaty planets. They take raw ore as payment. Valentina had to take one of the ore carts all the way to a landing pad. She saw a different species of alien unload crates and load up the raw ore from the carts, so that provides some corroboration."

Henry, who stood unnoticed several steps away, overheard his aunt's name, Valentina, and made his way closer to the apparently private conversation.

"Do they load the whole cart or just the contents?" asked Mrs. Storm.

"Let's find out." Captain Jack looked up and called over to Valentina, who was sitting in quiet contemplation. She rose and made her way over, nodding at Henry, who was pretending not to listen, lying on his back and staring at the ceiling.

"They take the full carts into the hull of the ship, and they come out empty. That's all I know," she shrugged..

"That is good enough; it's worth taking the risk," resolved Mrs. Storm. Seeing her collaborators' inquisitive expressions, she continued. "If one of us can hide in the bottom of a cart, covered by enough ore, they might make it onto the alien ship without being noticed. If they can stow away to another planet and get us some help, we might have a chance to get out of here."

"There are many unknowns here," said Haruka. "If our mole were to be discarded into a large hold, they could be crushed during the fall, even if they are not discovered. The air in the holding compartment may not be suitable for humans to breathe. I think there is a high risk of getting injured, caught, or killed."

"All risks, I agree," said Captain Bask. "However, if they are loading the ore onto a ship, it's more likely to go into a room rather than a hold. The atmosphere is the same for us and these lizard people. Maybe it's the same for the other aliens as well?"

"The aliens from the cargo ship were not lizard people. They were not wearing any sort of protective headgear," said Valentina. "They were far away, but their skin was pink, and they had large ears with snouts resembling an Earth pig, but narrower and longer."

"Haruka is right. It is very risky. Sara is also right. It is worth the risk," said Captain Bask.

"What do you think, honey?" asked Mrs. Storm.

"Who's going to go?" questioned Mr. Storm. "I would volunteer, but there won't be enough room to conceal me. It would have to be Haruka or Captain Jack or...."

"Or me," interrupted Henry. "I'm the skinniest one here."

"Out of the question," said Valentina. "I already promised your mother I would keep you safe during the space cruise. I've clearly failed at that, but at least you're alive. I won't allow you to put your life in jeopardy."

"But...."

"I agree," said Captain Jack. "I have military training designed just for these situations."

"You have military training to escape lizard aliens from a mine on a foreign planet in space?" asked Henry.

"I have been trained for escape and survival in hostile foreign environments," Captain Jack defended. "Even if it's not specifically for this situation, it's more training than you've had. Why are we even discussing this?" he pleaded with the group. "I'm going. That's final!"

"No, Captain," disagreed Haruka. "You are the only one who can understand the aliens. Your absence would be noticed immediately. You may be a Marine, but I am Haruka Moriyama. Also, I am smaller than you and fit better in the mine cart." Captain Jack opened his mouth to argue, but Mr. Storm beat him to it.

"She's right, Captain."

"Jack, she's our best shot," agreed Captain Bask.

"All right. All right. You make good points," Captain Jack relented. "Except the Japanese/Marines comparison. I don't agree with that."

"Agree to disagree," said Haruka laughing. Everyone chuckled and relaxed into the plan.

"I don't mean to be a downer, but we still have the guards and the chains to deal with," said Captain Bask.

"We'll have to position someone in the cart during a break," said Mr. Storm.

"It won't work, darling," said Mrs. Storm. "Look around. No carts. The guards usually take breaks after the carts are sent. If they are not completely full, they take the carts with them on their break. They'll be here when the carts are being filled."

Mr. Storm turned a little red.

"Don't be embarrassed, dear. It's an easy thing to miss." Mrs. Storm was good at a lot of things, but comforting her husband when he was embarrassed was not one of them.

"Okay," said Captain Jack. "We need a distraction, and we need to figure out how to get the chain loose so we can reposition ourselves."

"How do we get loose?" asked Mr. Storm.

"I could pick the lock on my ankle restraint," answered Captain Jack.

"You can do that?" asked Captain Carlie Bask. "And here I thought I knew everything about you."

"I wasn't always a Marine," Jack said.

"You joined when you were seventeen!" rebutted Carlie.

"Before that I, umm, worked as a locksmith," he winked.

"Oh really," said Carlie.

"Look!" Jack unloaded. "I have a lot of experience opening locks and right now it doesn't matter why. I'll tell you all about it when we get back to Earth. Does that work for everyone?"

"That works fine," said Mrs. Storm, giggling.

"Does anyone have a paperclip?" Captain Jack asked.

"Who carries around paperclips?" Carlie snorted.

"I'm on the end," said Henry. "I can do this."

"No!" the adults shouted in unison.

"I think I might have something that works," said Valentina. She pulled out a bobby pin from her hair and handed it to Captain Jack.

"This works fine," he said smiling, "just dandy." He knelt down and began to work it around in the keyhole on his ankle restraint. It took several minutes, but everyone remained silent with anticipation. "Got it!" he grinned. The brace fell to the ground, freeing his leg.

"This will work," said Mr. Storm. "It gives us a good shot. Now how do we distract the guards?"

"Oh, Babe," said Mrs. Storm. "I think this one is all you. They only have whips and cattle prods, no other weapons that I have seen. They rely too much on these chains. Why don't we put you at the end and Haruka second?"

Mr. Storm could not contain his excitement.

"I like this plan. I'll slip off and have some fun with the guards while Haruka gets into position. We can have one or two large rocks already in there to bear the weight of the rest of the ore and bury Haruka while the guards are distracted."

"Okay," said Captain Jack. "We'll share the plan with everyone this evening before bed when we're all together. We're going to need everyone's support on this."

The guards returned and cracked their whips. Everyone got back to work, energized with hope at the possibility of escape.

CHAPTER 10

Hanna and Blue Visit the Zoo

Hanna jolted awake. She was in some uncomfortable form of transport. Her head felt groggy, and her body ached. She reached up to rub her forehead, but her hands were restrained. She moved her legs; also restrained, but she did feel her pack against her shin. Why would they restrain her but bring her pack?

She heard Blue's familiar voice, "Hanna, are you okay?"

"I think so," she said, blinking her eyes and trying to locate Blue from the sound of his voice. "It was Gambrio, that one-armed creep."

As her eyes grew accustomed to the dark, Hanna noticed that she wasn't alone in the compartment. There was an assortment of aliens, all restrained. Hanna caught the eye of a tall, muscular humanoid with a shock of red hair running over the center of an otherwise shaved head and down her back, ending at her waist. Her furious appearance was magnified by the feral look in her eyes and her bared teeth, which Hanna was confident should not be interpreted as a smile. Her restraints were enormous and glowed with some blue energy, nothing like the plain metallic clasps securing the rest of the prisoners. This was the single most intense, intimidating being Hanna had ever seen. She didn't scare easily, but all alarms possessed by the human body were screaming. Fight? No. Flight? She wouldn't make it. Freeze? A quick death. Fawn? Hanna never fawned. She took a deep breath, braced herself, and mustered her best glare. Teeth chattering, she met the impressive specimen's gaze.

"Hi. I'm Hanna," she said, voice trembling.

No response. The alien eased her posture and turned away her gaze. Hanna looked over to Blue.

"Are you okay? Where are we?" asked Hanna.

"I don't know for sure, but I think Headmistress Blurch got rid of us," said Blue.

"That's right!" came a familiar voice over the intercom.

"Gambrio!" shouted Hanna. "You're gonna get it, you hear me?"

"Yes, I am, Earthling!" Everyone in the hold turned to stare at her. "The zoo is paying a pretty penny for you. And a Makaran that hasn't turned? Maybe even more rare! Headmistress Blurch and I have an arrangement. A very profitable arrangement. Ah. We're here."

"Oh no," said Blue. "I knew it. We're going to the zoo. This is bad."

"Do you mean like a *zoo* zoo? Where they keep exotic animals?" asked Hanna.

"It's more like exotic species," said Blue, "that have gotten into some kind of trouble with the Galactic Police Force. They carry out their community service by living at the zoo, especially if they are from rare planets or habitats or sometimes if they are endangered."

"Oh. I see," answered Hanna, not sure that she fully understood the implications. Blue was clearly worried though, and that worried her.

The back of the transport vehicle opened to bright, blinding lights. Through squinted eyes and the shade of her hand, Hanna witnessed Mr. Gambrio accepting some sort of payment. He turned to Hanna and flashed a creepy smile.

"Have a good life. Just think of it as a permanent detention. Hahaha," he laughed as he sauntered away.

The alien with whom Mr. Gambrio had transacted business was green with tusks—or were they horns?—covering his face and arms. He looked at the group and uttered some words that were untranslatable—cuss words, Hanna assumed. He pressed a button, and the cords that held the prisoners' legs slackened enough for them to stand and walk if they all went together.

"All right. Out you go," came a rough and grumbly voice. "Let's get you cleaned up and present you to the Zookeeper," said the tusked alien.

He ushered them into a building and led them to a room with a large drain in the middle. While they were still chained, he turned on a hose and sprayed some unknown liquid that stung a little when it hit Hanna's skin. She shivered in her wet clothes, but a giant air dryer blasted her in the face with warm air. She was dry within seconds, her hair frizzled into a poof. Their captor shuffled the aliens into a room with a small stage. They stood as though in a police lineup with a bright light shining in their faces. Hanna could not see the tusked alien, but she recognized his voice.

"Here they are, Zookeeper Beb. An Aglozyte, a Bimber, a Haglerath, an unturned Makaran, and an Earthling."

There was a gasp that could only be Zookeeper Beb. "Remy, you fool!" he scolded. "How could you bring a Bimber here?"

"It's just a female, sir," answered the tusked Remy.

"Just a female!" shouted Zookeeper Beb. "Just a female! Are you serious? Do you have any idea what they are capable of? You weren't here four galactic standard years ago when a male got loose and in less than two hours killed 3,570 guests *including* a Bandalar. He killed a Bandalar!" Zookeeper Beb slowly enunciated each word. "With his bare hands! This one's *only* a female! What does that mean? She'll only kill 2,000 guests? Take her back."

"I can't take her back, sir," sighed Remy, blandly. "No returns."

"Then take her to the kill box," he ordered.

The alien with the shock of red hair turned her intense gaze toward Zookeeper Beb, who jumped back with a squeal. This must be the Bimber.

"Kill box broke down yesterday sir," Remy said dryly. "Overheated from too much use and the engine fried. Repairman is coming tomorrow, but it may take a few galactic standard days."

"Fine, put her in the ice box *until* the kill box is repaired. *Then* take her to the kill box. Move her to the top of the list." Zookeeper Beb waived his hand with a nervous, forced confidence. What could go wrong?

"Yes sir," said Remy. "What about the Earth person sir?"

"Does it come with any items?" asked the Zookeeper.

"Just this bag with a few things supposedly from Earth."

"Let's put her and her bag into exhibit A and see what she makes of it. Be accommodating. We need people to believe she is from Earth, even if we don't."

"I am from Earth," Hanna shouted. "Let me out of here. I know the Corridor Patrol." Remy and Zookeeper Beb both laughed raucously. Surprisingly, so did the Bimber.

"Good," said Zookeeper Beb. "Let Remy here know what kind of items you may need. We want to show the people your natural habitat, so if you need us to synthesize something like sleeping or dining furniture, just describe it to him. Do you have any Earth clothes?" He turned to Remy before Hanna could answer. "Make sure she wears something unique that could pass as Earth clothes."

"I have clothes in my pack!" Hanna said furiously before realizing she was actually accommodating them. She started to protest but was interrupted.

"No more talk. Remy, go and get them settled," commanded Zookeeper Beb, "and make sure she puts on those Earth clothes."

"Yes sir!" Remy marched them off the stage.

#

Hanna was released from her shackles and placed in an empty square room with three clear walls, like glass, and a side that opened onto a large, winding path. It was dark outside, and the path was empty, but she presumed it would soon be filled with visitors who would file past to view her in her natural "Earth" habitat. The cage directly next door had some strange-looking furniture but no occupant. Beyond that, she could see different species in similar cages lining both sides of the path. Why nobody just walked out was a mystery to her, but she thought twice before making the attempt herself. Hanna walked up to the path and carefully extended her hand, anticipating some resistance. Her hand met with an invisible barrier, but there was no shock or discomfort when she touched it. She could feel the breeze from outside but couldn't reach beyond the edge of the two side walls. It was as though the air itself was solid.

She didn't know what to make of this latest development, but her goals remained the same. She was going to find her parents, and if she had to go through the zoo to do it, that's what she would do. She saw her pack and was suddenly relieved, thinking it strange that something inanimate could bring so much comfort. She took out the carefully folded shorts and t-shirt she wore the day the *Eloise* launched. She was going to change into them, not because they wanted her to, but because it was something familiar in this strange place.

She took her drumsticks from her pack and sat on the floor to tap out a rhythm. After a few minutes of contemplation, she took out her towel and folded it into a pillow. The temperature was perfect, and she lay down to sleep in the brightly lit room. When she opened her eyes again, there was a Dorian staring at her from the cage next door.

#

"I'm sorry but she is not here," growled said Headmistress Blurch.

"Help me understand," said Mung. "This is the Sendori Sanitarium for Homeless, Lost, and Discarded Children, is it not?"

"Obviously!" huffed Headmistress Blurch.

"I am certain that Boother and I left the Earth person here only a few galactic standard days ago. Is that your recollection as well?"

"I don't know every student that comes through here," grumbled Blurch.

"Mzzz. Tzzzarana rezzzeived uzzz," said Boother, his bumps a concerned purple.

"Then you should take this up with her," said Headmistress Blurch, immediately regretting her suggestion. *What to do? Gambrio needs to fix this.*

"Let me call in their, eh, her teacher, Mr. Gambrio." She reached down and pressed a button. "Gambrio! Get in here. Now!."

Moments later, Mr. Gambrio entered and greeted Boother and Mung with his large red hand. Following the introductions, he offered his explanation.

"Regrettably, young Ms. Hanna Storm has run away," Gambrio said. "I'm afraid she befriended a Makaran, and they ran off after a tussle with some of the other children. We haven't been able to locate them. It's tragic, really. If you find them, could you please safely return them? We are so worried."

"We'll do our best to locate them, we assure you," said Mung.

As they left, Boother shared his impressions. "They were lying. I'm zzzure of it."

"How brazen!" said Mung. "I could not tell." As they neared the exit, Mung heard a familiar melodic voice.

"Mung, Boother, please wait," said Tsarana.

"Tsarana! So lovely to see you again. I hope you are well," beamed Mung.

"Thank you, Mung. It is nice to see you as well. You have come for Hanna, correct?" came the melodious question.

"Mr. Gambrio said she ran off with a Makaran. Do you think that is true?" inquired Mung.

"She did befriend a Makaran," answered Tsarana. "However, I do not believe they ran off. I believe Mr. Gambrio and Headmistress Blurch are involved in something far more nefarious. These are not the first children to disappear. When inquiries are made, 'they ran away' is the standard response."

Mung stood silently as Boother's bumps turned an angry black.

"Please excuse us," said Mung, mustering all of the strength he could to hide his rising anger.

When Mung burst into Headmistress Blurch's office, Blurch was laughing with Mr. Gambrio, both of them sucking in smoke from long tubes protruding from some small spherical contraption. Boother reached up and grabbed Mr. Gambrio's arm, holding it fast. Headmistress Blurch fell backwards over her chair and was trying her best to lift her behemoth self off the floor. Mung stood face to face with Mr. Gambrio, their noses almost touching.

"You have upset me," rasped Mung. "I am going to launch an investigation into the youth that have gone missing from this hallowed institution. You see, I promised Hanna she would be safe here. I suspect you may have turned me into a liar. I don't want to be a liar." Mung pulled out his hand cannon and pointed it squarely at Mr. Gambrio's nose as Boother's bumps turned a dark, almost black purple.

"Tell me where she is. Now," Mung threatened calmly. .

"I'd tell him now," said Boother. "I've never zzzeen him like thizzz. No telling what he might do."

"All right! She's at the Galactic Species Zoo," cried Mr. Gambrio. "Please don't hurt me. It was all Blurch's idea. I was just following orders. It's her you want."

"Our investigation will sort all of this out. I will make sure to note your exceptional cooperation in my report," said Mung, fully intending to do so, perhaps without the little detail of having aimed a hand cannon at a suspect's face.

"Plot a course for the Zoo as soon as we get back to the ship," Mung barked to Boother as they made their exit.

"With pleazzzure, zzzir."

CHAPTER 11

A Day At the Zoo

Hanna slowly rose from the ground, fixing her gaze on the Dorian in the neighboring cage. He sat in an elaborate, throne-like chair, reading from an electronic tablet. An orange mist floated upward around him, and he inhaled it deeply with his scaly snout. He glanced up ever so briefly to acknowledge his new neighbor before returning his attention to his tablet reader.

Hanna pounded on the wall.

The Dorian exhaled and set the tablet reader on a stand next to his throne. "Welcome to the zoo," he greeted. "The occupants of this fine establishment have very little privacy and it is considered impolite to stare. We try to accommodate each other by minding our business," he hissed.

Hanna continued to stare.

You're a Dorian," she announced with great conviction.

"How perceptive!" came the sarcastic reply. "I'm afraid you have me at a disadvantage. You know what I am, but I do not know what you are."

"I'm from Earth, you weasel." Hanna noted the look of surprise on his face, but she wasn't thinking rationally. "That's right. I'm from Earth and I want to know where my parents are being held. Tell me where my parents are!" Hanna demanded, banging on the transparent barrier between them.

The Dorian recovered from his brief surprise.

"My, my. I haven't the foggiest. What makes you think I would know?"

Hanna did not respond.

"Let me guess. They were captured by Dorians, and since I'm one of several million Dorians in Galaxy Prime, you assume that I have knowledge of where all laborers are at all times."

Hanna still did not respond, but she was starting to regain her own composure. She analyzed the situation. She had no idea how long this Dorian had been at the zoo. It was unlikely that he had been involved in the attack on the *Eloise*. She knew nothing about this individual. In Hanna's fourteen years of life on Earth, she had seen entire races of people judged solely on their appearance. It was a plague on Earth, and it disgusted Hanna to think she was now doing the same thing to this Dorian. "Benefit of the doubt for the individual is often the most strategic move, at least until someone gives cause for doubt," her father had preached. Nonetheless, surely he must have some information about his fellow Dorians that would be enlightening.

"You're right," Hanna apologized. "I'm sorry. Our ship was attacked by Dorians, and I was the only one to escape. They took my parents and I'm trying to find them. It was unfair for me to take it out on you. My name is Hanna, Hanna Storm."

"Apology accepted," responded the Dorian cautiously. "I am called Saldo. I'm sorry to hear about your parents, but I am glad that you were able to escape. It is exceedingly rare that someone escapes a Dorian attack. I'm impressed. We value our laborers a great deal."

"How long have you been here?" inquired Hanna.

"Many, many galactic standard years. Since I was a youth," lamented Saldo.

"I'm so sorry," said Hanna.

A bell rang and a door in the rear of Hanna's habitat opened up.

"Time for first meal and entertainment practice," explained Saldo the Dorian. "You will have orientation today and will select an area of entertainment. Try to avoid the balancing acts or water dancing. They have an extremely high mortality rate."

"Thanks," Hanna nodded as she exited the doorway. A long hallway that stretched behind the habitats was filled with exiting residents. Hanna followed Saldo down the hallway, which emptied into a large courtyard where all of the inhabitants were congregating. Hanna spotted the tusked Remy, who motioned her over to where he was assembling the new recruits. As she made her way over, she saw Blue standing alone off to one side, his head down and his hands in his pockets.

Hanna altered course and threw her arms around Blue's neck, squeezing so tightly that if he hadn't already been blue, he soon would have been. Blue tensed, arms straight to his side. It took a moment, but he relaxed into the hug, lifted his arms, and squeezed back. Everybody ceased their conversations and stared. Very few aliens had seen a Makaran, but nobody had never seen someone willing to touch one.

"Blue! I'm so glad you're okay," squealed Hanna.

"It's good to see you too, Hanna. Are you okay?"

"I am. My neighbor is a Dorian. I hope that he can give me some clues about where my parents might be."

"Be careful, Hanna. You can't trust Dorians," warned Blue.

"Oh, I'm sorry," she answered sarcastically. "I also hear that I shouldn't touch Makarans."

"I just don't want to see you get hurt. Please be cautious," Blue murmured.

"Look, I get it. I really do, but he gets the benefit of the doubt like everyone else. Give people a chance and they can surprise you."

"Or betray you," mumbled Blue.

Hanna furrowed her brow.

"You have surprised me though," recovered Blue, "so you may be correct."

Remy, having gathered all the newcomers, began their orientation by grumbling from a notecard.

"Every day, you will rise on time and come to the yard for first meal and exercise. You will then spend one galactic standard hour practicing your assigned entertainment routine. Afterward, when the guests arrive, you will return to your habitats until called upon for your scheduled entertainment routine, which will occur three times throughout the day. After the zoo closes, you will report to the yard for your second meal and socializing for one hour, after which you will return to your habitats for rest. Are there any questions?"

Silence.

"Very well," continued Remy. "We'll now hear a few words from Zookeeper Beb."

A sausage-shaped alien about half as tall as Hanna strolled into the yard. Bristly hair above his lip resembled a mustache and small, beady eyes sunk back into his bald head.

"Thank you, Remy," he said formally. "There is only one rule here. Do as you are instructed. Is that clear?" Affirmative nods all around. "Good. There is only one punishment for breaking the one rule: the kill box. Break a rule, and I will wipe you out of existence. Nobody cares that you're here. Nobody will care if you're suddenly not here. Now please form a single-file line so that Remy can assign you to your entertainment group."

Pale looks of concern descended upon the newcomers, but they hustled into line. Hanna was first.

"Do you have any special skills?" asked Remy. Hanna racked her brains.

"Nothing that I can think of," she said.

"Do you have any musical talents? Can you sing or play an instrument?" persisted Remy.

"I can play the drums," she answered. "I started lessons when I was eight."

"You're a percussionist?" he asked.

"Yes, sir," she answered, almost cheerfully. Hanna always felt restored when she was thumping out a rhythm with her sticks.

"Great. Our last percussionist was sent to the kill box. I hope you can keep a tempo. Report to the Music Master at station twelve."

Hanna dallied, looking back over her shoulder, waiting for Blue, who finally caught up to her.

"I got the music band," said Hanna. "What did you get?

"The high wire balancing," he grinned. Hanna stopped, a look of concern on her face.

"It's fine. Makarans are known for their exceptional balance and agility. This won't be at all challenging," Blue reassured her.

Hanna, though still skeptical, nodded her acceptance.

"I should get to station twelve. I'll find you at dinner," she said. She leaned over and kissed Blue on the cheek. "Be careful, okay?"

"You too," he smiled.

#

The Music Master lifted six batons with six skinny, stick-like arms. The antennae on top of his beetle-faced head twitched nervously.

"Welcome percussionist! Welcome!" the director beamed at Hanna. "I'm Perto. I will direct you using my top right arm." Perto wiggled the baton in his top right hand. "I don't have to impress upon you the seriousness of what we do here. Our lives depend on the audience's reaction. We must impress them each day or we all end up in the kill box."

Hanna glanced around at her rag-tag alien bandmates with their rag-tag assortment of alien instruments. She recognized some of the musical devices and mentally categorized them into high strings, low strings, high horns, low horns, and percussion. There were a few aliens without instruments, and Hanna concluded that these were vocalists. Though empty-handed, each wore a small metal disc centered with a red dot, bright, like a red laser pointer. For some, it hung on tight necklaces around various-sized necks. For others, it hung over alien parts unknown to Hanna.

"These are your percussion blocks," clicked Perto. "Manufactured by Bleezlesnats. Top of the line! Familiarize yourself with them. Care for them as if my life were at stake! Ahem...I mean as if your life were at stake, of course. Because it is." Perto's antennae twitched wildly.

Hanna surveyed her percussion kit. Single black cubes balanced atop stands of various heights and a few large black boxes on the ground with some sort of foot pedals attached to their bases. Everyone was blowing or strumming or picking or singing. Melodious voices were amplified by the small metal discs with laser-like dots. Hanna grabbed a small stool and plopped it down behind the drum kit. She scooped up a pair of sticks lying on the ground. They were made of some unusually light material, but they felt comfortable as she spun them between her fingers. She tapped one of the squares, and it produced a raspy thump, not unlike a snare drum. She went through each square carefully and found ones that sounded familiar. Within a few minutes, she had identified her high hat, tom toms, cymbals, and bass drum—everything she needed in a trap set. She positioned them in the order she was used to just in time for Perto to begin.

"Okay. Percussion, please give me sixty beats per galactic standard minute." Not yet knowing how long a galactic standard minute was, Hanna began tapping the drum at what she thought was a pretty reasonable rate.

"No! No! No! Do you want to get us all killed? Slow that down demonstrably," ordered Perto.

"It would help if I knew how long a galactic standard minute was," she retorted.

"A galactic standard minute is forty-two galactic standard seconds or one-forty-second of a galactic standard hour," said Perto.

"That doesn't really help," said Hanna. "What is a galactic standard hour? How is it calculated?"

"You really must be new to the galaxy," said Perto, flustered and nervous. With one of his hands, he pulled out a handkerchief and wiped the sweat from his forehead. "I hope you don't get us all killed. A galactic standard hour is the average of all the hours on all the Galactic Treaty planets. On some planets, an hour is longer; on others, it is shorter. So the standard is simply the average," he clicked. "Most citizens know the formula to translate their native hours into galactic hours, but clearly you do not. I'll make this easy for you. Give me a beat."

Hanna lightly tapped her drumstick on one of the small squares.

"Slower!"

Hanna slowed it down.

"Slower!" Perto shouted.

Hanna had never played the drums this slowly before, for any song, ever. Not even for smooth jazz.

"Perfect! Keep that tempo please," Perto said. "Now, high instruments." Alto and soprano strings and horns began a long steady note. "Good. Now, low instruments." The bass and baritone strings and horns echoed the note an octave lower. "Excellent!" exclaimed Perto.

To Hanna, the music was awful. She looked around, and from what she could tell, others were in agreement. "Now, vocals," he finished. The voices boomed over the instrumentals.

With everyone playing, it sounded like thirty different performers all vying for supremacy in the listener's ear. She went with it because Music Master Perto had a pleased look on his face and Hanna had no idea what passed as music in this galaxy. She would do her job and hope nobody would be sent to the kill box. An alarm rang.

"That's it people," said Perto. "Back to your habitats. I'll see you at our first performance of the day."

#

Hanna sat on a stool in front of her alien drum kit and slowly, monotonously tapped out the required rhythm. The previous two performances had been uneventful. She did not understand how anyone could appreciate such monotonous music, but to her dismay, the alien visitors cheered. The insect-like species who looked similar to Music Master Perto cheered particularly loud and complimented the orchestra vociferously. They had just finished a set when the previous crowd left, and a new crowd was ushered in.

Music Master Perto gasped. Hanna thought he looked nervous. Indeed, he was beginning to perspire, or leak, or whatever that was dripping down his face. The aliens in the crowd were all of the same species. They were humanoid but had enormous ears and reminded Hanna of a herd of elephants. All were wearing the same bright purple shirt with some alien writing on it, like a family reunion group at a theme park.

Hanna looked at the strange lettering on their clothing, and the words "Happy Birthday Glabor" popped into her mind. She marveled again at the technology in her tiny ear translator. The other members of the band started murmuring, and, boy, did they look worried!

"Why is everyone so nervous, Music Master Perto?" Hanna inquired.

"Oh dear! Oh my! Those are Faramorathians. They are very musically discerning. If they are displeased in the slightest, they will lodge a complaint with the Zookeeper, and we'll all be sent to the kill box! Let's see. We have to start. We have to start."

Perto tapped all six of his batons and readied the musicians. One of the horns let out a nervous squeak. Perto dropped his batons and the music started. The audience immediately began to murmur, whispering in hushed tones to one another. Several of them covered their ears. Music Master Perto looked over his shoulder and slowed his batons until they came to a stop. He froze.

Hanna recalled her mother's words: "In any emergency, it is always better when someone takes charge, not because they know what to do in that particular situation, but because they inspire others to action when action is needed." Several days after her mother had spoken those words, Hanna had been in school when a classmate had fallen and hit his head on a rock, splitting it open. The teacher attending the students had almost passed out at the sight of the blood, but Hanna had sprung into action, instructing the teacher to call 911 and a nearby student to hand over her sweater. The scene was under control when the paramedics arrived, and the injured boy had made a full recovery.

Hanna took charge. She would not sit idly by and wait for the others to be sent to the kill box. She grabbed a microphone disc from one of the vocalists and placed it on her neck.

"Ladies and Gentlemen, we have a special treat for you. Today, we'll play you a classic Earth piece by a very special band known as the Clash. Please give us a moment." Murmurs of complaint turned into murmurs of curiosity that spread through the crowd of the music-discerning Faramorathians.

Mrs. Storm had fancied the Clash in her youth, and Hanna had had ample exposure to their music. She hoped that the musical lingo she used would translate correctly as she made her rounds of the different sections, quickly conveying her instructions while the crowd listened.

"The key is A major. Low section horns and strings, I want you to give me a baseline that sounds like this: Boom! Boom! Boom!" The low section horns and strings started repeating the notes as Hanna had sung them. She signaled them to stop and continued through the rest of the band.

"Now high section strings, I want you to repeat this rhythm: Dunh! Dunh! Dunh!" She walked them through a few rounds until she was satisfied and cut them off. "High section horns, you play this: Wah! Wah! Wah!" All were obedient.

"Outstanding. Vocals, you can sit this one out. I've got it." She took her seat, adjusted the disc on her neck, and counted them off while banging her drumsticks together.

"One, two, three, four." Hanna attacked the drum set with vigor. Each section came in by turns and Hanna sang out the lyrics.

The Faramorathians were on their feet dancing and clapping along to the beat. Their ears bounced up and down in rhythm to the music. To Hanna's surprise, the vocalists picked up on the words and began to sing along with her, joining in on parts of the chorus. Music Master Perto even perked up and took charge, furiously swinging his batons at each of the sections.

Hanna ended the song with an impressive drum solo. The crowd had doubled in size with a variety of aliens. Everyone was screaming and shouting the musicians' praises. Hanna stood up and bowed.

"That was amazing," she thought to herself.

#

At dinner, Hanna found Blue and took a seat next to him. Each thought that the other looked exceptionally pleased as they eagerly munched on the crunchy pellets and ate their gray paste.

"How was your high wire act?" Hanna asked.

"It was good. Well, more like amazing," Blue gloated. "I think the crowds were impressed. How was your concert?"

"I taught the band to play an Earth song and, dare I say, it was well received, thank you."

"I guess it wasn't such a bad day," said Blue. "Could have been much worse."

Hanna felt a pang of regret. She felt safe and somewhat comfortable, forgetting for a time that she was a prisoner here and that she had a task to focus on. Her parents were out there somewhere, and she had to find them.

"We have to get out of here," Hanna declared. "I need to find my parents."

"If you even try to escape, it's straight to the kill box," answered Blue. "It's too risky. This isn't a bad life for a Makaran, by the way," he said defensively.

"You won't come with me if I go?" Hanna sounded alarmed.

"I'll join you," said a familiar voice coming from over Hanna's shoulder. It was the Dorian.

"Saldo!" grinned Hanna..

Blue chimed in. "She doesn't trust you enough to plan an escape with."

"Excuse me, Blue, but I'll decide who I trust," corrected Hanna.

"What do you mean escape? I meant I would join you for second meal," explained Saldo, "but I'm intrigued. Tell me more about how you plan to escape," he said, taking a seat next to Hanna.

"Dorians can't be trusted, Hanna," repeated Blue.

"I've been thinking about it, and I'm sure I can help you find your parents," offered Saldo in response to Blue's skepticism. "I have a contact in the Dorian Empire who should know where they are, but I would have to get home first. If you really think you can escape this place, I will come with you and help you find your parents."

"Don't believe him, Hanna," pleaded Blue, glaring at Saldo.

"Not all Dorians are bloodthirsty conquerors, Makaran," challenged Saldo. "Almost half of the Empire is against violence and wants to join the Galactic Treaty. Many of us want to travel the galaxy and meet new people and experience other cultures."

"Enough of this," intervened Hanna. "Blue, I appreciate your concern, but we need to give Saldo a chance. I'm breaking out of here, and I'll take Saldo with me. What about you?"

Blue eyed Saldo carefully. "If he's going with you, I'm going too."

"Good. It's settled then," said Hanna. "Now, how do we get out of here?"

The Dorian spoke first. "At night, they have very few guards and rely mainly on the habitat's solid screen to keep us locked in, but there is no way past it that I have been able to find. Each habitat has a manual emergency override on the outside wall that the staff can use to release us, but otherwise, the solid screen is impenetrable. During the daytime, we are free to walk about during our shows, but the guard presence is more substantial. Furthermore, the likelihood of a Dorian, Earth person, and Makaran being spotted in a crowd is very, *very* high. We would most certainly be caught prior to reaching the exit."

The Dorian was very thorough in his analysis. This would require more thought.

The tusked Remy appeared and encouraged everyone back to their habitats.

"Let's all think this over tonight and share our ideas tomorrow," suggested Hanna. Each headed back to their habitat, hoping that they could find a way out.

CHAPTER 12

To Flee or Not to Flee

Hanna couldn't sleep. She paced back and forth in her prison cell habitat, thoughts of escape swirling through her mind. Night time meant sparse guards and Hanna itched to figure a way out. She could see the Dorian sleeping in the next cell over and considered the panel Saldo had mentioned. Hanna decided to look closer. She searched for the emergency release and saw it just outside her habitat on the wall. If not for the barrier, she would have been able to easily reach it. She put her hand against the solid, clear wall and pushed. It moved about as much as a cement wall. She had no idea what kind of technology was at play. Was it some sort of particle field? Was it really compressed air, as it seemed? She looked to see what might be generating the barrier but found no sign of any technology other than the switch.

Hanna's hands ached a bit from her effort on the drums. She looked down and noticed that her skin was dry and cracking, almost to the point of bleeding. Who knew what kind of bacteria this planet had! She reached in her pack and pulled out the tube of petroleum jelly and gave both her hands a healthy coating, like lotion, and resumed her pacing.

She was growing increasingly frustrated. Why couldn't she figure this out? She went to the clear barrier and punched it as hard as she could.

"Mama pajama!" she said out loud. Her hand punched right through the barrier and stopped at her wrist. Hanna pulled her hand back in and slowly tried again, sliding it through the barrier up to her wrist where the petroleum jelly stopped. "Escaping alien prisons," she breathed excitedly. "Yet another use for petroleum jelly."

She ran back to her pack and coated her arm with a thin layer of the jelly up to her shoulder and went back to test it. Her entire arm made it through the barrier, and if she could just stretch far enough...Success!

She stretched so hard that she almost fell when the barrier dropped. Hanna froze, expecting to be caught at any moment. No alarm. No sound. Zookeeper Beb and his sidekick Remy must have thought the invisible wall to be a sufficient deterrent. Or perhaps the threat of death was enough to keep most inhabitants in line.

Hanna had no intention of waiting until tomorrow. She grabbed her pack and engaged the emergency release on the Dorian's cage.

"Saldo!" she whisper-shouted. "We're leaving, now! Grab whatever you need."

Saldo was out the door in an instant. They silently strolled down the row of habitats until she found Blue's and released his barrier. He embraced Hanna with an amazed smile.

"Excellent! Let's go," said Saldo.

"Wait!" said Hanna. "I'm not leaving anybody here. Plus, it will cover our escape." She started back up the row and opened everyone's barrier. Several occupants ran. Others stayed put. Blue ran to the other side of the path and opened the cages there, keeping in time with Hanna.

"Great. Everyone is free. Let's go," demanded Saldo.

"Not everyone. Not yet. Where is the ice box?" Hanna asked Saldo.

He hesitated.

"Where is it?" she demanded. "I'm not leaving without her, and the longer we debate it the more likely it is that we'll get caught." Hanna was insistent.

"Follow me," sighed Saldo in defeat. They ran up the path away from the main exit to a cluster of buildings. "It's in there," he said, pointing to a small square building with a single door.

"Okay. I'm going in. Stand guard here with Blue."

Blue started to protest but was cut off by a blaring alarm as lights flooded the area. Four alien guards, all dressed in combat gear, moved in to surround the three escapees before Hanna could take a single step. Behind the soldier guards came Remy and Zookeeper Beb.

"I knew it!" shouted Beb. "Remy, how did I know the Earth girl would be one of the runners?"

"I don't know, sir," grumbled Remy.

"It's the kill box for all of you," shouted Beb. "Earth girl or not, I will not have anarchy in my zoo. Guards! Lock them up and ready the kill box." Remy and Zookeeper Beb disappeared after the other freed inhabitants.

The guards bound their hands and marched them into the same building where the ice box was. Hanna could see the Bimber looking at her through a transparent glass window that was frosted around the edges. Her face was expressionless. This was a precarious position and Hanna did not see an immediate way out of it. Different scenarios raced through her mind. Could she rush the guards? They obviously preferred the kill box for some reason; maybe it left no evidence. She decided against it for now. Maybe as a last resort. She felt the panic begin to rise inside and took a few deep breaths to calm herself but had to swallow a scream when the lights went out suddenly.

Hanna heard four thuds as four bodies crumpled to the ground in succession. Just as suddenly, the lights turned on, and Hanna found herself staring directly at a small, frog-like creature standing upright. He reached almost up to Hanna's shoulders. He peered at her from behind a black ninja-style mask.

"I'm Stiggs. I'm here to rescue you," he croaked and began unlocking Hanna's restraint. "The Monarch wants to see you."

Hanna looked to Saldo and Blue.

"Anywhere gives us a better chance than here," said Blue. Saldo agreed.

"Okay, Stiggs was it? I'll go with you, but I won't go anywhere without these two." Stiggs reluctantly unlocked Blue's and Saldo's restraints.

"This complicates matters, but we can do it if you follow me exactly," Stiggs explained.

"I need to do something first." Hanna marched past the three of them to the ice box.

"Stop!" yelled Stiggs.

"Are you insane?" yelled Saldo.

"What are you doing?" yelled Blue.

All pleas went unheeded. Hanna stood in front of the half-frozen glass.

"Don't you dare!" said the Bimber.

"I'm not leaving without you," answered Hanna with determination.

"Let me die in dignity. Don't open the door," she yelled back.

"I can't do that," Hanna insisted. She opened the door, unlocking the Bimber's restraints. The Bimber released a bloodcurdling scream and stepped out through the door, brooding and defeated.

"We have to go. Now!" croaked Stiggs.

"Lead the way," said Hanna. She followed Stiggs out through the door and they made for the exit, staying in the shadows as much as possible. It wasn't enough; a guard spotted them, and it seemed as though fifty more appeared out of the darkness to converge on the exit. Hanna, who had some training in mixed martial arts, adopted a fighting stance. She heard the Bimber snicker quietly as she put her hand on Hanna's shoulder and pulled her backward, walking to the front of the group.

"Just follow me," was all she said quietly, resigned to her newly found freedom. The Bimber walked forward. The first few guards attempted to restrain her, but she picked one up and threw him the length of a football field. She punched another with a solid uppercut, and he disappeared straight up into the dark sky. Hanna didn't see where the guard landed but noticed it took a while before she heard his screaming reentry and subsequent thud.

As soon as the other guards realized that it was a Bimber, several tried to use hand cannons to blast her. She ignored them. Her body would stop for a moment, stunned, but she moved so quickly that anyone who got off one or two shots found themselves looking her in the eye shortly thereafter. A few more guards went flying. The rest simply parted as the group followed the Bimber to the wall surrounding the zoo.

"Stand back," the Bimber said to the group. "You all look very fragile, and I wouldn't want you to get hurt," a touch of sarcasm in her voice. Having given fair warning, she performed a short breathing routine while an orange light gathered around her arm. She punched the wall, releasing a burst of energy, and a hole large enough for all of them to walk through appeared amid the residual dust and debris.

Feeling safe, Hanna stopped the Bimber. "Why are you helping us? I thought you were upset that I freed you."

Stiggs interrupted with a plea of urgency. "Please!" croaked Stiggs. "We must go now. There's a shuttle waiting."

Hanna mustered her most confident look for the Bimber. "We'll continue this conversation in a minute."

Stiggs led them to a launch pad where a very fancy-looking shuttle was waiting. They all piled in. The interior was the most elegant and plush space Hanna had ever experienced, and that was saying something, given that Hanna had rubbed elbows with Earth's wealthiest.

"What's your name?" Hanna asked the Bimber.

"I'm yours. Call me whatever you wish," the Bimber said morosely.

Hanna was dumbfounded. "You're mine? What's that supposed to mean?"

"I am honor-bound to serve you as long as I live because my life would have ended in the kill box if you hadn't robbed me of my death." The Bimber stared down at Hanna with a look of resignation

"You're upset I rescued you? Are you serious? I don't understand," Hanna said incredulously.

"I am upset. My life is no longer mine to live on my terms. It belongs to you. I am...."

"I relieve you of your commitment," interrupted Hanna.

"You have no authority to do that. Whether you like it or not, I am yours. Until now, my greatest shame was being born a female, but this," she paused, "this is worse."

"Excuse me?" chastened Hanna. "Being a female is awesome!"

"You're not a Bimber," came the sullen response.

"Hey!" Hanna shouted. "Bimber, Human, it doesn't matter. Females are the best and we need to help each other. There is no shame in being yourself."

The Bimber did not respond.

"I'm Hanna Storm. What should I call you?"

"I'm yours. Call me whatever you wish," the Bimber repeated.

Hanna rolled her eyes. "I want you to answer my question honestly," she said, trying to assert the authority that the Bimber had ascribed to her. "What do you wish to be called?"

The Bimber stared back. "Prior to my death, my name was Mera."

"Then your name post-death is also Mera," insisted Hanna. Did Mera smile? Or was she growling? Either way, Hanna felt satisfied that she understood the Bimber's cultural requirement to become Hanna's property, as strange as it seemed. Hanna was no stranger to cultural differences, but she maintained the philosophy taught by her parents. "Wrong is wrong," she said to the Bimber, "whether in your galaxy or mine, and owning another person is wrong." The Bimber gave no response, and Hanna decided it was time to turn her attention to the next mystery.

Hanna's curiosity emerged when she recalled the Monarch that Stiggs had referenced. She was grateful for the assistance, of course, but was at a loss as to what this Monarch's agenda was. What was he the Monarch of anyway? A planet? A system?

"So, who is this Monarch?" Hanna asked her companions.

"Everyone knows the Monarch," answered Blue. "He's the greatest businessman in Galaxy Prime."

"And the wealthiest," added Saldo. "Even the Dorians know of his fame. Rumor has it that some Dorians defy laws and do business with him, importing certain luxuries from Galactic Treaty planets."

"There is no evidence for that," croaked Stiggs. "He is a celebrity of the highest caliber and has many talents. Business is just one of his pursuits."

"So, he's not the Monarch of any planet or system?" asked Hanna.

"He is known as the Monarch on many planets and in many systems," responded Stiggs. "He may be the greatest being in the Galaxy since Erthe united the planets against the Dorian invasion."

"Are we headed to New Meadows?" asked Blue excitedly. "I've always wanted to go there."

"That is our destination," answered Stiggs. "We will arrive shortly." Hanna was intrigued. This Monarch sounded very important, and it was Hanna's experience that important people often behaved as though they were the only people that mattered. She wasn't sure what to expect.

Hanna looked out of the window as they approached a large city in orbit around the planet they had just departed. The structure was bursting with light and bright neon signs that were likely visible from a million miles away. The whole vibe felt familiar to Hanna. It reminded her of the bustling metropolises she had visited on Earth. One of the signs showed an advertisement for the zoo, and she saw a picture of her and Blue advertised as the newest exhibits. Words in alien writing that Hanna perceived as "Makaran" and "Earth Person" flashed beside their images. The whole thing looked like a giant floating Las Vegas in space.

She had made the drive with her parents, coming down I-70 from Colorado and connecting with I-15 in Southern Utah. Descending from the mountains and seeing the Las Vegas skyline all lit up had been quite an experience, one that Hanna now felt as though she was reliving. They parked, and a doorman greeted them on their private landing platform.

"Welcome, Earth girl," said the alien doorman. Others waiting in a very long line looked on with jealousy. When the Makaran stepped out, the doorman jumped back, but quickly regained his composure. The people waiting in line gasped audibly. However, this was mild compared to their response when the Dorian stepped out: double gasps at double the volume. The doorman, however, remained professional. When Mera the Bimber stepped out, there was outright anarchy. People screamed and ran in all directions. The doorman managed to extend his hand to help her out of the ship, but he was shaking tremendously.

"Welcome, ma'am," he choked out. Mera glared at him, and he fainted. She hurried to catch up with Hanna.

Stiggs led them into an opulent lobby with a crowd hustling and bustling about. The longer they were there, the fewer gasps they heard, but everybody continued to give them a wide berth. This was surely a casino. Hanna had walked through the Bellagio once, and this had a very similar appearance and atmosphere.

"What is this place?" Hanna asked Stiggs.

"The Monarch has established a large conglomerate of gaming institutions and has developed many very popular games of chance."

Hanna saw a game that resembled roulette and another that was played with cards. She was pondering the familiarity of all this when she heard music coming from somewhere ahead. There was a concert going on and she recognized the music. It was Earth music! She immediately split off from the group and headed toward the sound. Stiggs and the others followed.

She saw the entrance to the concert hall and quickened her pace. Was her translator responsible for this? It had to be. She started singing along to the lyrics.

Ignoring the door attendant, Hanna burst into the concert hall. There must have been a hundred and fifty thousand aliens in there, all cheering and clapping. Down on the stage, she saw a familiar human face in a familiar human outfit singing a familiar human song, just as she had seen in Las Vegas.

The song ended and the crowd erupted in cheers. "Thank you," came an iconic voice. "Thank you very much."

It suddenly all made sense. The Monarch. The New Meadows, or in Spanish, the New Las Vegas. The translator must have been in overdrive for her to hear it as "the New Meadows." The ambiance reminded her of Las Vegas because it was Las Vegas, or a copy of it. The gambling, the concert hall, the opulence, all of it! The performer may or may not be "the Monarch," but whoever it was, they were definitively from Earth.

"That is the Monarch," croaked Stiggs. "He still does two shows a week. His music is very popular throughout the Galaxy. He'll be waiting for you in his library. I'll inform him that you have brought, eh, guests with you." Stiggs eyeballed the motley crew.

Hanna could not believe it. Could it really be him? She was here in the Andromeda Galaxy, so why not him? He looked young; shouldn't he be much older? Once again, Hanna had so many questions, and she couldn't wait to ask them.

CHAPTER 13

A Daring Escape

Captain Jack focused intently on the lock of his ankle restraint. He had practiced picking it every time the guards took a break and could now do it in under ten seconds. The guards had just departed with the ore cart, giving the prisoners a brief respite. The captured passengers and crew of the *Eloise* were on edge, waiting to see if the guards would come running.

Captain Jack made his way over to Haruka and got to work on her restraint. It popped open without much effort, and they both strolled over to the end where Henry crouched. Captain Jack anticipated one last plea from Henry to let him be the one to escape, but it never came. When Henry's restraint was released, he quietly walked over and took Haruka's place. Haruka was now on the end, with Mr. Storm next in line. Captain Jack made quick work of Mr. Storm's ankle restraint and returned to his place in line. Captain Jack left his own restraint unlatched; he wanted to be able to move quickly if these blasted lizards overreacted to Mr. Storm's distraction. He was fairly certain, however, that the guards had gotten the message from the large lizard with the scar on his eye that the prisoners were not to be harmed.

It was the last shift of their work day, and the human prisoners were diligent in performing their mining duties. The raucous guards burst in and casually surveyed their captive laborers. If anyone exhibited signs of nervousness, the guards did not notice it. It helped that the humans were dripping with sweat and covered in dust, masking any observable signs of anxiety. They were careful to fill all of the carts except for the one closest to Haruka. She took charge of filling that one herself, placing two large stones on the side that could serve as braces for other rocks.

It was almost time for the carts to be taken to the surface.

"Hurry and get that last cart filled, you filthy worms," ordered one of the two guards, his comments directed at Captain Jack, the only one who could understand them. "The transport is about to leave."

Captain Jack relayed the message. Taking this as his cue, Mr. Storm bent down, half hidden behind a boulder, to fully release the ankle restraint Captain Jack had unlocked earlier. When he stood up, there were four guards instead of two, all focused on him. He looked at Mrs. Storm. She shrugged her shoulders. Mr. Storm turned to Haruka.

"We're still a go. Be ready," he whispered. Haruka nodded. The four guards approached Mr. Storm, sneering and grinning. He jumped into action with a speed that surprised even Mrs. Storm. He had a few meters of free ground to gain momentum. He dropped his shoulder and plowed into them, knocking all but one to the ground.

Haruka saw her chance and went for it. The guard who had barely missed being tackled had his attention on Mr. Storm, but as soon as Haruka took a step, he turned and ran toward her. The alien guard grabbed Haruka by the waist with his clawed hands, heaved her up over his shoulder, and carried her off down one of the tunnels.

Two of the three guards tackled by Mr. Storm had been knocked out cold. Mr. Storm grappled with the third guard and placed him in a fairly wicked front chokehold. It took longer than it would for a human to pass out, but Mr. Storm could feel his struggling opponent start to slow down.

It was during this brief moment of uncertainty that Henry looked over at his aunt Valentina and quickly unloosed the ankle restraint that he had not fully latched. He slid quietly into the cart where Haruka would have gone. Captain Jack looked over at Valentina. There was a moment of uncertainty when Valentina gasped at Henry, but the look on Henry's face told her all she needed to know, and she gave her nod of approval to him and then to Captain Jack.

"Do it," she said, knowing that this was the best chance for everybody. In truth, she was worried that this little stunt would get them all killed and that getting Henry out of there might be the only way to save him. Captain Jack and the others quickly filled the cart, finishing just before a contingent of ten other guards and their merciless leader marched into the mine.

"You four," barked the commanding officer, pointing to some of the guards. "Get the big one out of here and into the isolation cage with the other."

"You four," he sneered at the other guards. "Get this ore to the launch pad. They are about to leave."

"But that is a job for laborers," said one of the guards. His commander pulled out a hand cannon and shot the complaining guard in the arm.

"It is a job for you. Now you can do it with one arm," replied the commander. "Now move!"

The guards performed their duties, the last two staying behind with the captives. Mr. Storm resisted the urge to continue fighting. He rationalized that compliance now was the best way to keep the attention of the four guards escorting him to who knows where.

Captain Jack De La Vega kept waiting for the guards to count the prisoners, but this never happened. They were marched back to their holding area and fed as usual. No Mr. Storm. No Haruka. No Henry. He hoped that this attempt wouldn't cost them their lives, but they had no indication as to whether or not Henry had succeeded.

#

Mr. Storm was thrown into a dark room.

"Who's there?" came Haruka's hushed voice.

"It's me, Sebastian," said Mr. Storm. Haruka cautiously felt around for him and embraced him.

"I'm sorry I failed. That dirty *tokage* grabbed me before I could even reach the cart."

"It's not your fault, Haruka. It's mine. I missed one of the guards. I mean, I did get three of them," Mr. Storm said, impressed with himself. "Haruka, Henry took your place and got away. At least, the guards took the cart out of the tunnel with him inside it. I think he may have made it onto the alien ship."

"But we can't be sure," said Haruka.

"We can't be sure," said Mr. Storm, "but we can be hopeful," he said through sniffles and tears. "I hope my Hanna is okay. I hope Henry will make it. I hope we all do." He needed a hug and was glad Haruka was there.

"I need a hug," he admitted. Haruka reached her arms as wide as she could but couldn't quite manage to get them around his back.

"Yes sir," Haruka said through her own sniffles and tears. She considered herself very stoic and took pride in the fact that she rarely cried in difficult situations. Her one weakness—well, it was a weakness in her mind—was when someone else started to cry. She couldn't stop herself from feeling their pain and crying with them, which is what Mr. Storm would have labeled the strength of empathy. "We can be hopeful," she agreed.

Light burst forth into the dark room as a contingent of scaly guards forced Haruka and Mr. Storm out into a brightly lit hallway. Once out of the room, the alien lizards bound their prisoners' hands and marched them down a long corridor onto a loading platform that led to the surface. Mr. Storm could see the orange sky and wondered whether it was natural or due to the pollution caused by the mining facility. Until that moment, he could hardly believe they were on an alien planet, but he now confirmed it with his own eyes.

"It's beautiful, in a way," said Haruka. The strange wind tingled her skin and the scent on the air was refreshing but foreign and strange. Their brief moment of reverie was interrupted by a shove in the back and the harsh sounds of the alien lizard language. Their march took them to a large, blocky building covered in shiny glass windows that reflected the blinding sunlight. Once inside, they made their way down a seemingly endless hallway and into a small waiting room, where a Dorian with intricate features sat at a small reception desk. This Dorian looked very different from the guards that Mr. Storm and Haruka had seen so far. Its snout was slender and its frame smaller. The scales on its exposed arms were more brilliant and diverse in color. Even its smell was less pungent, almost pleasant.

"A female?" Haruka inquired of Mr. Storm.

"That would be my guess," he responded.

The alien looked down at her desk, uncomfortable under the human stares. She stood up and led the guards and prisoners into a room where a lone Dorian was seated behind a large, intricate desk. He waived his claw rudely toward the female Dorian and she departed with a bow. He turned his attention to the two prisoners and began hissing and growling as he leaned back in his giant chair. Haruka and Mr. Storm exchanged barely visible smiles. The alien bureaucrat stopped making sounds and pushed a button on his desk. The female Dorian returned and placed a tiny, almost microscopic metal ball in each prisoner's ear. Mr. Storm shook his head as the foreign object tickled its way down into his ear.

"All right, let's try this again. Can you understand me now?"

"Yes, I can understand you," replied Haruka.

"I can too!" said Mr. Storm, excitedly.

"Good. Do you know…"

"A universal translator! This is amazing. Captain Jack wasn't kidding. I have so many questions. What decryption algorithm do you use? Is it adaptive? Are they connected to a central database?"

"Shut up!" screeched Administrator Serno. "Close your mouth! It is time for you to listen, not…not…not babble on. You're a laborer. For the love of Lady Lakanar!"

"You don't have to be rude about it!" retorted Mr. Storm.

"Do you know how many aliens have escaped this facility under my leadership? None. Zero."

"Impressive!" said Haruka sarcastically.

"Do you know how many aliens have even, even, even, attempted it?" he asked.

"Twenty-seven?" replied Mr. Storm.

"No! Not twenty-seven. Zero. You two are the first. Now I have to come up with a way to…to…to discourage your kind from escaping. That is okay, because I love discouraging aliens from trying to escape," he said menacingly. "Now, I could have you both tortured in front of the others to set an example, but I don't know if that will be a strong enough deterrent."

"That should be strong enough, I think, right, Sebastian?" Haruka asked. The only thing worse than torture was death, and she could survive torture.

"That would work really well," agreed Mr. Storm.

"No, no, I don't think so," replied Administrator Serno. "I could torture you in front of everyone and then kill you. That might do it."

"Uhhh, not sure that would work," said Mr. Storm.

"That will just make everyone want to escape even more, I think," agreed Haruka.

"Hmmm. You may be right," mused Serno. "I find it more effective when you don't punish the perpetrators. You see, if you punish the perpetrator, they are more likely to try escaping again because they think they are risking only a bit of pain if they are caught." Administrator Serno let the idea sink in. He could tell that the captives knew where this was leading, and he relished these little moments. "The guards report that your mate is also captive here," he smirked at Mr. Storm.

"If you touch her, I will kill you with my bare hands. That is a promise. You won't be able to stop me." Mr. Storm stood calm, collected, and intense. The fear that descended upon Administrator Serno's face lasted only a brief moment.

"There it is. That is what will keep you from trying to escape again. Now, I can't kill her. That would clearly provide you with great motivation to escape. I can, however, make you watch as she suffers." Serno's tone was malicious, sinister. He moved in close toward Mr. Storm and looked up at him with a glare of superiority. "That should be just enough motivation to keep you from escaping again. You will also help ensure that the others don't escape because, if they do, I won't take it out on them, or their partners, or you. I will take it out on your mate. Her screams will haunt you."

Administrator Serno was not nearly as tall as Mr. Storm, but he stood confident in his command and control over his prisoners until Mr. Storm delivered a head-butt that bloodied his face and knocked him unconscious.

Mr. Storm and Haruka walked out of the office door and into the waiting room where the guards stood ready. The receptionist sat at her desk watching intently.

"We're done in there," said Mr. Storm to female Dorian. "We won't be needing a follow-up appointment."

"He's going to need a doctor," giggled Haruka.

#

Two short, pink-skinned alien pilots were reviewing their pre-launch checklist. They had round bodies and limbs with pig-like snouts. The Dorian guards had brought up the last load of ore, something neither of the pilots had seen before. It had always been one of the laborers, but these two weren't in the habit of asking questions of the Dorian guards. The Dorians had left, and it was time to take off.

"Hey Bart, did you notice that we have a guest in the cargo hold?" snorted one of the pilots, his narrow, pig-like nose twitching.

"I sure did, Veemo" answered Bart. "I overheard the guards talking about Earth people. This might be one of them."

"I heard that too. Maybe it's one of them. You know the Monarch has a pretty sizable reward for anyone claiming to be from Earth," explained Veemo.

"Very sizable," said Bart. The two exchanged grins as they pulled away from the Dorian mines.

CHAPTER 14

On the Trail of Hanna Storm

Boother and Mung arrived to a chaotic scene at the Galactic Zoo. Some of the zoo's inhabitants moped back to their enclosures while others scurried about, hoping to escape. A contingent of guards scurried back and forth, uncertain as to which group they should pursue. Mung grabbed one of the frazzled guards.

"Who is in charge here?" he demanded. The guard gestured toward a short, sausage-shaped Korilan who paced nervously back and forth. Next to him fidgeted a tusked Teloran trying to reassure his boss—or perhaps himself—that everything would be fine.

"That would be Zookeeper Beb and his assistant, Mr. Remy." the guard smiled. Mung and Boother made their way over.

"Excuse me, Zookeeper Beb. I understand that you are in charge here. I am Officer Mung, and this is Officer Boother. We are with the Corridor Patrol."

"You have no jurisdiction here," shouted Beb. "We're in the middle of a catastrophe. A catastrophe! Be on your way."

Mung exchanged a surprised look with Boother's orange bumps.

"Let me handle thizzz one," said Boother. "It'zzz my turn to play bad cop." He turned to Zookeeper Beb and grabbed the collar of his tunic with stubby, gelatinous arms.

"We are the Corridor Patrol on an official invezzztigation. Everywhere izzz our jurizzzdiction. You can anzzzwer our quezzzztionzzz or we can arezzzt you for obzzztruction."

"How can we help you?" grunted an intervening Remy. "We need to get back to managing this crisis as soon as possible."

"What happened here?" asked Mung.

"That horrible, horrible Earth girl and her Makaran friend released all of our exhibits. That's what happened. We're ruined," lamented Zookeeper Beb.

"We don't know it was them," corrected Remy.

"Oh, I know it was them. Who else but that horrible Earth girl and her disgusting Makaran companion? Everything was fine before they arrived. It was them. I know it! I know it!" screamed Zookeeper Beb.

"How did you come by an Earth girl?" asked Mung, knowing very well that he had purchased her from the Sendori Sanitarium for Homeless, Lost, and Discarded Children. "Only low-level criminals are sent here when so ordered by the Galactic Courts, correct?"

"That is true," Zookeeper Beb laughed nervously.

"Interesting," said Mung. "Boother, have you seen any reports of an Earth girl being sentenced to this facility?"

"No zzzir," answered Boother.

"Nor have I," rejoined Mung.

"Lizzzten up Beb," said Boother, grabbing him by the collar again. "We already have an invezzztigation going on. It would be in your interezzzt to anzzzwer our quezzzztionzzz. Where izzz the Earth girl?"

Zookeeper Beb remained silent, despite the fear that he could not hide. Remy, however, groveled before the Corridor Patrolmen; he did not want to end up an exhibit in this place himself.

"She escaped. Witnesses say she was with a Dorian, a Makaran, and a Bimber," grumbled Remy honestly. "My name is Remy; please note my cooperation."

Boother's bumps darkened to a concerned purple. He released Beb, whose collar he had been holding this entire conversation. "Great Galadaria'zzz Girdle!" exclaimed Boother. "Did you zzzay a Bimber?"

"And a Makaran and a Dorian," said Remy.

"Which way did they go?" asked Mung.

"There is a hole in the south gate where the Bimber broke through. That's all I know," Remy complied.

"Let's go Boother. We need to find her," said Mung. "If we can't find an Earth girl, a Dorian, a Makaran, and a Bimber traveling together, we should turn in our badges." Mung turned to address Zookeeper Beb and Remy. "Thank you for your time gentleman. Someone from the Corridor Patrol will be along shortly to arrest...ahem, I mean, assist you. Yes. To assist you with your crisis here."

Boother and Mung briskly left the chaotic scene and continued their search for the Earth girl Hanna Storm.

CHAPTER 15

The Monarch and the Cosmonaut

Hanna Storm sat on a plush couch in a library that resembled one that you might find on Earth. There were a few old tomes, scrolls, and books but also a variety of discs, cubes, and other alien media that Hanna could not identify. Blue sat next to her on one side and Saldo on the other, while Mera sat on a couch that was meant for two. She was not quite as tall as Mr. Storm, but Hanna was in no doubt as to who would be victorious in a match, no matter how much she admired her father's fighting abilities. A large, throne-like chair directly across from Hanna's couch stood empty. Stiggs, who had changed into a tuxedo that made him look like a frog butler, stood next to the empty chair.

The door to the library opened, and the Monarch walked in. Hanna stood, and her compatriots followed suit. He had changed out of his white, bedazzled jumpsuit and was wearing matching dark jeans and jean jacket, collar upturned. He sported large sunglasses, a gold chain, and several rings. His shirt was unbuttoned down to just above his navel. He moved toward Hanna, hand outstretched; Mera jumped between the two.

"Whoa!" the Monarch paused. "Relax Ms. Bimber," said the Monarch. Hanna nodded to Mera, and she backed away, keeping her gaze fixed sternly upon him.

"Uh-huh. You are definitely from Earth," declared the Monarch, sizing Hanna up and down. She did the same. He reached out and embraced her. "We don't get too many Earth folks out this way," he said. "It does my heart good to see you."

"How did you get here?" Hanna marveled. "Are you really him?" She had so many questions.

"I'm me," he chuckled. "The real deal, young miss. You'll get a kick out of this. Stiggs, what's my full title?"

"You are known throughout Galaxy Prime as the Monarch of Mineral and Rotation," came the proud response. Hanna giggled. These translators!

"Let's swap stories. I'll go first," offered the Monarch. He took his seat on the throne and invited the others to sit back down. "Stiggs, go fetch us some sodas."

"As you request," said Stiggs, disappearing through the door.

"In 1971, I met with President Nixon, and we sort of hit it off. I told him about the UFOs I'd seen at various times throughout my life, and a few years later he invited me out to Area 51. They had a spaceship that had crash-landed on Earth, and he let me take it for a spin with one of his Area 51 pilots. We were up there in space when a large green wall just swallowed us up. I ended up here in Galaxy Prime and have been building my business empire ever since."

Hanna's mouth had fallen open about two words into this story and remained open. Her inability to speak was soon overtaken by her curiosity, but she was finding it hard to think straight.

"Why haven't you aged?" was the only response she could think of. Start working, brain!

"One of my science-type friends explained it to me once. I don't really remember the details. Stiggs!"

Stiggs entered with some colorful and bubbly beverages. Hanna selected a purple one and took a long tug on the bottle. She swished it around in her mouth as she had seen her mother do with a newly opened bottle of wine. An exotic, fruity bouquet rushed her senses of taste and smell. She had expected a grape flavor, but it was something else entirely, a flavor she could not put into words, even to herself.

"Stiggs, why don't I get any older?" asked the Monarch.

"You are from Sister Galaxy and won't begin to age until the gluon particles from your time in your galaxy reach you here in Galaxy Prime. That will occur in about 10 million years."

"Thanks, Stiggs. I don't get how the whole space-time continuum works, but I don't think Earth scientists have found that space rays cause aging yet," said the Monarch.

"That actually makes some sense," said Hanna, "but only if there is some sort of undetected subatomic radiation produced by gluons that drive the aging process. This is big."

"It's groovy all right, but my brain can't fit it in for some reason," said the Monarch, tapping his noggin.

"Where is the person who piloted your ship?" Hanna asked.

"Dwayne? He met a Florangian and settled down with her in some system somewhere. Stiggs?"

"The Florangian system, sir, like the species," he croaked.

"How did you know about me?" asked Hanna.

"Word travels fast, little lady," he said. "When I heard the zoo had an Earth person, I wanted to make sure she didn't end up in the kill box."

"Thank you for sending Stiggs," she said. "Thank you Stiggs."

"What's your story, young miss?" asked the Monarch.

Hanna recounted her entire story, beginning with the first commercial space cruise on the *Eloise*; her encounter with the Corridor Patrol Officers Boother and Mung; her stay in the Sendori Sanitarium for Homeless, Lost, and Discarded Children, where she had met Blue; and her escape from the zoo, where she had picked up Saldo the Dorian and Mera the Bimber.

"I know Tsarana well," said the Monarch. "She has the voice of an angel," he sighed with starry eyes. "Sorry to hear about your parents. From what I know about Dorians, they are probably stuck in a mine somewhere. Going after them would be dangerous."

"Extremely dangerous without someone like me to help," interrupted Saldo.

The Monarch looked at him suspiciously and continued. "With that many humans, I'm inclined to help. People in this galaxy think we're a myth, so we have to stick together. Those Dorians can be nasty though," said the Monarch. "No offense," he said, directing it at Saldo.

"None taken," responded Saldo graciously.

"It won't be easy. No ma'am, not easy at all. Plus, I'm respected in this galaxy, and I have to retain my completely legitimate businesses." The Monarch stared off into the distance over Hanna's shoulder. She could almost see the wheels spinning in his head. "I'll send you to Vlad. He'll take care of it. He's got a good mind for things like this. Stiggs! Where is Vlad these days?"

"He is usually at his club, sir," answered Stiggs.

"Vlad?" said Hanna. "He's human?"

"He's more Soviet cosmonaut than human," laughed the Monarch. "Stiggs! Take Hanna and her crew and get them to Vlad. He'll know what to do. Stick around and help them out as much as you can."

"As you wish sir," croaked Stiggs.

#

Hanna, Blue, Saldo, and Mera stood in line at a swanky night club. The line was filled with aliens of every variety dressed in colorful and fancy clothing. Bright blues and oranges with long flowy material were clearly in fashion. Hanna recognized instantly that the patrons here were of high social and economic status, or, as Hanna called them, snobs.

Hanna brushed off the crowd's stares but was surprised when nobody ran from the Bimber. The potential patrons visibly shook in their bright blue and orange shoes, but nobody exited the line.

"Majestic!" Hanna said aloud. "Popularity over safety at this club."

"How is that majestic?" asked Stiggs.

"Never mind," Hanna deflected. Explaining her repertoire of Earth exclamations to Stiggs may require several days.

"As you wish." Stiggs hopped off to the front of the line to negotiate their entry. He began speaking with a beefy-bodied bouncer that stood at least seven feet tall and had three pairs of equally beefy arms. A ring of eyeballs encircled its head. Without pausing the conversation with Stiggs, the bottom arm on its left side shot out to catch a small bug-like patron trying to sneak in without paying the entrance fee.

Hanna had never been in a nightclub before, but she had seen plenty on television. She didn't really understand the appeal of it, but some of the kids she knew on Earth were already trying to make fake identification cards and gain entry to places like this. It was noisy and crowded, and the fact that everyone was staring at her and her companions began to weigh on her.

"Where are we at with our entry?" she interrupted Stiggs and the massive bouncer.

"On target, young miss," rumbled the bouncer. He opened the chain guarding the door and personally led them to a room in the back where she saw a human dressed in an orange flight suit, laughing, drink in hand. He was sitting down, but Hanna could tell right away that he was shorter than she was. She remembered that the Soviet cosmonaut Yuri Gagarin, the first man to orbit the Earth, had been five feet and two inches tall and had worn an identical orange flight suit. Those first cosmonauts had to be short to fit inside the rocket! There was enough room in the booth where the human sat to accommodate Hanna and her crew, but Mera remained standing and alert. Hanna noticed that she was tapping her feet to the music but wasn't sure if drawing attention to it would embarrass the Bimber.

"I'm Vladyslav Evgenyevich Zelenko. You can call me Vlad. You must be Hanna Storm. Welcome to Galaxy Prime." Hanna marveled at how the translator not only translated his words but also conveyed his thick Ukrainian accent. Ukrainian and English must not be very compatible according to the universal translation algorithm. "Monarch say you have problem. I help fix problem."

"How did you get here, to the Andromeda Galaxy?" Hanna asked.

"That is easy. Easy peasy. I was first man in space. Suddenly my ship was surrounded by green light, like Aurora Borealis on Earth. Few days later, I am here in this galaxy."

"What year was that? I thought Yuri Gagarin was the first man in space. That was on April 12, 1961." Hanna was well versed in the history of Earth space exploration.

"Ha! Little Yuri? First man in space? He was just junior officer when I went up in August 1959. Nobody knows of me on Earth then?"

"No, not really," Hanna said apologetically.

"The devil take it. Yuri Gagarin! Those ungrateful communists!" exclaimed Vlad, his brown eyes flashing as he ran his hand through his dark, curly hair. "They are too embarrassed by mistakes, so they do not admit them. They just bury mistakes and forget."

"We should get to the task at hand," Saldo sighed.

"Right," said Vlad. "Let's get down to business, as Americans say. So, you want to find your parents. First, we need ship, one that can no be tracked."

"I have a ship," said Hanna. "The *Eloise*."

"This ship comes from Earth?" asked Vlad.

"Yes."

"Good. It will not be registered and will be difficult to track," Vlad said.

"I don't know," said Hanna. "The Corridor Patrol found me pretty easily."

"Yes, because you are object that exited outside of corridor. They did not know you were ship until they found you," Vlad explained. "Plus, Dorian technology is not advanced. They will no be able to track you, but your ship will need modification."

"One small problem," interjected Hanna. "The *Eloise* is currently in the hands of the Galactic Police Force."

"This is not problem," said Vlad. "Stiggs can steal anything. Also, Galactic Police impound is near mechanic I know. Very good mechanic. Can make modifications to your—what is it?—*Eloise*?"

"That's right," Hanna confirmed.

"This is ludicrous," said Saldo. "Stealing from the Galactic Police Force? Modifying an Earth ship? This plan is doomed. Thinking Dorian technology inferior? Stupidity! They'll find you as soon as you cross the border into Dorian space."

"You have better idea?" asked Vlad.

"Yes. Let me contact my people and arrange for a ship to meet us at the border," insisted Saldo.

Vlad paused to consider, as did the others.

"No. My plan is better," said Vlad. Saldo was about to rebut, but Hanna placed her arm on his.

"Saldo, if that's what you want to do for yourself, that's fine. You have no obligation to stay with us," Hanna explained.

"I won't stand a chance on my own," said Saldo. "A lone Dorian in Galactic Treaty space is too suspicious. I'd be back in the zoo within a galactic standard week. A Dorian with an Earth person, a Bimber, and a Makaran? That is actually less suspicious, for each of us, but especially me."

"This is true," said Vlad. "Better to stick together."

"So, let's say we get this ship stolen from the Corridor Patrol," said Mera, "and let's say we get it properly modified. How are we going to find her parents?"

"Pirates," said Vlad.

"Pirates?" Blue asked. "No. No. I can't handle pirates." Blue stood up and paced nervously, eyes on the floor and hands gesticulating wildly as he mumbled to himself something about "never again."

"Relax," said Vlad. "Is simple. We need pirate for to sell Hanna to Dorian mine."

"Excuse me?" said Mera.

"It's okay, Mera. Let him finish," Hanna intervened.

"Dorians do only business with pirates. There are moons, two or three, where maybe humans work, but pirates know with which one Earth people are." His Ukrainian accent was coming through thickly. "Pirates know these things. We choose right mine and use Hanna for bait. You sell Hanna to mine. She look for parents. When you find, you rescue. Is simple," said Vlad matter-of-factly.

"Nothing about this is simple," said Mera.

"How do we get pirates to help? Ask politely?" said Blue, still exhibiting disbelief at the fact that this was actually being discussed.

"Is simple," said Vlad. "Pirates have code, no? Challenge for leadership. You win, get information, and ask for few pirates to help you."

"A code? What code?" gasped Hanna. "I've been listening carefully, Vlad, and want to give you the benefit of the doubt, but this sounds nuts. Butts and nuts! Code or not, you want me to pick a fight with pirates? And you think I will win?" asked Hanna. "I mean, I can take care of myself, mostly, but I am *not* confident of winning a fight with anyone from this galaxy."

"Of course you win," said Vlad, "obviously. You will no fight, Hanna. You have Bimber. She win, for sure. Is simple. Keep Bimber hidden when you make challenge. Then bring Bimber out for fight. That is all."

"This is insane," said Blue. "Even if we win and the pirates help us sell Hanna to a mine, how do we get her out if something goes wrong?"

"Take secret weapon," said Vlad.

"What secret weapon?" asked Hanna.

"Stiggs. He can steal anything, even person from mine. Just do what he say, and you will be fine. Everything is fine. You go with them, right, Stiggs?"

"That is the Monarch's wish," Stiggs croaked.

"Good. Is settled. Everything A-okay. Let's drink," said the Ukrainian in his thick accent. "I teach them how to make vodka. That is why this place so popular. Only place in galaxy with good vodka."

"I'll pass," said Hanna.

"I'll have a double," said Mera.

#

"Boran, report!" instructed Master Slythe, who was standing resolute, gazing through an observation window from his ship. Dorians did not name their vessels. Rather, the vessel was an extension of its master and was considered part of his being. Slythe's rise to power had been prolonged and difficult. His was a lesser clan which suffered much humiliation at the hands of the large and powerful Clan Midoka. As a youth, Slythe had watched his father grovel and plead for his life during a very public execution at the hands of elite Midoka soldiers. He had sworn vengeance and spent years scheming in disguise within Clan Midoka. When Slythe had sown the seeds of discontent among enough of the populace, he led the revolt against Master Midoka. During a very public execution, he had relished watching Master Midoka grovel and plead for his life. Now Slythe stood on his own ship, meticulously supervising a fleet of spacecraft under his command. The spacecraft were delivering and connecting pieces of equipment to an enormous semicircle structure floating above a small moon somewhere in the Kamal-Etet system in Dorian-occupied space. It was here that Dorian lore placed a corridor to another galaxy, and it was here that Slythe launched his first attempt to open a corridor to Earth.

"The corridor engine is on schedule for completion in three galactic standard days," growled Boran. "Shifts are doubled, and the mines are producing at capacity." Boran's only working eye focused on the construction taking place outside his Master's window.

"Good! Let me know as soon as it is operational. Are the first construction vessels ready to mobilize?"

"As you instructed, I have appointed Master Rabard to organize and lead the entire fleet. Construction and material vessels are now being outfitted under his command," answered Boran.

"Master Rabard is perfect for this mission. He is both ruthless and efficient. He'll get the most out of the Earth laborers." Slythe was content. "Speaking of laborers, how are our Earth prisoners faring? Are they productive?"

"There has already been an escape attempt by the warrior among them, but it was easily quashed," growled Boran.

"Interesting," considered Master Slythe. "It's good that they have some fight in them, unlike the spineless globules of the Galactic Treaty planets." He paused to reflect. "We shall have to make an example of him."

"Administrator Serno is already taking measures."

"Serno? Excellent," he chuckled. "I should like to see it myself. Prepare my shuttle."

"If I may, Master? What of the Royal Court?" inquired Boran.

"So far, they remain in the dark about our plan, and I intend to keep it that way. In fact, you have some business to attend to. Follow me." Boran raised his scaly brow in curiosity. He followed Slythe out the door and to the brig of their ship. In one of the cells quivered a small, weedy Dorian.

"This is a spy from Clan Moradan, the Emperor's most loyal supporters. I want you to make inquiries as to what he knows and root out any other insurgents. Word of our little project cannot get back to the Royal Court until we have the Earth people working our mines and Earth resources supplying our factories. Only then will I be able to unite the clans against the Emperor." Master Slythe paused and smiled, a distant look in his eyes. "After we secure the Empire, we will no doubt be able to crush the Galactic Treaty planets and conquer the entirety of Galaxy Prime. I will rule and Clan Slythe coffers will overflow," he hissed menacingly.

"All hail the new Emperor," Boran bowed. "If you will excuse me, Master Slythe, I am eager to begin my interrogation."

"Of course," Slythe grinned. "I know how much you enjoy your work. I look forward to your report. I'll take my shuttle to the third moon and pay a surprise visit to Serno. Join me there when you're done with your...recreation."

"As you wish, Master Slythe."

#

"There izzz an incoming tranzzzmission Mung. It izzz from Command."

"Put it through Boother," replied Mung. Boother pressed a few buttons and rotated a knob until the picture on the screen came through clearly. It was the image of the Lady of the Chamber at Galactic Police Force Command.

"Lady of the Chamber!" said Mung, with a great deal of surprise. "How may we serve you?"

"Have you found the Earth girl yet?" asked the Lady of the Chamber, a touch of urgency in her voice.

"She was not at the Sendori Sanitarium for Homeless, Lost, and Discarded Children," explained Mung. "It appears that the Sanitarium is illegally selling students to the Galactic Zoo."

"What? How can that be?" asked the Lady of the Chamber, with genuine surprise in her voice.

"We've launched an official investigation, but Boother and I are still on our primary mission to find and return the Earth girl. We followed her to the zoo, but she had escaped by the time we arrived."

"Escaped? Escaped where?"

"We don't know for sure, but witnesses place her with a Makaran, a Dorian, and a Bimber, all of whom have escaped from the zoo. We're sifting through tips, but the most promising is a sighting of said subjects at one of the Monarch's properties. We're en route to investigate now."

"Great Maken's Meat! Did you say a Bimber?"

"And a Dorian and a Makaran," said Mung without emotion.

"How is she still alive?" asked the Lady of the Chamber. "Never mind," she said, responding to her own question. "Our intelligence operative in the Dorian Empire has reported unconfirmed rumors of the construction of a giant corridor engine near the Kamal-Etet system. We need the Earth girl back here immediately for questioning."

"Understood. We'll collect her from New Meadows and bring her directly to Command."

"Acknowledged," said the Lady of the Chamber. "I suggest you make haste. Oh, and please bring me back an autographed picture of the Monarch for my daughter. She just loves his music. End transmission."

Boother and Mung looked at each other.

"If they are building a corridor engine that can reach Earth, we have to warn Hanna," said Mung.

"We have to find her firzzzt," asserted Boother.

CHAPTER 16

Eloise Gets a Makeover

Stiggs slowed his sleek limousine-like spacecraft to a gentle stop. They were now in the seediest part of the entire Capital system. The Capital system stood at the cross-roads of several space corridors within Galaxy Prime. Every species in the galaxy could be found here. Galactic Treaty system embassies were here along with most galaxy-level government administration buildings. A good mechanic could make a decent living in this sector, but some modifications were more legal than others, and it was to this part of town that someone seeking less-than-legal modifications could go. They pulled into a large field that contained an enormous, rusty, run-down, old hangar. The sign at the entryway was poorly lit and looked like paint on metal rather than the fancy holographic signs that Hanna had seen in New Meadows. Hanna's universal translator kicked into gear, and the meaning of the strange writing on the sign coalesced in her head. "Haranda Su's Spaceship Repairs and Modifications."

"I believe we have arrived," croaked Stiggs. "Haranda Su is the best mechanic in Galaxy Prime," he explained. He led the Earth girl, Bimber, Dorian, and Makaran toward the hangar entrance. Upon entering, Hanna could see that the hangar was largely empty with the exception of a small ship that looked as though it could seat just two or three people. A small creature approximately half Hanna's size was welding metallic poles to a metallic sheet.

"Welcome!" came a cheerful voice through the thick welding mask covering its face. "You must be the clients Vlad sent over. Make yourselves at home."

The team looked around. There was no part of this hangar that would ever be in any of their homes, and they wondered just how they would make themselves feel at home in this place.

"That should do it." The alien hopped down from its workstation with the grace of a gold-medal gymnast. It approached Hanna and lifted its mask. "I'm Haranda Su. You must be an Earth female. Never seen an Earth female before. I'm female too. A Rinarian female." The Rinarian put forward one of her four hands for a human-style handshake. "This is how Vlad taught me to do it." She had two arms, but each arm had two hands and wrists.

"Yep. I'm a female from Earth," replied Hanna. "My name is Hanna Storm. These are my friends Mera, Saldo, and Blue. You know Stiggs I guess."

"Sure do! Hiya Stiggs!" she waved. "Wow, a Bimber," she said enthusiastically, "and a Makaran?" she said quizzically. "Don't steal my soul now," she laughed. "I'm just messing with ya. And a Dorian," she said suspiciously. "Where'd ya dig this one up?" she asked Hanna.

"Saldo was a prisoner at the zoo with us," she answered.

"Wonder what he did to get tossed in there," Haranda Su said sarcastically.

"He's going to help me find my parents. They were kidnapped by other Dorians. I helped him escape and now he's going to return the favor. We help each other out," Hanna defended.

"Dorians only help themselves," Haranda Su said, giving the Dorian a suspicious look.

"You can't judge all Dorians by the actions of a few," insisted Hanna.

"Maybe so," said Haranda Su, still trying to read the Dorian. "Maybe so."

"I don't need you to trust me," said Saldo. "I just need you to modify the ship so I can get back home and take Hanna to her parents."

"The ship!" croaked Stiggs. "I'll go retrieve Hanna's ship from the Galactic Police Force impound yard." Stiggs leaped up and disappeared out the hangar door.

"All we can do now is wait," said Haranda Su. "I'll put on some Dutherian tea. My living area is up in that loft. Follow me." The team followed Haranda Su up the ladder and into a comfortably sized loft area with a sofa and a few chairs and cushions on which to sit. Everyone found a spot and settled in. Mera looked particularly out of place sitting on a Haranda Su-sized stool, her knees almost to her chin. Haranda Su disappeared through a small screened-off corridor and returned with cups and a steaming pitcher of Dutherian tea. She distributed the cups and poured everyone a good measure. The aroma was unfamiliar to Hanna, but it was very pleasant, and she blew on her tea and sipped. Delightful!

"So, what's a Dorian doing out here in the zoo," asked Haranda Su.

"I was working in logistics at a mine when a smuggler hit me over the head and loaded me in the hold. I woke up in my zoo habitat, and that was it," explained Saldo. "I hope they received a fair price for me."

"I thought you had been there since you were a kid," said Hanna inquisitively.

"That is also true," he said without missing a beat. "I started working at the mine when I was very young, even for a Dorian, and was young when I arrived at the zoo."

"A likely story," scoffed Blue.

"Oh?" responded Saldo. "What about you? How did you end up at the Sendori Sanitarium for Homeless, Lost, and Discarded Children?"

"I was discarded," said Blue sullenly. "The Sendori Sanitarium for Homeless, Lost, and Discarded Children was the only place that would take me. Even they almost didn't. Said I was too old. If Tsarana hadn't intervened and pledged to Headmistress Blurch that she would take personal responsibility for me..."

"How old are you Blue?" interrupted Hanna.

"Three hundred and fifty-seven galactic standard years," said Blue. Shocked looks all around!

"Wow," said Hanna. "I would have put you at fifteen, tops."

"In my species I'm still an adolescent, okay?" Blue defended. "Evolution gave us plenty of time to find our adopted species. Once we undergo metamorphosis, we inherit their physiology and live on average the same length of time as they do." As far as Blue was concerned, it made perfect sense. Very efficient. He decided to throw the spotlight on someone else. "What about you, Mera? What's your story?"

"Yeah, Mera," seconded Hanna. "How did you end up in the zoo? I can't imagine you being taken by force."

"We're not invincible, you know. I'm just a female," she said.

"What does that have to do with anything?" Hanna gasped.

"Everything!" shouted Mera. "For a Bimber, if you're a woman and want to be a warrior, you can only fight other women or other species. You can't fight the best because you would lose." Mera increased in her intensity and an orange-colored energy began to form around her body. "And if you do want to fight boys, your parents are disgraced, and they are forced to get rid of you." She smashed her hand against the thick metal wall of the hangar, and blew a hole right through it. The orange energy dissipated, and she sat down.

"Your parents sold you because you wanted to fight the best? Mera, I'm so sorry." Hanna said, throwing her arms up around the Bimber. She squeezed as tight as she could.

"On my planet, boys are stronger than girls, on average," explained Hanna, "but when it comes to you, an individual person, on average doesn't matter." Hanna really wanted to get this point across. "My dad told me a story about how he wanted to be a distance runner when he was young. Try as he might, he never reached the top ten of his boys' team. He even compared his fastest times to the girl's team and was slower than the top seven female runners. So even though the fastest boys were faster than the fastest girls, the best girls were faster than most of the boys. Does that make sense?"

"Great," responded Mera. "Even in Sister Galaxy the girls are worse than the boys." All she took away from Hanna's speech was that the fastest boys were faster than the fastest girls.

"I think you missed my point," said Hanna. "That maybe wasn't the right story to make it. Let me tell you about my neighbor Tamika. She is a few years older than I am and she loved to play American football. Football is a sport usually played only by boys. Tamika loved football though, and she was good—so good, in fact, that she was the first girl to play on her high school football team." Hanna paused for effect. "You see, Mera, people may think a woman can't do certain things until she stands up and shows that she can. That's what you were doing, and that makes you my hero. Earth's history is full of women like that," Hanna explained.

"I get it," sighed Mera. "You're technically right I guess," she acquiesced. They all sat in silence for a moment and then the tiniest spark lit up in Mera's eyes. "I may not ever be the best fighter in the galaxy, but just because something has been done a certain way for thousands of years doesn't mean that is how it has to continue." The spark grew and started to fill her whole being with an orange glow.

She stood forthright and declared triumphantly "I will be the first female Bimber to defeat a male in combat. That much I can do."

"Exactly!" said Hanna. Mera picked her up in a big bear hug.

"Rinarian females aren't usually mechanics," joined in Haranada Su, "but I'm the best in the galaxy, better than any male Rinarian," she stated confidently. "I have my father to thank for that." She leaped onto Mera's shoulder and joined in the hug. Saldo sat back and laughed.

"Oh, please. Dorian women would never behave like this. They understand their purpose is to create and raise the next generation. Imagine! A Dorian female warrior or mechanic. How absurd! I don't think I'll see that in my lifetime." Mera started her cycle of intensity, but Hanna put an arm on her shoulder and Mera inhaled a slow breath of restraint.

"I guess we have some work to do in the Dorian part of the galaxy," was Hanna's only response.

It was a brief and awkward silence, broken by a curious Mera.

"How do women on Earth fight?" she asked.

"Well, they fight the same way as men. It's not always the strongest who wins. It's the most skilled and the most clever."

Mera gasped in suspicious unbelief. "On my planet, it is always the one who hits the hardest that emerges victorious," she explained, as though any other path to victory was a ludicrous impossibility.

"On Earth, there are a lot of different styles of fighting. My dad trained me a little bit in what we call mixed martial arts because it combines boxing and wrestling," Hanna explained.

"Show me!" Mera begged.

"Okay," giggled Hanna. She had helped her father teach a few self-defense classes and confidently stood up to demonstrate what she had learned.

"If you really want to defend yourself," said Hanna, "you need to be willing to shove your thumb into someone else's eye socket."

"I have no problem with that," said Mera matter-of-factly.

Hanna showed Mera a few boxing combinations, which Mera had already mastered of course. She was particularly interested when Hanna showed her a few blocks and other defensive moves. Apparently, Bimber fighting was all about offense and brute force. Where Mera really became excited was in the grappling portion of the lesson.

"Brazilian jiu jitsu was pioneered by a few brothers," explained Hanna. "They figured out ways to get people on the ground and control them. They could snap arms and break legs of competitors twice their size," Hanna boasted. "I'll show you a few basic moves. Hey, Blue, come here."

Blue reluctantly came over and Hanna coaxed him into a fighting stance with fists raised.

"First thing you want to do is distract your opponent, and then you take them to the ground." Hanna slapped down one of Blue's arms and lunged to her knees, wrapped both arms around Blue's legs, lifted him into the air, and gently laid him down onto his back.

"Ummm, what are you doing, Hanna?" queried Blue calmly.

"Showing Mera some Earth fighting moves," she answered. "Now, if at any time you are in pain, you need to tap my arm and I'll let go."

"I don't think that will be necessary," said Blue.

"Okay, Blue. Whatever you say. Prepare yourself," Hanna warned.

Blue smiled. Hanna had placed her chest on top of his and her knee up into his side with his arm pinned down. He wasn't going anywhere. "This is called 'side control'," explained Hanna. "Now, I'm going to get on top of him." Hanna swung a leg over Blue's torso and was on him in an instant. "I like to throw a few punches here." Hanna simulated some punches to Blue's face, but he did not flinch...at all. Haranda Su giggled.

"From here you can also do a number of different arm breaks," Hanna smiled, unperturbed. "This one is called the Americana," she gleamed. Hanna wrapped her arm through Blue's and bent down over his side. "Once you have control, you put the arm in this position and bring it down to your opponent's waist like this." Blue laughed.

"That tickles!" shouted Blue.

Hanna paused, then applied even more pressure. "You have to calmly whisper something to intimidate your opponent at this point, like 'I'm taking you down to the train stop and putting you on the pain train' or 'I'm going to break your arm and there's nothing you can do to stop it,' something like that." Blue laughed again. His arm was like rubber. Try as she might, she couldn't get Blue to submit. He just kept laughing and asking Hanna to stop tickling him. Frustrated, Hanna finally released him.

"Well, it works on humans," she defended.

"It probably works on most species," explained Blue, "but Makaran physiology is very pliable. We morph, remember?"

"Okay, Blue. you win," she conceded. "Now you try Mera. You can practice on Saldo."

Saldo held up his hands to resist but was on his back before he knew it. He was also on his feet before he knew it when Mera jerked him up. Now back on the ground. This happened four or five times before she moved into the Americana. She executed it flawlessly on her first try. "Show me more!" Mera demanded.

"Okay. This is my favorite move," Hanna said. She rolled Blue over onto his stomach and laid down on top of his back. "Once you have the advantage, you grab them from behind in a headlock like this." She wrapped one arm under Blue's neck and grabbed the bicep of her other arm, squeezing her elbows together. She rolled over onto her back and squeezed with all her might. Blue continued smiling. "You have to lock your legs in like this," she demonstrated, wrapping her ankles around Blue's inner thighs. "Usually they pass out, if they aren't a Makaran," Hanna clarified. "It's called a rear naked choke."

"Naked? You just did it clothed. Is it more effective to be naked?" Mera asked, starting to remove her trousers. Hanna held up her hand and quickly intervened.

"I don't know why it's called that. Probably because it makes you feel vulnerable, like when you're naked," she guessed.

"I don't feel vulnerable when I'm naked," said Mera. "I feel invincible!"

Haranda Su jumped to her feet.

"Stiggs is back." She slid down the ladder and pushed a big red button on the wall. The hangar doors opened slowly. Hanna and the others followed, and Hanna felt a surge of hope as the *Eloise* came into view. The enormous shuttle moved forward into the bay. Haranda Su leaped and clapped all of her hands several times when she saw the Earth ship.

"I've never seen a ship like this before. It's got a solid shape. Good structure. But it's going to need a lot of work," Haranda Su said to Hanna. "If you're going to captain this ship, you'll need to be familiar with all of the upgrades, and I am going to need your help."

"That would be awesome!" responded Hanna. "I have so many questions."

"Good. Walk me through your ship," Haranda Su smiled.

Hanna and Haranda Su spent the next hour going through the ship. Hanna showed her the manuals and schematics. Haranda Su was very excited about the Wolverine rocket.

"This is an excellent design. It will only take a few modifications to turn this into a sublight engine."

"A sublight engine?" Hanna inquired.

"It runs on a special fuel and can reach speeds of up to point nine-nine the speed of light. Great for getting away in a pinch.

They aren't common, but like I said, it will only require a few modifications."

"I don't think an entire tank of fuel could generate enough thrust to reach those speeds," Hanna observed doubtfully.

"Not this fossil fuel you're using. You need something far more dense and already oxygenated. Have you ever heard of a tagaf?"

"Can't say that I have," responded Hanna.

"A tagaf is a small, non-sentient herbivore that lives for a million galactic standard years. This animal puts all of its waste into a single organ where it is stored and compacted over time. Right before it dies, it poops a single pellet that contains all the energy it has gathered over a million years. This pellet has enough energy to keep this ship flying at max sublight speed for an entire galactic standard year."

Hanna's jaw dropped. "It must be very rare," she said.

"It is for most people, but not for me," Haranda Su smirked. "I have a pretty good supply stockpiled."

They continued their walk through the ship. Hanna was surprised every time Haranda Su opened her mouth to say things like "Here's where we'll put the energy-based weapons," or "Here's where we'll put the projectile-based weapons." She decided to leave the main cabin and retractable viewing window as it was but added a smuggling compartment, fortified energy shields, a secondary Talrisian metal retractable shield, a more aggressive steering system, an oxygen maker, food and matter synthesizers with healthy supplies of source material, vertical takeoff and landing engines, a brig, a new navigational array with the latest star maps, a voice activated central computer with access to all of the ship's systems, and upgraded toilet with a seat warmer and temperature adjusted water sprays.

"Is this a gravity engine?" Haranda Su asked.

"It is," said Hanna.

"Pretty risky, I'd say. They don't mix well with corridors," warned Haranda Su.

"Yeah, you know, I experienced that. Almost tore the ship apart."

"It does more than that. It tears the whole corridor apart. They are illegal on most interstellar ships, but I'll leave it intact and integrate an automatic shutoff with the central computer system."

"Great," said Hanna.

"I'm also going to integrate a miniature corridor engine into the main computer system," stated Haranda Su, "so that you can make jumps wherever you are. The range will be limited, but it gives you a lot more flexibility in charting an efficient course."

The repairs progressed far more quickly than Hanna had anticipated. Blue proved to be a useful mechanic and picked things up quickly. Haranda Su was exceptionally clear in her direction and guidance, but Hanna still struggled to keep track of all the changes being made.

#

As the third day dawned at Haranda Su's Spaceship Repairs and Modifications hangar, the repairs and modifications to the *Eloise* were almost complete. The Monarch footed the bill, as Haranda Su mentioned more than once, so no expense was spared. Hanna grew increasingly anxious to be on her way to find the pirates. She was getting closer and closer to her parents. She could feel it in her bones. She felt a tap on her shoulder. It was Blue.

"Can we talk for a minute?" he asked with some concern in his voice. "Somewhere private?"

"Sure. Of course," Hanna answered, leading him to a small locker room in the back of the hangar. It had a few locker compartments, a shower, and a toilet. "What's on your mind?"

"I really like you, Hanna," admitted Blue. "You are the only friend I've ever had, and you mean a lot to me. I don't want to see you get hurt."

"Is this about Saldo?" she asked.

"I have a really bad feeling about him. I don't trust him," Blue said. "It's bad enough with just him, but when you combine a Dorian with pirates? Hanna, something bad might happen. Please just think about it," Blue pleaded.

"Blue, you're a great friend. I care about you so much, but Saldo hasn't done anything. He's a chauvinistic pig, but I will continue to give him the benefit of the doubt until he gives me a reason not to trust him. That's just how I operate."

"I admire you Hanna," Blue said. "but I can't go with you."

Hanna frowned and took a step back. *She and Blue were friends, of course, and she couldn't picture going forward in a strange galaxy without him, but she was embarking on an extremely dangerous quest that was hers, not his.*

"I understand," she sighed, stepping back in to hug Blue.

"I don't know if you do," halted Blue. "I just can't face pirates again. They're dangerous and I'm terrified, and I don't want to be there to get hurt. I don't want you to get hurt either."

"Where is all this fear coming from, Blue?" asked Hanna.

Blue breathed deeply and quivered as tears formed in his eyes. "They hunt Makarans," Blue whispered. Hanna stood silent, her mouth struggling to find the right words, but Blue wasn't finished. "Makarans that haven't turned, like me, are easy to spot and kill. But Makarans like me are also the only ones who can spot a Makaran that *has* turned." Understanding descended upon Hanna, and she raised a hand to her mouth in disbelief.

"Oh Blue," she said, stepping in to embrace her troubled friend. "Did they use you?"

Blue held her tight. "I don't know who, but someone hired a band of pirates to kill Makarans," Blue managed. He took a deep breath. "They killed so many. So many died because of me." Blue broke down. "I barely escaped," he stammered, sucking in shaky gulps of breath.

"Oh Blue! That's awful. So awful," Hanna empathized. "It wasn't your fault, Blue. I know it. I understand why you can't go with us" lamented Hanna. She squeezed Blue even tighter and kissed him on the cheek. "Where will you go?" she asked, still holding on to him.

"I'm not sure. Probably back to the Monarch. He was so helpful; I thought I could return the favor somehow. Plus, I know that's where you'll go once you rescue your parents."

"I thought you believed that I would get hurt and wouldn't make it," Hanna frowned sarcastically.

"I know you'll make it," Blue declared. "I don't doubt that. I just can't go with you."

"How will you get back?" Hanna asked.

"I'll turn myself in to the Corridor Patrol and they should send me back to the Sendori Sanitarium for Homeless, Lost, and Discarded Children ," Blue answered. "I'll see if Tsarana will help me contact the Monarch."

"That's a solid plan. We're leaving soon," said Hanna, tears forming in her eyes.

"I'm leaving now," replied Blue. "I'll head out the back. I don't want to see Saldo again. Will you tell the others?"

Hanna nodded and gave Blue a departing hug and kiss on the cheek as tears streamed down her cheeks.

#

Hanna made her way back to the others. Saldo and Mera were engaged in a heated discussion about interspecies gender dynamics. Stiggs was observing with some interest, but they all fell silent when Hanna approached the ship.

"It's all done," said Haranda Su. "You're ready for takeoff. You have the coordinates to an area of space where pirates are active. Your ship is unregistered and unique; they will assume it's a ship with valuable cargo that someone has gone to great lengths to hide. You only have to sit there, and they'll find you." Hanna embraced Haranda Su.

"Thank you for everything," she said. "I'll miss you."

"Same here. I hope you find your parents," said Haranda Su.

"I will." Hanna was determined. "Everyone ready?" Mera, Saldo, and Stiggs all nodded in agreement. Hanna mustered her courage. "Then, let's ride."

"Wait," croaked Stiggs. "Where is the Makaran?"

"He's not coming; he already left," Hanna slowly whispered. "He's going back to Sendori and then hopefully to the Monarch to wait for us."

"What a coward!" declared Saldo. "You're all weak." He grabbed Hanna and pulled out a small hand cannon he had been concealing, pointing it directly at Hanna's head. Mera had already covered most of the ground between her and the Dorian, but stopped when the weapon was raised; she wouldn't make it in time if he fired. Saldo took out two discs, slapped one on Hanna and the other on his own shoulder, and they disappeared.

#

Boother and Mung waited quietly in the plush library. A servant with spindly arms and snakelike legs offered them tea and crackers, which Mung declined and Boother munched enthusiastically. The door opened and the Monarch swaggered in. Mung jumped to his feet and Boother scrambled to follow as he hastily shoved a cracker into his vertical mouth hole.

The Monarch raised his hand and said, "Whoa there!" gesturing for them to be seated. "No need to get up on account of me." He plopped into his throne-like chair and turned to the officers.

"Hello, fellas. How can I help you?" asked the jolly man. His face shone with civility and a hint of curiosity.

"I am Officer Mung, and this is my partner Boother. We are looking for an Earth person named Hanna Storm. We have reason to believe she came here after escaping from the zoo. She was traveling with a Dorian, a Makaran, and a Bimber."

"Well, cut my arms off and call me handy! What a sight that gang was!" exclaimed the Monarch.

"Then you've zzzeen them?" asked Boother, his bumps transitioning to an excited yellow.

"You know, back on Earth, I loved to entertain, but I have always admired law enforcement. I admire you boys, and I'm happy to perform my civic duty."

"You are an Earth person?" said Mung incredulously. "I had no idea." Boother's bumps burned a blazing bright orange.

"I usually don't admit to it because nobody believes it, but you two know better, don't ya? I did see those kids here. That Hanna Storm is quite an adventurer. Said her parents were taken by Dorians. I sent her over to Vlad to help them with a plan to bust them out."

"Where can we find this Vlad?" asked Mung, "and can you please sign this photograph? It's for our captain's daughter."

A small, hairy servant resembling a large caterpillar scuttled through the door and whispered something in the Monarch's ear.

"Well, uh, bring him in and make sure they get paid." The Monarch turned back toward the Corridor Police. "Looks like we found ourselves another human from Earth."

The servant escorted Henry in and presented him to the Monarch, who stood up and put out his hand. "I'm known around these parts as the Monarch. What's your name son?"

"I'm Henry," he said with surprise. "You mean you're from Earth? How is that possible? Never mind," he answered his own questions and hurried on. "That's not important right now. We were kidnapped by a bunch of lizard-looking aliens, and they have everyone working in some mine. Those smugglers who brought me here know where they are. We have to rescue them!" Henry's voice cracked.

"Whoa, son! Slow down there," said the Monarch. "This is Officer Boother, and this is Officer Mung from the Corridor Patrol."

"Henry, were you on the same ship as Ms. Hanna Storm?" asked Mung. Henry did not respond.

"I don't understand what they're saying," Henry said to the Monarch. "Are they speaking to me?"

"You need a translator," explained the Monarch. "He needs a translator," he repeated to Mung and Boother. Boother reached into his belt and pulled out the tiny metal ball.

"Go on over to Boother, son, and let him stick that thing in your ear. It'll tickle a little, but everybody's got one. It'll help you understand what they're saying," clarified the Monarch.

With the translator properly installed, Mung repeated his question.

"Were you on the *Eloise* with a Ms. Hanna Storm, about your age, when it was captured by Dorians?"

"You know Hanna? We thought she made it back to Earth!"

"She attempted to follow you in the *Eloise* and ended up stranded out here," Mung explained with a hopeful gleam in his eyes. "We are searching for her. Have you seen her?"

"No," Henry said incredulously, consternation smearing his features. "Hanna didn't make it back to Earth? I guess I'm not surprised. I mean, I just met the Monarch and can now understand aliens. This is too wild." Henry mumbled. He looked up hopefully at Mung, "You'll help me rescue the others and Hanna. You are the police, so that's your job right? You have to help me rescue them!" Henry pleaded.

"We have no jurisdiction beyond the border with the Dorian Empire. Our primary objective is to find Hanna Storm and take her to Command for questioning," replied Mung. Henry's shoulders slumped and he looked down at the floor.

"Well, that little lady is going to find her parents," declared the Monarch authoritatively. "When a teenage Earth girl is determined to do something, it gets done. I bet that hasn't changed. You find her parents, you find her. That's your best shot."

Henry straightened, and hope returned to his face. "Right," Henry muttered. He looked at Boother, then Mung, at the floor, up at the Monarch, and back to the floor. "I'm going with you then," Henry swallowed. "Which one of you is Boother again?" he asked, raising his gaze.

"I'm Mung. This is Boother. Come with us Henry. Command will want to ask you questions about your experience in the Dorian mines. You should know that despite what the Monarch said, we are going to find Hanna, not mount a rescue mission in Dorian space for these other Earth people." Henry looked at the Monarch, who winked at him.

"Right," squeaked Henry. "Good. That sounds good. I'll come with you to find Hanna."

"Excellent! Now where can we find this Vlad?" Mung asked of the Monarch.

"And can you zzzign thizzz photograph?" added Boother.

CHAPTER 17

A Fight for Freedom

Master Slythe sat patiently in Administrator Serno's office as Serno burst through the door huffing and puffing, his forehead bruised and nostrils slightly out of alignment.

"I came as quickly as I could, Master Slythe. I've been attending to some miscreants," said Serno stiffly and breathlessly.

"So I've heard," said Master Slythe, his tone edged with disdain. "I'd like you to bring the Earth warrior to me."

"Of course, Master Slythe. Zora!" he shouted through the doorway. She hurried in and awaited instructions. "Have five—no, ten—guards bring me the warrior."

"As you command," obeyed Zora, bowing intricately.

"Administrator Serno, tell me what you are doing to address the attempted escape," said a stone-faced Slythe.

"Of course, Master Slythe. I considered executing the warrior, but he is so large and productive in the mines. His death would likely invite greater attempts to escape on the part of the remaining Earth people," explained Serno.

"Interesting. I concur. Please continue," said Master Slythe placidly.

"I then considered executing his mate," grinned Serno. Slythe returned the evil grin.

"Oh, I like that," agreed Slythe.

"Yes, yes," said Serno excitedly, "but, ultimately, I determined it would only serve to strengthen his resolve and inspire feelings of vengeance."

"Too true. Too true," responded Slythe.

"I finally settled on public torture of the mate," declared Serno harshly.

"Excellent! I like it. I see you have earned your reputation, Administrator Serno. When will the torture take place? I would like to witness it."

"It will commence this evening, Master Slythe. You shall have a front row seat."

The office door opened, and ten armed guards shoved Mr. Storm inside, his hands cuffed in front of him. He stood quietly, observing his surroundings.

"Leave us, guards!" barked Master Slythe. They obeyed with haste, leaving the room to the three occupants, one of whom was quivering with fear, and it was not Mr. Storm. "So, this is the great Earth warrior. You are indeed a specimen," mused Master Slythe. "What is your name?"

"Sebastian Storm," he said. Mr. Storm eyed his captors warily. Dispassion and a cool, relaxed stance greeted the Dorian leader.

"I'm Master Slythe. I captained the ship that captured you and your friends."

"Good to know," said Mr. Storm with a hint of malice in his voice that was not lost on Slythe or Serno.

"You attempted to escape, but you should know that you will never return to your precious Earth. You will live out your days as a laborer here in the mines."

"If you say so," shrugged Mr. Storm.

"I do say so," Master Slythe bit out through clenched teeth. "Right now, I am building an engine large enough to sustain a corridor with Earth. With this new technology, I will be able to harness the natural corridor between our galaxies at will." Slythe hissed spittle onto the desk in front of him and slammed down a clenched claw, creating an indent in its surface. "That corridor will endure until our forces conquer Earth. I will enslave your people and strip your tiny planet of all its resources. Then, I will return to rule Galaxy Prime." Pride, confidence, and triumph rang out as Slythe concluded his monologue.

"Good for you," patronized Mr. Storm, a slight smirk on his lips. "Your mother must be very proud."

Master Slythe sprang up and pointed a single claw at his captive. "*You* are going to watch while *I* torture your mate," he spat. "Serno! I won't be joining you in the front row." He locked eyes with Mr. Storm. "Sebastian Storm can have my seat."

Zora burst through the door.

"Administrator Serno, a priority message is coming through for Master Slythe," she said, breathlessly.

"Don't just stand there! Put it through!" bellowed Serno, glaring at her.

The transmission came with some static, but Slythe recognized a familiar voice on the other end.

"Saldo! Is that you cousin?"

"Slythe, you old wacklar. I finally made it out of that confounded Galactic Zoo," said Saldo. "I'm bringing you a gift too. An Earth person."

"I am very pleased, Saldo. We are undertaking an impressive quest and I need you here. Bring the Earth person. We have a crew of them here working the mines."

"I thought you might," said Saldo. "When she said her parents were captured, I was almost certain it was you. I always knew you would find the corridor to Sister Galaxy." Mr. Storm's heart dropped into his stomach. He had thought perhaps they were talking about Henry, but when he heard "she said her parents were captured," a more ominous thought entered his mind.

"Please, don't be Hanna," he whispered to himself.

"Her parents? What is her name?" asked Master Slythe with a hopeful voice.

"Hanna Storm," came the reply. "Her name is Hanna Storm." Mr. Storm flushed red. Anger seared through his veins as he clenched both his teeth and fists and shock raced through his body and mind. How was Hanna here? She ought to be safe on Earth. Her skills in all things space should have landed her back home. A chill ran down his spine as he realized what she had chosen instead. Of course, she would launch a rescue mission—it was a no-brainer! Why did she have to be so much like her mother?

"Excellent. Bring her to me as soon as you arrive," commanded Slythe.

"I will, cousin. See you in a few galactic standard days," responded Saldo.

"Administrator Serno," said Slythe, as he leaned back in his chair and clawed his snout in contemplation. "As long as the mate survives, do you believe the execution of the daughter would encourage compliance or encourage further dissidence?"

"As long as the mate lives, I believe the execution of the daughter would be an excellent deterrent for all of the Earth people."

"Excellent," responded Slythe, his face betraying both mischief and delight. "I concur. Torture followed by an execution. How satisfying!"

Mr. Storm stayed silent. His mind raced as he considered the implications. His muscles tensed and relaxed. He breathed quietly and deeply but could not stop the tremors that radiated throughout his chest. Hanna was in grave danger. All his training and all his experience in staying cool under pressure abandoned him. The bonds mocked him, and a cold, dark depression extinguished his characteristic hope. The slightest of tears inched its way down his cheek as he tried to contemplate a universe without his daughter somewhere in it. Mr. Storm grasped at the thought of his daughter, and it slowly became the seed of his determination. Finally, he glanced around the room, calculating and assessing his options. He needed to plot his next moves carefully. Hanna's life depended on it.

#

Boother and Mung stood outside the club where Vlad was supposed to be. The line meandered up the street for at least a galactic standard kilometer. They did not have time to wait, but the bouncer ignored their attempts to get his attention. He just stood there, silent, letting in the next guests in line. Even when Boother and Mung pulled their badges, he looked at them carefully and said his partner would verify their authenticity, but his partner never came. Finally, an Earth person popped his head out through the door and addressed the trio. "I am Vlad. Welcome to club," he said, the thick Ukrainian accent penetrating even Mung's universal translator. "Monarch mentioned you guys are coming. Please, come inside, please." Low ambient light greeted their over-dilated eyes, and the heavy scent of soil and algae hung pungent in the air. Vlad led the way down a faded red carpet to a bare gray table surrounded by hard chairs. The lighting near the table shone a little brighter and carried exotic colors that dispersed throughout the club. The walls were adorned with nostalgic symbols of the Soviet Union: a bust of Lenin, a hammer and sickle, the old Soviet flag. An impressive symphony of sound marched through the air, with a voice singing out "the great and powerful Soviet Union!" Vlad motioned to the hard wooden chairs, and the three guests took their seats. Mung made quick work of introducing himself, Boother, and Henry. Vlad gave a special welcome to young Henry and was explaining his past as a Soviet cosmonaut when Mung finally interrupted.

"Thank you for the backstory, but where is Ms. Hanna Storm?" he chafed.

"She leave. She already go. I send her to Haranda Su to fix up spaceship."

"What zzzpazzzeship?" asked Boother.

"Quite right," said Mung. "Where would she acquire a space-ship?"

"From Galactic Police Force impound yard. She retrieve her own ship," Vlad said without emotion.

"She broke into the impound lot and stole her ship?" Mung asked, flabbergasted.

"No, no, no," answered Vlad. "She no steal anything. She take her own ship. How can you steal what is yours already?"

Mung paused, uncertain how to respond. "Never mind that," he said. "Where is she going after repairs?"

"Modifications," corrected Vlad.

Mung took a tense and slow breath. "Fine! Where is she going after modifications?" he corrected, eyes wide with frustration.

"To find pirates," said Vlad bluntly.

"Pirates!" screamed Mung. "What in the four Belthian Maidens does she want with pirates?"

"Don't worry. Is very simple. Is all part of plan," Vlad smiled.

"What plan?" shouted Mung, incredulous. The club's patrons straightened up in their hard wooden chairs and strained to see who was making such a fuss. When they saw the uniforms, they quickly turned back to their drinks. "You know what? Never mind," said the bristling Mung. "Until we find Hanna Storm, you are coming with us, Vlad."

Vlad smiled. "No. This is not part of plan," he declared..

"This is not a debate! This is an official Corridor Patrol investigation! You will come with me now or I'll have a dozen officers down here checking everyone's identification and searching for illicit materials." Mung breathed heavily as the threat rolled off his tongue. A tinge of insanity laced his words. Boother's bumps were a concerned purple. Vlad just sat quietly, pondering the threat.

"I come with you. Is good plan. Is simple. I like simple," he said. "Let's go." Vlad stood and gave directions to a bushy-tailed uniformed servant no larger than a squirrel who was standing on a pedestal nearby.

"Good," said Mung, pleasantly surprised. "Boother, once we get to our ship, radio the impound lot and see if Hanna's ship is still there. If it is not, we will set course for Haranda Su's. She has to be there. If she's not there, Boother, I cannot be held responsible for my actions. I owe the Galactic Police Force Chamber of Commanders some answers," he huffed. "Hanna is also my responsibility," he continued passionately. "If anything, untoward happens to her, Boother...."

"I'll go radio the impound," Boother blurted as he hurried away to avoid the glint of hysteria in Mung's gaze. If they didn't complete this wild goose chase of a mission soon, even Boother's notable patience would run out.

#

Mrs. Storm stabbed her shovel into a pile of ore and heaved it into the mine cart. Over an hour had elapsed since ten gnarled guards had escorted Mr. Storm away. Concern for her husband chiseled at her nerves, but she concentrated on the fact that profit was derived from living miners, and these aliens seemed to hold profit in high regard. She also knew how productive her husband was with a sledgehammer; this wouldn't be lost on the guards, either. He was valuable. In her peripheral vision, she noticed Valentina wiping her eyes.

"I'm sure Henry is okay," soothed Mrs. Storm. "If he had been caught, they would surely have returned him here by now."

"You don't know that for sure," Valentina snapped.

"No, I don't," Mrs. Storm concurred, "but the evidence points in that direction."

Valentina took her pickaxe and banged it against the wall, the vibration echoing through the cavern. "You know his parents didn't want him to come," she said, through her repeated and vigorous swings. "They thought it was too risky. I had to convince them to let Henry come. I promised them he would be okay." Sweat ran down her brow, and her chest heaved from the effort, or was it from the emotion?

"I don't think anyone could have predicted being kidnapped by aliens," reasoned Mrs. Storm. "This is not your fault and Henry will be okay. Don't give up hope." Mrs. Storm knew from past experience that stating possibilities or hopes as facts was sometimes the only way to push through impossible situations.

"It's so hard to stay positive," Valentina grunted.

Mrs. Storm looked around. Everyone seemed so dejected. Even the ever-positive and cheerful Marie spoke less than usual. "Do you like to sing?" she asked Valentina.

"I love to sing. I haven't even thought of music since these monsters turned our world upside down," she responded, her eyes lighting up. "It feels strange to remember; music has always been such a major part of my daily routine."

Marie chimed in. "Everything feels surreal, like I'm in a nightmare and I can't wake." Her countenance washed dark as she contemplated her own words, contradicting the bubbly demeanor she had displayed at the beginning of the space cruise.

"Know any good songs?" asked Mrs. Storm of the two women. On their long adventures, she and Mr. Storm would often sing around the campfire with their clients. It served to bond them together and ease some of the tension that was generated during the intense itineraries of an Extreme Adventure.

"I think I know one that might fit," Valentina said. She unleashed a powerful, clear note and sustained it for several seconds before descending into an upbeat old classic country song about working the mines.

"I like it," said Mrs. Storm. Recognizing the song, she joined in on the chorus. Soon, everyone had joined in, and the gloom began to ease. Valentina had a beautiful singing voice, so much so that even the guards were mesmerized. Spirits were lightened, and the singing resonated until a new sound clashed with it from somewhere down the tunnel. Silence. Mr. Storm walked in surrounded closely by ten guards. Blood dripped from his brow and his swollen face was bruised red, purple, and blue.

Mr. Storm bore an uncharacteristically stormy expression. His wife tried to recall whether she had ever seen him look this way, but nothing came to her. She had seen him injured, bruised, and bleeding, but it was his mood that frightened her. The extra guards shoved Mr. Storm to the ground and hastily retreated. The remaining guards passed around some water to the other prisoners, sent off the loaded carts, and took a break, leaving the laborers to rest.

Mr. Storm approached his wife slowly, head down. She threw her arms around him, and he broke down in her arms, tears coursing down his cheeks. Great, wracking sobs shook his body as she sat him down and held him close. After several minutes, he sniffled his last sniffle and regained enough composure to tell his wife what he had overheard about their daughter..

"Hanna is coming here," he said. The news hit Mrs. Storm like a rock hitting a window. She slumped, jaw gaping but speechless.

"I overheard a radio transmission that confirmed a human named Hanna Storm is on her way. She was looking for her parents." Mr. Storm's eyes met his wife's gaze, and he lost it all over again.

Mrs. Storm had begun to tear up herself. "I don't know what to say," she mustered.

"It gets worse," said Mr. Storm gulping in deep, shaky breaths of air. "Because they think I tried to escape, they are going to torture you publicly in front of the rest of us. They know you are my wife."

"I can handle torture. They aren't going to waste a laborer. I'll be fine," she shushed.

Mr. Storm straightened suddenly, grabbing his wife by the shoulders and looking her squarely in the eyes. "They are going to torture you...and execute Hanna," he cried.

"No!" screamed Mrs. Storm. Shock. Disbelief! "No, they can't. I'll take her place. They can execute me." Mrs. Storm fell into his arms and sobbed, Mr. Storm holding her tiny frame as he cried along with her.

The other captives looked on in concern but held their peace. After a few moments, Valentina broke the silence. "Sebastian?" she asked gently. "Any news of Henry?"

Mr. Storm wiped his tears and stood up. "No word on Henry. They think I was the main culprit. They want to punish me by punishing my family. That means Henry probably made it to safety. If they had caught him, they would have made his punishment public, and they probably wouldn't have waited." Valentina took courage from this, and her concern turned to the Storm family. Mrs. Storm rose to her feet and whistled for everyone's attention.

"Tell them what is going on, Sebastian," she said. "We need to come up with a plan." Everyone gathered around and listened closely.

"Hanna didn't make it back to Earth. She followed us somehow. I overheard them talking. She's been captured and is on her way here." Gasps. Mr. Watts sank down on a rock, his knees weak and shaky. Marie put a comforting arm around his shoulder.

"I'm pretty sure Henry got away," Mr. Storm continued. Valentina heaving a sigh of relief. "They think I masterminded the escape. To punish me, they're going to torture Sara and execute Hanna, publicly." More gasps! "They mentioned flogging, so I'm pretty sure Sara is getting whipped, but I don't know how hard or how much," Mr. Storm explained. "They are keen to keep her alive, though, because of her value as a laborer. That goes for all of us and works in our favor."

"I can take my licks," said Mrs. Storm. "Our priority has to be saving Hanna. I cannot let my baby girl die," she stated bravely through tears.

"Any ideas you come up with over the next work rotation we can discuss at the break," Mr. Storm said.

"Count us out," interrupted Rory King. "I can't risk having them flog my Genevieve, or me for that matter. I have very sensitive skin."

"Can it, Rory!" yelled Captain Bask.

"Grow a spine, you jellyfish," said Haruka.

"We won't win," Rory solemnly defended. "All this will do is get us killed. We need to go along with things to survive until we can find a way to buy our freedom."

"The price of freedom can be very high, Mr. King," interjected Donovan Watts. "Many brave souls sacrificed their lives to grant you the freedom you had on Earth. What will be the price of freedom for us here, I wonder, as slaves in a foreign world?"

"True," pondered Mr. Storm, "but Rory's right too. This will be dangerous. Some of us could be seriously injured or killed. We appreciate any help we get, but we don't want to endanger anyone else. Please consider carefully whether you want to get involved."

"How do we know your actions won't put us in danger?" said Rory. "Why should we suffer because your daughter got herself caught?"

Mrs. Storm stomped up to Rory and Genevieve. "I won't let them execute my daughter as long as I draw breath," she declared, her intensity permeating the air. "I don't condone violence, let alone murder," she warned, "and my husband is no killer, but, so help me, I will not stop him if he has to snap the neck of anyone who tries to prevent us from rescuing our daughter. Including anyone who might be tempted to reveal our plan to these aliens."

"Snitches get stitches," said Mr. Watts, tapping his cane loudly for emphasis. Marie chuckled silently to herself. Rory and Genevieve made no response. The tension between the Kings and the Storms endured as the guards returned and everyone resumed work.

On the next break, Valentina, Mr. Watts and Marie, Captains Jack and Carlie, Haruka, and the Storms huddled together to plan Hanna's rescue. Urgency permeated the rescue planning as time ticked away toward an unknown execution date.

"Okay," began Mrs. Storm. "What do we have?"

Captain Jack raised his hand. "They will be expecting Sebastian to cause trouble, right? Or perhaps you, Sara. I think we should oblige them. If there is a distraction that is big enough to draw the guards' attention, I can drop to the ground and crawl to Hanna." Captain Jack paused for responses.

"It's clear we'll need a distraction of some sort," said Mr. Storm.

"I don't think any distraction will last that long," said Mr. Watts. "Will you be able to pick the lock fast enough during that commotion?" he asked Captain Jack.

"I'll practice it a few more times, but now that I know how the lock works, it will go much quicker. I can get it down to fifteen seconds," assured Captain Jack.

"Fifteen seconds can be an eternity," mused Mr. Storm, "but this is our best shot. We keep the guards' eyes up while you pick your lock and make your way to Hanna."

"Why are these locks so simple?" asked Valentina. "I mean, they have spaceships, for crying out loud! You would think they could find a more effective pair of restraints."

"It's a simple question of economics," opined Mr. Watts. "On Earth, we have the technology to build amazing restraints, perhaps electrified or magnetized, that would be virtually impossible to break. The cost of producing those, however, would be prohibitively high. Do you know what our local police have started using instead of handcuffs? Little strips of plastic. Their effectiveness is not always guaranteed, but they get the job done most of the time, and they are very, very inexpensive."

"I hated economics," said Valentina, "but you just made more sense than any of my professors ever did."

"Well, I'm more a businessman than an economist," chuckled Mr. Watts. "Back to the topic at hand, there are still a lot of unknowns. First, we don't know where the venue will be or if we'll all be seated and chained together. Second, we don't know if there will be any cover between Captain Jack and wherever Hanna will be. Third, let's say he gets to Hanna and frees her; what happens next? How do they escape these mines and this planet? Finally, if we fail, or even if we succeed, what will the consequences be for those of us who remain? I don't ask these questions to discourage our efforts. No. No. I only wish to maximize our chances of success."

As the truth of Mr. Watts' words hit the group, they fell silent, each of them pondering the consequences of planning a rescue with so little information.

Mr. Storm finally broke the silence. "All I know is that if we do nothing, Hanna dies," he began to weep, "and I cannot stand by and do nothing," he sobbed. His wife put her arm around his waist and held him close.

"We take the mines," said Captain Jack with the most sober and serious of expressions. Everyone paused. Mr. Storm stopped weeping. "Have you ever heard of Sergeant Alvin Cullum York?" Nobody responded. "He wasn't a marine but a corporal in the Army during World War I. At first, he was a conscientious objector, but he joined later when he reconciled his faith with Army service. He was one of a small group of men instructed to breach enemy lines and take out German machine gun nests. They had captured some German troops when they were ambushed and some of the soldiers in his unit were killed. He became the highest-ranking officer and ordered the remaining men to guard the prisoners while he went to deal with the Germans. He was from Tennessee, and he could shoot. He started picking off Germans in their trench until he ran out of bullets. He was charged by German soldiers with bayonets and killed them all with his pistol. The German officer in charge offered to surrender after shooting at Corporal York and missing. Corporal York and his men returned with over 130 prisoners; after that he was promoted to sergeant. The odds were against him. He was vastly outnumbered. He didn't want to kill but wanted to protect. The odds are against us. We are outnumbered. We don't want to fight, but we have to if we ever want to see home again. If they are going to kill Hanna, we have to fight back, not just for her, but for all of us. We may be outnumbered, but we've proven that we are not outsmarted. They don't want us dead, which gives us an advantage. They've been hesitant to even harm us. We take their weapons, and we hold our ground. I don't think we can rescue Hanna without rescuing all of us." Not a single person interrupted his motivational speech. Hope and inspiration glowed in the faces of his listeners. Marie was the first to respond. "I'm in," she said, putting her hand forward.

"As am I," said Mr. Watts. He shifted his cane and put his hand on top of Marie's.

"Me too," said Haruka.

"Me three, I mean four," said Carlie.

Mr. and Mrs. Storm each put in a hand, followed by Valentina and Captain Jack.

"This won't be a walk in the park," said Captain Jack, "and we may not all make it, but we have to fight. There's no viable alternative…"

"Let's go talk to the others," said Mr. Storm. "Rory and Genevieve may not want to go along with this, but once we have the keys and are free, they can go wherever they want," he said, disdainfully. His wife threw him a reproving glance. "Oh! I almost forgot," Mr. Storm continued. "There's a chance I may be seated next to the administrator of this place rather than with all of you."

"If that happens, Captain Bask can lead the others and we can have two points of distraction," responded Captain Jack. "Either way, your targets remain guards with keys and guns. Don't bother with the whips." They all looked hopefully at one another.

"Oohra!" Captain Jack yelled.

"Oohra!" they all echoed.

#

A tense and uneasy week passed before Hanna's spaceship was to arrive. Mr. Storm furiously pondered his wife's upcoming torture and his daughter's upcoming execution. He imagined every possible angle, developing contingency plans for every action. Mrs. Storm paced, deep in thought, pausing every few moments to cast a worried glance at her husband. She wasn't concerned about her own torture, but she could sense that her husband was in a dark place. Captain Jack reduced the time it took him to pick his lock and, with the help of Valentina's bobby pins, taught Mr. Storm and Captain Bask how to pick the locks. Captain Bask had it mastered within a few minutes, delicately twisting the bobby pin until the latch clicked to unlock. Mr. Storm, on the other hand, fumbled the tiny bobby pin between his huge fingers until he finally got it to enter the keyhole. Getting it to unlock required a mental exertion of determination that Mr. Storm typically reserved for particularly daunting tasks. Eventually, he was able to do it in under a minute.

When the time finally came, a large contingent of guards ushered everyone up from the dark, dank caverns into the tunnel and out onto the surface. The humans shrank back, squinting in surprise at the brightness of the outdoor world. The guards pushed and shoved them forward. Haruka stumbled, and Mr. Storm gently picked her up and set her back on her feet, the distraction giving him momentary relief from the heightened anticipation surging through his body.

Mrs. Storm's eyes adjusted first. She saw a small, raised platform with two tall metallic posts glinting under the bright orange sun. One loomed empty. To the other, a prisoner was shackled, her head down. Mrs. Storm froze when she saw the tan cargo pants and white tank top.

"Hanna!" shouted Mrs. Storm. Mr. Storm jerked around, desperate to see his daughter. Hanna lifted her head and searched in the direction of the voice.

"Mom! You're alive!" she shouted, relieved. "I was coming to rescue you, but someone I shouldn't have trusted double crossed me," shouted Hanna evil-eyeing Saldo, who was standing next to Administrator Serno, Master Slythe, and a large Dorian with a patch over one eye. Saldo laughed and approached Mrs. Storm.

"So, you're the mother I've heard so much about," he said. Without a universal translator, she could not understand anything he said, but his mannerism oozed ickiness and reminded Mrs. Storm of those old-timey villains with a cape and mustache who would tie young women to railroad tracks. Saldo turned to Mr. Storm. "You are clearly Hanna's father. She did not exaggerate your size. You're even bigger than Boran. It's incredible!" Saldo looked on with some awe, disbelief, and even a smidge of respect. Mr. Storm understood everything, but it was Mrs. Storm who spoke.

"You will regret the day you ever saw us," she warned, locking onto Saldo's eyes with more solemnity than Mr. Storm had ever seen her express. Saldo smiled, pleased, and returned to his Dorian friends.

"I tried my best to find you and really hoped I could rescue you. I'm so sorry," Hanna cried.

"You found us and that's no small feat. You continue to amaze me, daughter. I love you so much," said Mr. Storm.

"I love you too, Dad," she returned.

"How sweet," Master Slythe mocked. He raised his hand and contemplatively clawed at his chin. "Guards!" he commanded. "Bring me the mother." The joy of anticipation dripped from his reptilian smile.

One guard reached down and unlocked Mrs. Storm's ankle. Before he could stand back up, he lost several teeth, which had inadvertently come into contact with Mrs. Storm's knee. It wouldn't fix anything, but it did ease the tension in her shoulders.

While everyone's attention was focused on Mrs. Storm being dragged to the platform and chained up next to Hanna, Captains Carlie Bask and Jack De La Vega were doing reconnaissance on the guards. They had spotted two with guns and keys that stood close by. The remaining twenty or so guards had only whips.

The guards cautiously chained Mrs. Storm up next to her daughter, steering clear of any appendages, especially her legs. Nobody else wanted to lose teeth from an errant knee to the face. They pulled the chain, raising her hands high above her head with her back toward the crowd. The guard ripped the back of her shirt, exposing her bare skin.

"Right then," said Slythe. "Shall we begin?" He walked over to a guard and demanded his whip, which the guard immediately handed over. Slythe turned to address the crowd of Earth people.

"This is what happens when one of you tries to escape." He pulled back the whip with a venomous smile and a grace that indicated experience. He let it fly with a mighty crack and Mrs. Storm screamed, her back trickling red. All the guards were transfixed on the public flogging. While Slythe cocked his arm for another release, Captain Jack dropped to ground. Mr. Storm clenched teeth and fists. He looked for Captain Jack but could not find him in the crowd.

Crack! The whip struck a second time. Master Slythe searched out Mr. Storm's face and bellowed out a victory laugh. When Slythe turned back for his third blow, Mr. Storm bent down over his ankles and worked furiously to unlock his restraints.

Mrs. Storm gritted her teeth in silence for the third delivery as drops of sweat began their journey down her cheeks. Resolved to give the others more time to complete the rescue, she hoped to keep it going as long as possible. Hanna screamed after the third strike.

"Stop it!"

"You must wait your turn, little one," patronized Master Slythe. He was preparing to deliver a fourth blow when he paused, noticing a commotion among the Earth captives. He watched in shock as Mr. Storm, free of his ankle harness, took out one of the guards with a huge right-hand blow.

Mr. Storm dropped on top of the motionless guard, grabbed his keys, and tossed them to Carlie Bask, who caught them with one upraised hand and a nod of approval. He grabbed the guard's weapon and fired relentlessly at the lizard army standing between him and his wife and daughter. The weapon discharged a bright blue and white energy blast that left huge, gaping holes in the alien soldiers with charred skin surrounding the edges.

Captain Jack had simultaneously taken out the other target guard. He threw the keys to Rory King, who stood frozen like a deer in the headlights. Haruka grabbed the keys from the motionless billionaire and rushed through the row of prisoners, unlocking everyone's restraint. The freed captives sprang into action. Carlie Bask proved formidable as she sped past two Dorian's she had knocked to the ground. She grabbed a whip and wrapped it securely around a guard's neck until he passed out. The small-framed Haruka was no less effective in her assaults, thanks to her judo training. The reptilian guards never saw her coming. Every time a Dorian guard attacked her, she stepped lightly out of the way, grabbed their uniform, and introduced their face to the ground. Two or three attacked at the same time and Haruka weaved in and out, leaving a trail of guards behind her. She looked up to see a guard making its way toward Rory and Genevieve, who stood placidly in place.

As Rory caught sight of the guard, he dropped to his knees and pleaded. "We aren't with them. We can work in the mines," he offered. "We don't want to fight."

The lizard soldier sneered while raising his whip to Genevieve. Rory jumped in front to protect her, but the crack of the whip never came. Haruka had blindsided the guard and taken him to the ground. Gracefully, she stood up.

"You have to fight, Rory. There's no choice."

Rory nodded and raised his hands in a fighting stance, Genevieve standing behind him. The next guard who approached found himself socked squarely in the snout.

"You've still got it, darling!" exclaimed Genevieve King.

"Of course, darling. Third place in the regional amateur championships, you know. I could have gone professional," he beamed. Genevieve rolled her eyes but watched as her husband danced around another alien throwing a combination of punches that knocked the creature to the ground.

Valentina, Mr. Watts, and Marie formed a gang hell bent on taking down any guard that they could grab. Valentina jumped up on an unsuspecting guard's back and clawed at its face while Mr. Watts found strategic targets to jab with his cane. Even the gentle Marie relentlessly punched and kicked to help take Dorians down.

Amid the commotion, Boran and a few guards approached Master Slythe, urging him to follow them to safety. Saldo and Administrator Serno responded immediately, but Master Slythe stood his ground.

"Why are the females fighting?" asked Slythe of Boran.

"I am uncertain, but we must depart," answered Boran.

"Why are the females defeating your soldiers, Boran?" Slythe mocked with a smile.

"The shame is mine to bear, Master Slythe, but we must go now," Boran bowed.

Captain Jack caught sight of the Dorian leadership and laid down heavy fire.

Slythe stood immovable and untouched. He glared at Mr. Storm, raised his hand cannon, and aimed it at Hanna. Mr. Storm raised aloft his own weapon and took aim. Crack! Mr. Storm's ear rang as he felt a sharp pain on the side of his head. Blood ran into his eye, obscuring his vision.

"I've got you, Sebastian," Carlie Bask yelled, taking down the guard that had attacked Mr. Storm and punishing him with relentless blows to his face until he went limp.

Mr. Storm wiped the blood away, only to see Slythe retreating toward Boran, Saldo, and Serno. Slythe smirked wickedly.

Mr. Storm turned to Hanna. She hung limply, eyes closed, a gaping round hole in her chest with charred, smoking skin around the circumference. Mrs. Storm let out a bloodcurdling scream. Mr.

Storm ran to the platform and wrapped his muscular arms around his daughter's lifeless body. He froze there, stunned. He knew she was gone. Tears streamed down his blood-stained face.

In a rage, he grabbed the chains that bound Mrs. Storm and pulled until they broke from the pole. She fell into his arms. He steadied his wife until she could stand on her own and then pulled on Hanna's chains until they jerked loose. Mrs. Storm collapsed again from the effort, but Mr. Storm caught her with one arm before she hit the ground, scooping her gently up over his shoulder, stomach down so as not to aggravate her back injuries. He squatted down by Hanna's body and, with his free arm, picked up his precious daughter and threw her over his other shoulder.

Captain Jack and the others formed a perimeter around the Storms. He searched desperately for possible escape routes before settling on the building where Administrator Serno had his office. It looked well fortified, and he organized their retreat.

"We have to move," ordered Captain Jack, his Marine training coming through. "Everyone on me!" he shouted, and safely led the group of humans toward the building.

CHAPTER 18

Blue's Journey

Hanna nodded and gave Blue a departing hug and kiss on the cheek.

She held him tight, and he returned the hug. Something started to feel different. Hanna tried to disengage the hug, but Blue held her tight. She could feel his body changing shape. When she finally broke free, he was in the final stages of turning human, but not just any human; except for the clothing, it was like looking into a mirror, down to the last detail. Hanna was speechless.

"I won't let him hurt you. You refuse to listen to me, but I know you are in danger," he pleaded. Hanna opened her mouth to speak only to inhale a strange purple powder Blue blew from his palm to her face. Blackness engulfed Hanna as she fell into her friend. "I love you, Hanna. You're the only friend I've ever had, and friends protect each other. You taught me that." Blue swapped their clothing and leaned her up into a locker, closing and locking it tight. He leaned his forehead against the cold metal door and sighed. "If I die, it's no less than I deserve, but if you die, Hanna..." Blue couldn't finish the thought. He walked out as Hanna Storm to face the others.

Saldo and Mera were engaged in a heated discussion about inter-species gender dynamics as Stiggs looked on with a bland expression. They fell silent when Blue, in his new Hanna Storm costume, approached the ship.

"It's all done," said Haranda Su. "You're ready for takeoff. You have the coordinates to an area of space where pirates are active. Your ship is unregistered and unique; they will assume it's a ship with valuable cargo someone has taken great lengths to hide. You just have to sit there, and they'll find you." Blue embraced Haranda Su.

"Thank you for everything," he said in Hanna's voice. "I'll miss you."

"Same here. I hope you find your parents," said Haranda Su.

"I will." Blue was determined. "Everyone ready?" Mera, Saldo, and Stiggs all nodded in agreement. "Then let's ride."

"Wait," croaked Stiggs. "Where is the Makaran?"

"He's not coming; he already left," answered Blue. "He's going back to Sendori and then hopefully to the Monarch to wait for us."

"What a coward!" declared Saldo. "You're all weak." He grabbed the Hanna Storm impostor and pulled out a small hand cannon, moving it toward Blue's head. Mera had already covered most of the ground between her and the Dorian but froze as the weapon made contact; she wouldn't make it in time if he fired. Saldo took out two discs, slapped one on Blue and the other on his own shoulder. They were gone.

#

Mera, Stiggs, and Haranda Su stood there in shock. Mera broke the silence.

"I'm going after them," she proclaimed. "I owe Hanna my life, and I really, really want to punch some Dorians."

"I agree," croaked Stiggs. "The Monarch would not appreciate it if we returned without her. To think he entertained that...that...that slime ball Saldo. How awful!"

"Good," said Mera, "because I can't fly Hanna's ship."

"Oh, it's very intuitive," said Stiggs.

"How will you find them?" asked Haranda Su. "I can hack the traffic records for this area, but it's a long shot."

"Still worthy of an attempt," voiced Stiggs.

Thump!

Stiggs put up a silencing webbed hand. "Do you hear that?" he inquired.

"Hear what?" asked Haranda Su.

Thump!

"That," said Mera.

Thump!

"It's coming from back there," said Stiggs. The three of them cautiously made their way to the locker room near the back of the building, the thumping growing increasingly loud and desperate as they neared. When they arrived, they realized that one of the locker doors was being struck from the inside.

"Let me out of here!" came a familiar voice.

Haranda Su opened the locker, and, to everyone's surprise, Hanna Storm jumped out dressed in Blue's clothing.

"Where is Blue!" she demanded. She paused as her eyebrows creased, then continued, "I mean me. Where am I?"

"You're at Haranda Su's in the locker room, but how did you escape from Saldo?"

"Saldo? What are you talking about?" said Hanna, confusion and anger exploding across her face.

"What are *you* talking about?" demanded Mera, matching Hanna's tone.

"Blue turned into me, knocked me out with some purple powder, and then put me in that locker," Hanna said angrily. She looked down for the first time. "And he undressed me!" she said with some shock, "that turd!"

"Then, it was Blue who was taken by Saldo," reasoned Stiggs. Hanna looked bewildered.

"You came out from the back and said Blue was going back to the Monarch," explained Mera. "Right after that, Saldo called us all cowards, pulled a hand cannon on you, and used transport discs to disappear with you."

"So Saldo took Blue, thinking he was me," said Hanna. She reflected for a moment, the weight of Blue's perfect prognostication weighing on her heart. "We have to go after him," she whispered, almost to herself.

"We agree," said Mera. "Haranda Su is going to try and track them."

"That's a real long shot," said Haranda Su. "I don't know if we'll be able to."

Hanna took a few deep breaths. "I need to think," she said, pacing the floor with her head down. After a moment's pause, she voiced her thoughts out loud. "Saldo knew our plans and that I was looking for my parents. Now he thinks he has me. Why does he want me if he has his own way home?" she asked.

"The most likely reason is that he plans to sell you—or Blue, rather—himself," croaked Stiggs. "There is a reasonable probability that Blue will end up incarcerated at the same location as your parents."

"Bingo!" yelled Hanna.

"What is Bingo?" asked Mera.

"It means, if we can find them, Saldo won't think I'm coming because he already has me," Hanna said. "We can surprise them and save everyone. I say we stick to the plan. We find pirates and use their help to get across the border and find my parents. If we do, we find Blue."

"Bingo means all that?" Mera huffed. "What if Blue isn't there?"

"We free my parents and then we keep looking for Blue," Hanna answered. "I won't quit until I find him, especially since he turned out to be right about that turkey butt Saldo, who has now given me a very, very good reason not to trust him. He's getting checked!" Her entire being exuded an indignant determination.

Hanna grabbed her pack and returned to the locker room to change into the white linen outfit with magic pockets that Tsarana had gifted her. She carefully folded Blue's clothes and put them in her pack.

#

Boother steered the police cruiser onto the landing pad adjacent to a large hangar, passing the trash and refuse that littered the nearby alleys. Mung exited first, followed by Vlad and Henry, with Boother bringing up the rear. Mung knocked decorously on the front door and stepped back to wait for an answer, but Vlad walked casually past him and pushed the door open.

"Haranda Su," he called. "Is me, Vlad."

"Vlad!" Haranda Su screamed. "So good to see you!" She ran to the cosmonaut, and he leaned over to embrace her, lifting her off her feet and swinging her around. She caught sight of Boother and Mung, who had followed Vlad in.

"Corridor Patrol? Vlad, what did you do?" she asked, eyeing the officers warily.

"I do nothing," Vlad said innocently. "They look for Hanna. Did she come here?"

"Came and went," exclaimed Haranda Su. "Man, what a trip! She was unlike anyone I've ever met," her suspicious gaze returning to the Corridor Patrol. Henry stepped forward.

"Hanna was here?" he said. "How is she? Was she okay?"

"Another Earth person!" said Haranda Su. "Yeah, she was here. She sure is determined to save her parents."

"And I'm determined to save my aunt," Henry insisted, "and Hanna's parents and everyone else too," he added for good measure.

"You said she would be here, Vlad!" growled Mung, his body trembling. "We missed her again? Unacceptable! Unbelievable!"

"Undeniable!" laughed Haranda Su. Mung's pale face flushed purple, but Vlad interrupted.

"Never mind about him," Vlad advised Haranda Su. "Tell us what happen. Where did she go? She go for pirates?"

"Yes. Stiggs brought us her ship, and we made the modifications. She caught on pretty quick and helped me out. She also taught the Bimber a few Earth fighting moves. The Makaran finally decided to morph; he turned into Hanna!"

"What?" asked Boother, his bumps turning orange. Mung shuffled, his mouth gaping more than once as the conversation unfolded without him. Shock!

"It's true," said Haranda Su. "He morphed into Hanna, switched clothes, and shut her up in a locker in the back."

"Why would he do thizzz?" asked Boother.

"He thought he was saving her," answered Haranda Su. "He didn't trust the Dorian."

"You mean Saldo, from the zoo?" Mung finally broke in.

"That's the one," nodded Haranda Su. "Turns out, the Makaran was right. They were about to leave when the Dorian slapped some transport discs onto himself and Hanna, I mean the Makaran, and they were gone. Even the Bimber wasn't fast enough to stop them."

"What happened to Hanna?" asked Boother.

"We heard her banging in the locker and let her out," explained Haranda Su. "They decided to stick with the plan to find her parents. They should be reaching pirate territory within the next few galactic standard hours."

"Unbelievable!" said Mung, apoplectic. "Truly unbelievable! Haranda Su, you are coming with us," he screeched. "Everyone is coming with us until we find Hanna Storm!" he stomped. The flabbergasted bunch eyed Mung warily as he turned and marched back to his ship.

"Bezzzt to comply," said Boother. "I've never zzzeen him like thizzz." He followed Mung back to the ship. Haranda Su looked quizzically at Vlad.

"You should come. It will be fun," said Vlad, "and Hanna may need our help."

"Oh, I'm in," answered Haranda Su. "I haven't had a good adventure in a while. I would have gone with them already, but they didn't invite me," she smiled. "Lead the way!"

Haranda Su shut off the lights in her hangar, locked the door, and followed Vlad to the Corridor Police Cruiser. Henry followed, wondering what a Bimber was and how a macaroni could morph into Hanna.

When the growing search party boarded the cruiser, both Boother and Mung stood to attention. They faced a monitor full of uniformed aliens seated around a large circular table.

"That is our report," finished Mung. Mumbles and rumbles rambled around the table, but Vlad and Haranda Su could not make out what they were saying. The centermost alien with long antennae and large eyes grabbed the gavel in her pincers and banged the conference to order.

"Please! I think it is clear what must be done," she said authoritatively. "Boother and Mung, you must follow Hanna to these pirates, join her on her quest into Dorian space, and help free her parents and the other Earth people. Gather whatever intelligence you can on what the Dorians are planning. Bring the Earth people to us for debriefing."

"But, Lady of the Chamber," protested Mung, "this is highly unusual and of questionable legal standing. Are we not risking all-out war with the Dorians? I will do whatever it takes to find Hanna, of course, but entering Dorian space?"

"There is no law or agreement with the Dorians; there are no diplomatic relations," said the Lady of the Chamber respectfully. "From the perspective of the Galactic Police Force, there is no violation of any standing law. Further, we have reason to believe that they are planning for an assault on Galactic Treaty territories. We must gather as much information as we can."

"But..." started Mung, before being interrupted by Boother.

"We will follow your inzzztructionzzz Commander," he said "and report back on what we learn. Zzzigning out." Boother ended the transmission.

"I don't like this," said Mung, "but we have our orders." He threw a thankful nod to Boother, who, having no neck with which to nod, offered a jiggle of his head bumps in return. "Vlad, give us the coordinates," Mung ordered. "Let's go find some pirates."

The police cruiser lifted off and sped away.

CHAPTER 19

A Pause in the Battle

Inside the office complex, Mr. and Mrs. Storm knelt over their daughter's body and wept. Mr. Watts stood above them, leaning on his cane, his tears flowing freely. Having secured the office building, Captain Jack and Captain Bask led the other humans into the office. Captain Bask detoured to a jacket hanging on a hook by Administrator Serno's desk. She grabbed it and quietly placed it around Mrs. Storm to cover her torn shirt. Haruka Moriayama followed with a lone female Dorian prisoner. The captains looked quizzically at their navigator.

"She begged for her life and said she had information that could be useful if I spared her," Haruka mustered in her most menacing tone. She glared at the alien. "What is your name?" she asked.

"Zora," she quivered.

"Tell me something useful or I'll kill you where you stand," Haruka demanded, having no intention of doing so. In fact, the entire building had very few guards and the Earth people allowed the office workers to escape unharmed, but the captive Dorian had not witnessed it.

"I can show you the weapons storage," she stammered. "I can give everyone interpreters." She reached into her desk drawer; Haruka raised her weapon and Zora squeaked.

"Slowly," said Haruka. Zora complied and distributed the translators to the rest of the Earth people. Captain Jack explained their function to calm any concerns from his fellow freed prisoners. Zora approached Mrs. Storm, who looked up with a fierceness that made her take a step back. Zora handed her the tiny translator ball and Mrs. Storm put it in her ear as her husband and Captain Jack had described earlier. Zora continued to stare as tears formed in her eyes.

"I'm so sorry for your loss," the Dorian said humbly. Her apology met only with silence. She awkwardly stared at her captors before dropping her gaze. She breathed, hesitated, and remained silent. Haruka caught Zora's attention and led her away to the corner. Zora followed and curled up, humming quietly to herself.

"This is all my fault," said Mr. Watts. "I hope you can forgive me Sara, Sebastian." Marie put her arm around the mourning Mr. Watts, attempting to hold back her own tears.

"I have all of these feelings and emotions," Mrs. Storm started, her voice raw with emotion, "but we don't hold you responsible." She searched out her husband's face. "I know Sebastian feels responsible as well," she forced out, resting her hand on his shoulder. Resolve and anger crept into her voice as she continued, "The only people responsible are those aliens who took her life. Do you hear me Sebastian?" she implored. "We made the right decision. We weren't able to save her, but our plan saved everyone else."

Captain Jack overheard and made his way over to the grieving couple. "We all feel some responsibility," he admitted. "I can't imagine the grief you're experiencing right now, but I know the grief that I am feeling and the weight of responsibility and the role I played in this revolt." Deep breath. "I wanted to apologize. I know we did the right thing AND I regret it," he explained. "I have also been thinking about the urgency of our situation. I know you are mourning, but we aren't out of this yet, and we'll need both of you if we're going to make it," he explained as gently as he could. "I promise you, we won't leave Hanna behind, but we need you."

Mr. Storm wiped his eyes but otherwise remained motionless, his gaze never leaving his daughter's body. "When the time comes to act, you can count on us," he said solemnly. "Please give us a few moments with our daughter." Captain Jack nodded, and he moved away, followed by Mr. Watts and Marie.

"We'll make this right, Hanna," her father said. "I promise."

"As much as I want revenge, my precious daughter," Mrs. Storm cried, "I won't tarnish your legacy with it. I shall do my best to prevent others from sharing your fate, to the very best of my abilities." Mrs. Storm bent over and gently kissed Hanna's forehead. "I promise," she whispered.

Zora watched this tender scene from afar and marveled at the compassion of these Earth people. She herself had experienced the cruelty Dorians could impose on one another and knew it to be even worse for aliens. She motioned to her captor, Haruka.
"I have medical equipment for the mother. I can treat her injuries," she said. Haruka gestured with her hand cannon for Zora to stand up, and she rose and made her way to a wall cabinet from which she removed a small metallic box.

"Open it," Haruka commanded. Zora obeyed. Cloth bandages and gauze filled the container to the brim. Haruka called to Captain Bask and motioned her over.

"She wants to treat Sara," Haruka shared. "Does any of this look dangerous to you?" Captain Bask ruffled through the contents, leaving the contents askew.

"This looks like a standard first aid kit as far as I can tell" said Carlie. "Who knows what some of these ointments might do, but

I'm willing to bet they are medicinal. I say let her try. We don't want those wounds getting infected."

"Okay. I agree," said Haruka. She directed Zora over to where Mr. and Mrs. Storm had just risen from kneeling to standing over their daughter.

The first thing Zora pulled out was a thin, opaque white sheet. She spoke while the Storms looked down at their daughter.

"It is a custom with my people to cover our dead," She stretched out her arm with the sheet to Mrs. Storm, who hesitated before taking it. She handed one end to Mr. Storm, and they tenderly covered their daughter. Mrs. Storm turned to Zora.

"It is a custom among my people as well," she said.

"I have medicine for your back. If we don't treat it soon, it will become infected," said Zora. Mr. Storm eyed her with suspicion.

"I don't know if we can trust her," he said openly to his wife.

"I trust her," Mrs. Storm said.

Mr. Storm sighed. "And I trust you," he smiled. He looked at Zora and nodded with an expression clear of doubt.

Zora took out a tube of cream and gently applied it to Mrs. Storm's raw and wounded back. The patient let out a gasp of pain as the ointment touched her skin. Mr. Storm leaped to intervene, but his wife held up her hand.

"It only stings at first," Sara said. "Then the pain leaves."

"This will clean the wound and prevent infection," offered Zora to Mr. Storm.

"You are a mother, are you not?" guessed Mrs. Storm.

"I am," validated Zora. "I have three children. They were taken from me to be raised as laborers." Zora's head dropped. "I have not seen them for many years," she lamented.

"I'm so sorry," empathized Mrs. Storm.

"Aliens are not the only ones Dorians enslave," expounded Zora. "Dorian clans are at constant war, and the losing factions are considered fit only for hard labor. I was lucky with my appointment as First Secretary to a mining administrator. It is only because Administrator Serno fancies me. I don't receive the whip but would be glad to have it instead of the abuse that he supplies."

Some of the other Earth people made their way over to the conversation, including Carlie and Jack..

"How did they discover Earth?" Mrs. Storm asked.

"There have always been legends of a corridor that links to the Sister Galaxy. The system we are in now was once called Kamal-Etet. The Dorians conquered it in the Great Galactic War. Many have sought to find the corridor, but it is impossible to predict when and where it will open. Master Slythe developed a machine that attracts the natural corridor. On his first excursion, he returned with you," she explained.

"Is Slythe a Dorian leader?" Mr. Storm asked. Zora laughed.

"He is only the leader of Clan Slythe. He is not part of the ruling coalition." Her eyes narrowed, and a grave expression erased the laugh. "But his house is very powerful. If he enslaves Earth people to labor in Slythe mines and factories, he will become more powerful than the ruling houses. He could become powerful enough to conquer Galaxy Prime."

"How does he plan to enslave Earth?" asked Mrs. Storm.

"His corridor magnet device can attract the natural corridor, but it cannot sustain it. He must construct a giant aperture that will sustain the corridor long enough to send an armada of soldiers through. He must build a corresponding aperture on the other side for the return of Earth slaves. Once the apertures are completed on both sides, his armada of labor ships and battle cruisers will be able to travel back and forth with ease between here and your Earth."

"She must be lying," declared Rory King. "She's just the secretary! How could she know such detailed information?"

"She knows *because* she is the secretary," fumed Marie. "She hears everything!"

"How do we stop him?" interrupted Captain Jack with military seriousness. Zora paused the bandaging of Mrs. Storm and concentrated on her response.

"I don't know if he can be stopped. If you destroy the corridor engine before he sends his construction armada through, you will only delay the inevitable. He would just rebuild it. If you seek assistance from the ruling houses, they will only supplant Slythe and build the corridor engine themselves." She paused to think. "This system is the only place in Galaxy Prime where the aperture can be built because it is where the natural corridor manifests. If the Galactic Treaty planets were to retake this system and hold it, there would be no way to get to Sister Galaxy." Zora concluded her thoughts. "The only way to protect Earth is to take the Kamal-Etet system from the Dorians." Satisfied, she returned to the task of bandaging up Mrs. Storm while the Earth people stood quiet and contemplative.

"Why are you betraying your people? ?" asked Haruka suspiciously.

"Because I want to see vengeance rain down on Slythe and Serno and all of the Dorian clans that want to wreak pain and havoc on our people," she proclaimed bitterly. "There are many who thirst for power and have no regard for life. Many clans want peace with our galactic neighbors, but they lack the will to fight for it. My clan, Tempe, sides with those who want peace, but we are not powerful." Zora clenched her clawed fist. "Forgive me," she requested.

Valentina stepped forward and cleared her throat. "One of us made an escape attempt several days ago. It was a young boy, about this tall, named Henry. What happened to him?" she asked Zora.

"I only know the father Storm and this one," Zora motioned to Haruka. "They were thwarted in their escape attempt. No one else was captured, I am certain. If he is on this moon, I can help you find him."

"Sebastian and Haruka were merely a diversion," Valentina explained. "He was going to catch one of the spaceships that had different aliens piloting it."

"He may have been successful. We have had no word from the transport or seen any signs of an escaped Earth boy." The crease in Valentina's brow eased and her shoulders relaxed. It seemed increasingly likely that Henry had escaped.

Zora finished bandaging Mrs. Storm's wounds and Haruka took her around to tend to some of the other humans. A sense of victory filled the room; everyone had made it safely to the building, everyone but Hanna, that is. For the Storms, the cost was too high.

"Captain Jack," asked Mr. Storm. "We can stay holed up here for a while, but not forever. Zora seems knowledgeable and sincere. I don't trust her yet, but I trust my wife's instincts. Do you think she can help us get to a ship and get out of here?"

"That depends on our mission," responded Captain Jack.

"What do you mean?" yelled Captain Bask. "We would get the hell out of here!"

"You heard Zora," replied Captain Jack. "Our entire planet is at risk. We need to stop them from finishing that aperture."

"Insanity!" proclaimed Donovan Watts. "Even if we did, Zora said they would just rebuild it."

"No," interrupted Mrs. Storm. "Captain Jack is right. We have to stop them from getting to Earth, but we're at an extreme disadvantage here, and we've already lost someone." Mrs. Storm paused to try and check a fresh wave of emotion. "Our best chance of destroying this thing is to get to the Galactic Treaty planets and warn them of what's coming."

"She's right," said Mr. Storm. "We're not losing anyone else. We get to safety first and come back with reinforcements."

"I get it," said Captain Jack, "and you may be right. Situations like this are time-sensitive, though. We may need to act now before it's too late. If we have a reasonable chance to destroy the corridor engine, we should take it now."

"You led us to safety," Mr. Watts said solemnly to Captain Jack. "You inspired us to beat the odds and fight back, but we cannot press our luck on this. We can still stop them, but let's get everyone to safety first and then come back with numbers and equipment."

"All right," said Captain Jack. "Sometimes the prudent course is the right one. I just hope we don't lose our window of opportunity on this."

"There is one more consideration," said Marie. "That device the Dorians have may be our only hope for getting home." Silence. The weight of Marie's insight moved heavily through the room.

"If it means keeping these Dorians from Earth, I'm willing to make that sacrifice," said Captain Jack. "We have to protect Earth, even if we don't make it back."

"Contingency planning is wise," stated Mrs. Storm, "but we need not lose hope of returning to Earth in order to protect it."

"May I suggest we take each problem in turn," said Mr. Watts. "Let us first focus on getting everyone to safety. Then we can worry about thwarting the Dorians and, finally, how we get back home."

"I agree," said Captain Bask. "Time is not on our side here. We have to get to those treaty planets. I think Zora is our best bet."

"I think we're all agreed then," said Captain Jack. Everyone nodded.

"Haruka," called Captain Bask. "Bring Zora over here." Zora and Haruka made their way over.

"Zora, if we get to a ship, can you get us to the treaty planets?"

"I don't know how to pilot a ship," she said, "but I could show you how to get to a border crossing if we had someone to pilot."

"Between the three of us we'll figure it out." Captain Jack looked at Haruka and Captain Bask. "Right?"

"Of course," said Carlie.

"How hard can it be?" asked Haruka.

Everyone stopped as the sound of distant engines started to grow louder. Rory King came running into the room in a panic.

"Captain Jack! We have a problem." Rory led everyone to the window, where they had a view of the landing pad. Three ships landed, and Dorian foot soldiers poured out, weapons at the ready. There were hundreds of them.

"Butts!" said Mr. Storm. "All we have to do now is cut our way through a thousand Dorians, get on one of those ships, and hope the captains can fly it."

"They would be crazy to attack us here," said Captain Jack. "We have the high ground. We'd mow them down without giving up much cover."

"You should pass out the lawnmowers," said Mrs. Storm. "Here they come." Captain Jack distributed weapons from the storage locker that Zora had shown him. He directed each person to take up strategic positions around the building.

"Okay folks," said Captain Jack. "Light 'em up!"

CHAPTER 20

The Right Pirate

Hanna sat at the helm of the *Eloise* with Mera as copilot and Stiggs in the navigator chair. Mera looked a little comical sitting in a chair built for someone half her size, her knees higher than they should have been. Stiggs, who was familiar with the newly installed navigation system, had plotted a course within seconds of their lift off.

Hanna marveled at the new controls. Integration with the original system kept things intuitive, but the *Eloise* was now capable of vertical take-offs and landings. With the upgraded sublight engine, they had reached the nearest corridor and were on their way to pirate territory within minutes. Hanna took care to keep the artificial gravity off and her seat belt buckled as they jumped. It hadn't crossed her mind before, but now that she had some time to sit and think, she felt a surge of excitement at piloting her own spaceship. It wasn't really hers, she knew, but it felt like it in that moment. She had helped with the modifications herself, knew how to fly it, was learning how to navigate it, and took a moment to soak it all in. How many NASA astronauts dreamed of having something like this under their control? She was just barely fourteen and already living her dream—hers and everybody else's! This thought gave her the dual sensation of confidence in what she had achieved and fear at the thought of what she had yet to accomplish.

"I can't believe Blue morphed into you," said Mera.

"I know! Can you believe it? I feel so violated," said Hanna.

"Violated?" asked the Bimber.

"He saved your life! I can't believe he had the courage to do it," Mera clarified. "You should be thankful!"

"I am thankful, but it wasn't his choice to make. It was mine," said Hanna, defending herself. "Plus, he undressed me," she said.

"I don't understand Earth people. Are you ashamed of your bodies?" asked Mera.

"Humans are very concerned about propriety and connect nudity with mating," interrupted Stiggs. "The Monarch is very, very private," he added, as if that fact alone was enough to explain the behavior.

"Yes," said Hanna. "It's my body and I did not give Blue permission to look at it," she said.

"Maybe his eyes were closed," said Mera. "Look, if you had a wound from battle, I would have your clothes off as fast as I could trying to find the injury. Wouldn't that be the right thing to do?"

"It would be, but that's different," explained Hanna.

"Is it?" asked Mera. "Blue saved you. I would do the same for you. You know what? I think you would do the same for us." Mera paused to let her last statement sink in. "You're not as mad about the clothing as you are about the guilt you'll feel if something happens to him because he took your place."

Hanna started to tear up. "I don't know if I could forgive myself if anything happened to him," said Hanna.

"The Bimber warriors have a saying," said Mera. "I never know if the translators get it correct, but here it is: victory is not the fault of the defeated and defeat is not the fault of the victorious. Does that make sense?"

"I'm not sure I understand," admitted Hanna.

"It means, if I win, it is because of the decisions I made in battle, not because of the decisions of my opponent. The opposite is also true: if I lose, it is because of the decisions I made, not because of the decisions of my opponent. A warrior must take responsibility for their own actions, in victory or defeat."

"Okay, so, you're saying Blue made his decision and he is responsible for the outcome, not me." Hanna wrestled with the idea.

"Yes! Exactly. I might make a Bimber of you yet," Mera said jokingly. "When Bimber warriors go into battle, every one of them is willing to die honorably for two things, their cause and their fellow warriors. If a Bimber warrior went around thinking it should have been him, he dishonors the sacrifice."

"I understand," Hanna submitted. "I appreciate the perspective. Once we rescue Blue, I'll be sure to thank him," she assured Mera, "right after I punch him in his stupid face," she teased.

"We're reaching the corridor exit," announced Stiggs. "This is the very edge of the border between the Dorian Empire and the Galactic Treaty planets. It won't be long before we are found. I suggest that Mera hide in the smuggler's hold for now. If they know she's on board, they'll never agree to a challenge for supremacy."

"Ughhhh," grunted Mera, "as long as I get to fight."

"Take a communicator," instructed Stiggs, handing Mera a small round device. He handed one to Hanna and kept one for himself. "These are on the same frequency and work short-range," he explained. "We'll call Mera once the challenge has been accepted."

Mera left the bridge and entered the newly masked compartment situated under a pair of the fine leather recliners in the main cabin. The chairs lifted up, exposing a spacious compartment beneath. Mera sat down and began her pre-fight meditations.

Stiggs had understated things when he said it would not be long before they were found. The nose of the *Eloise* exited the green wall of light and immediately entered the cargo hold of a giant spaceship. It was positioned close to the corridor engine, presumably to catch anything that was exiting. Hanna reflexively tried to break free and was about to launch some of the *Eloise*'s new weapons when Stiggs put a hand on her arm.

"This is good. Remember why we're here. You're going to challenge their captain, our best fighter against theirs, and when you win, you are going to have them find out where your parents are being held and take you there."

"Right," said Hanna. "Thanks, Stiggs."

"I'm being very literal," Stiggs persisted. "You need to be assertive and tell whoever captures us exactly how things are going to go. That is the only way you will get an audience with the captain."

"Why don't you do it, Stiggs?" Hanna asked nervously.

"I considered that approach," answered Stiggs, "but you are a legendary species, the same as the Monarch, and the Monarch is respected among many of the pirate circles. We'll have a better chance if you are in charge. I am here to guide you. You will do fine. We will probably survive," Stiggs said matter-of-factly.

"Probably? Thanks for the confidence boost," Hanna said sarcastically. Hanna eased back on the power and landed the ship safely in the cargo hold of the enormous spaceship. She couldn't help but think how clever it was to position a ship this way—no time to react and too close to deploy weapons without endangering one's own ship.

"Here they come," said Stiggs. Two enormous aliens with large snouts sporting a single giant horn marched into the cargo hold. They each held enormous hand cannons, so big that Hanna imagined tugging on one and not moving it an inch. The aliens were gray and menacing and reminded Hanna of a rhinoceros or a thick gray unicorn that had consumed too many Twinkies. She wondered whether Mera would be victorious in a fight with just one of these creatures, let alone two. The larger of the two grumbled loudly, some device enhancing the volume of his voice, like a megaphone.

"Come out of your ship and you won't be harmed," it sneered in a low-bass voice. "Leave your weapons behind," it commanded.

Stiggs and Hanna put their hands up and exited the *Eloise* on the state-of-the-art retractable ramp that had been installed by Haranda Su. They approached the guards slowly.

"Is this everyone?" asked the smaller of the two rhinoceros guards. Hanna looked to Stiggs, who nudged her with his elbow. Hanna put on her best poker face and took a deep breath.

"Listen, you oversized herbivores," Hanna began, "here is what's going to happen. You are going to take me to your captain. I'll challenge your captain, your best fighter against ours. After we win, you're going to help me find my parents who are captive somewhere in the Dorian system." The passion in her voice combined with her confident posture brooked no argument.

The guards just stared down at her, dumbfounded.

"Do you need me to repeat myself?" Hanna quipped.

They suddenly burst out in low, grumbly laughter that lasted an annoying thirty seconds.

"The captain will love this," said the smaller of the two. "They think their best fighter will beat ours." The larger alien wiped a tear from its face and pulled out a small, round communication device and flipped it open.

"Captain," he paused.

"What is it, Grull?" came an annoyed, yet cultured and feminine voice.

"This lot wants to challenge you, our best fighter against theirs," he chuckled.

"Ooh. Exciting!" dripped her sarcastic response. "Throw them in the brig and search their ship. I want to know what treasures they've brought me."

The guards voiced their compliance and shoved Hanna and Stiggs down a hallway and into a room with no door. The larger of the two pushed a button located near the cell, and a sparkling, translucent wall of blue enveloped the entrance, blocking their escape. Hanna touched it and instantly flew backward, landing on her butt. Grumbly, slow laughs floated into the cell.

"Stay here," commanded Grull before wandering off.

"What now, Stiggs?" Hanna asked, panic in her eyes.

"You did well. Now, we wait," answered Stiggs.

They didn't have to wait long for the captain. Hanna gasped when she walked in with her entourage of pirates. The captain stood taller than Hanna by about a foot, with two arms and two legs in humanoid fashion. She wore her long dark hair slicked back past pointed ears, not unlike Blue's, but her skin was not blue. A deep brown complexion surrounded fierce, bright green eyes that met Hanna's stare. The captain wore a utility belt around her waist with various contraptions attached. Two more belts went up over her shoulders and crossed in an "X" centered just below her chest. Hanna pushed down the urge to fangirl over this captain's style and beauty. She forced herself to return the captain's gaze with a hard stare of her own, but it felt as though she was looking at the Mona Lisa or the Venus de Milo. This pirate captain was an exquisite work of art.

"I'm Captain Ternia," she said authoritatively. "Welcome to the pirate ship *Death Bringer*. What are your names and from where do you hail?"

"My name is Hanna Storm, and I am from Earth." Hanna straightened her shoulders and continued to return Ternia's intense stare straight on. "I'm here to challenge your authority, my best fighter against yours. After I win, you are going to help me find my parents; they're captive somewhere in the Dorian Empire."

A murmur rippled through the pirate captain's entourage. Captain Ternia, however, seemed unimpressed.

"And you?" the pirate asked of Stiggs.

"I am a servant to the Monarch. He has instructed me to aid Hanna on her quest." Another round of murmurs ran through the group, but Captain Ternia was still unphased.

"So you say," said Ternia. "Very well," she said, turning to her followers. "Go and prepare the feast. I'll decide whether or not I will accept this challenge after we've had our fill." The pirates gave a cheer and hurried off to make their preparations.

Ternia turned back to Hanna and Stiggs. "You'll join us for the feast as tradition demands," she commanded mischievously before exiting herself.

#

When the time came for the grand jollification, the rhinoceros guard named Grull and his enormous, smaller companion released Hanna and Stiggs from their enclosure. The guards were no longer armed with their huge hand cannons, but their physique spoke to the fact that they didn't need them. They led their two guests to a large dining room filled with noisy pirates seated at long rectangular tables, all of whom fell silent when Hanna and Stiggs stepped through the entrance. Ternia was seated on a raised platform with two empty chairs on either side. She stood up and the rest of the pirates followed her example. The guards guided them over to seats on either side of the Captain. Hanna confidently took her place as if she deserved the respect she was receiving, but her insides were a hot, jumbly mess and her tummy rumbled with unease.

Ternia raised her glass and the pirates solemnly stood, mugs of some alien beverage held to their chest in salute. Stiggs stood as well and mimicked the pirates. There was an awkward pause as Hanna stood empty-handed at her seat. Stiggs cleared his throat and motioned his head toward the mug on the table in front of Hanna.

"Oh!" Hanna said. "Sorry," she whispered to the Captain. She raised her mug.

"To our guests," said Ternia, "and the entertainment they bring." The pirates and Stiggs enthusiastically gulped down their beverages. Hanna hesitated at the smell but knew better from her many adventures on Earth that not to partake might constitute an insult that would lead to trouble. All eyes were on her. She bravely gulped down the fluid, which burned her throat and immediately made her light-headed. Cheers erupted all around, and Hanna sank back into her seat. Servants refilled cups and brought out the most elaborate dishes of food. The first real meal that Hanna had experienced in Galaxy Prime did not disappoint. This food had not been made in a food synthesizer, and it tasted so good! There were roasted meats along with strange, foreign fruits and vegetables. Hanna tried a bit of everything.

"I was disappointed to see you did not have any cargo," said Ternia, "but your ship itself is a worthy prize. Is it an Earth ship?"

"It is," said Hanna, "and the *Eloise* is not a prize unless your best beats mine."

"I haven't decided to accept your challenge yet," said Ternia. "I may decide to throw you two out of an airlock and keep your ship. It's not registered, almost impossible to track, and Haranda Su has put some work into it." Hanna dropped her spoon.
"How do you know Haranda Su?" she asked.

"She is the very best," said Ternia. "Everyone knows Haranda Su. It is easy to spot her work."

"She and I made a few modifications," Hanna said.

"You seem to be enjoying your farkle fruit," said Ternia. "Have you ever had anything so delicious?"

"It is the most amazing fruit I have ever tasted," said Hanna, "but it doesn't compare to chocolate." Hanna sighed dreamily.

"What is chocolate?" asked Ternia.

"Chocolate is a confectionary made from the cacao bean on Earth," Stiggs chimed in. "I've learned a great deal about it from the Monarch, but we've never been able to synthesize it according to his tastes." Hanna grinned as she ruffled around in her satchel.

"I have a chocolate bar in my pack. I'd be happy to share it with you," Hanna offered.

Ternia eyed the young Earth girl suspiciously but ordered Hanna's pack to be brought. "I doubt anything in the galaxy could be as delicious as farkle fruit," she mused, "but I admit I am curious, especially if it's a favorite of the Monarch."

Hanna took out the chocolate bar and opened the packaging before handing it to Ternia. Ternia broke off a piece and gave it to Hanna, who ate the piece without reservation to demonstrate that it was safe. Ternia then took a bite. Hanna had difficulty interpreting the look that came over Ternia's face. Was it one of enlightenment? Of splendor? Of gratitude? Of happiness? Hanna could not quite decide.

"I stand corrected," said Ternia.

"You're technically still correct. Nothing in *this* galaxy is as good as farkle fruit. Chocolate is from my galaxy," laughed Hanna.

"So, you really are from Earth," said Ternia. "Two of my men recently took a stowaway from the Dorian mines who claimed to be an Earth person and delivered him to the Monarch. They got quite the bounty for him too."

Hanna dropped a fork full of farkle fruit. Could it have been someone from the *Eloise*?

Ternia smirked and stood up. "Bart! Veemo! Get up here!" she demanded. Two pink aliens with long narrow snouts that resembled a pig's made their way up to the Captain's table.

"Yes, Captain!" they said in unison.

"Tell our guest what you know."

"We noticed someone hiding in the last shipment of ore from a Dorian mine," said Veemo. "Bart overheard the guards there talking about Earth people, so we figured it might be one of them. The Monarch sure thought so. He looked a little different from our guest here. His chest bumps were a lot smaller."

"Like many species here in Galaxy Prime, human females have larger chest bumps when they are fully grown than their male counterparts," said Stiggs. "This is a biological difference that..."

"We get it, Stiggs," said Hanna, turning red. "I am a female. The stowaway was male. What was his name?"

"Harry? Harvey?" said Bart.

"No," said Veemo. "It was something like Herby?"

"Henry?" shouted Hanna excitedly.

"That's it!" said Veemo. "It was Henry. He's with the Monarch now."

Hanna heaved a sigh of relief. Knowing that Henry was safe gave her much needed hope. It was also encouraging that these two knew exactly where her parents were being held.

"You have to take me back to that mine. I have to rescue my parents!"

"Just a moment," said Ternia. "I have not yet accepted your challenge."

"Then accept my challenge!" demanded Hanna, impatiently slamming her fist on the table. The room once again went silent. "The sooner we beat you, the sooner I can order these two to take me back to my parents."

"All right," said Ternia. "What say you?" she shouted to her audience. "Do we fight?" The crowd began to chant quietly. "Fight! Fight! Fight!" Then, the chant grew louder. "Fight! Fight! Fight!" The room went crazy as the chant gained momentum. One pirate with tentacle arms jumped up on the table and cheered on the chant. Others spilled their beverages as mugs pounded the table. The dining hall shook as a hodgepodge of alien pirates stomped wildly on the floor.

Ternia shouted to the group. "I accept this challenge on the following terms. If we win this fight, your ship becomes ours and you pledge lifelong loyalty to me and join our crew." Cheers from the crowd. "If you win, I will grant you your ship and our full support in rescuing your parents and any other human captives." Another loud cheer. "Finally, the battle is to the death!" This last condition elicited the longest and loudest shouts.

"I accept your conditions," said Hanna, smiling.

"Then choose your warrior. Who will it be? You or your Belafian friend Stiggs?"

"Neither," said Hanna. She reached for her communicator. "Mera, you can come in now." The rowdy pirates froze silently in place. Even Ternia could not hide her stunned expression.

There was a commotion in the hallway; one of the giant rhinoceros guards came flying through the dining hall and crashed into one of the tables, snapping it in half. Mera marched into the room in a rage. The entire crowd scrambled out of the way, terrified. Even Ternia took a step back.

"A female Bimber," burst out Ternia. "I never would have suspected. Oh well," she said matter-of-factly. The surprise vanished from Ternia's face just as quickly as it had arrived. "A deal is a deal. Melatar!" she shouted. "Please grace us with your presence."

The crowd erupted like Vesuvius as a large male Bimber entered the room. Hanna watched the courage slowly leak from Mera's face.

Melatar towered over Mera, and Hanna couldn't help but remember Mera's declaration that no female Bimber had ever beaten a male Bimber. Undeterred, Hanna also recalled Mera's declaration that she would be the first to do it. At least she was getting her opportunity.

"I can't fight a female," Melatar complained to his captain.

"The deal is made. It is to the death. You owe me your life, or have you forgotten?" said Ternia coolly.

"I have not forgotten," said Melatar. "As you command," he said. "A female. My shame is now complete." He began to flex, and his aura glowed red around his body.

"Mera! Remember your goals," Hanna shouted. "Remember my neighbor, Tamika. Just because it has never been done before doesn't mean it can't be done." Mera's orange glowing aura slowly began to grow. She stomped the ground and flexed her muscles.

"Mera, I know you can beat him. I've seen how tough you are. This is your time!" Hanna shouted. Mera's expression grew increasingly focused and intense. The people seated between the two Bimbers scrambled out of the way.

The warriors rushed toward one another, and the resulting blast of energy knocked everyone to the ground. Hanna stood up and saw Mera slowly exiting a gaping Mera-shaped hole in the dining hall's metallic wall.

Melatar laughed and was still laughing when Mera came flying back and drove her shoulder into his abdomen, pinning him against the wall. She unleashed a flurry of punches that brought Melatar to one knee. A ferocious uppercut from Melatar lifted Mera to the ceiling of the hall. She crashed back down, pulverizing the table and chairs that broke her fall. Melatar let fly a roundhouse kick that sent Mera flying across the hall into another wall.

"Mera!" shouted Hanna, running over.

"He's too strong," said Mera, bleeding through her nose and at the corner of her mouth.

"Remember Earth fighting! It's not always the strongest fighter who wins. Not always.

"Pantralak Poop!" cussed Melatar. "The fight always goes to the strongest."

"Stop babbling and finish her, Melatar," Ternia scolded impatiently.

Mera stood up and wiped the blood from her mouth. She bounded toward Melatar, who in turn started his charge. This time, when they clashed, Mera stood her ground. She clinched the back of Melatar's neck and delivered two swift knees to his midsection. He stumbled backward. When he came forward again, Mera fell to one knee and lunged at his legs. She wrapped both arms around his knees, picked him up, and slammed him to the ground. She quickly straddled him and began raining down punches. His nose broke and his eyes began to swell shut. She grabbed his right arm in the Americana hold that Hanna had taught her and slowly pulled his arm down to his waist.

"I'm going to break your arm," she taunted, "and there's nothing you can do to stop it." Snap! Melatar screamed in pain. Hanna looked over to see Ternia's worried face focused solely on Melatar. He used all of his strength to turn over and lie flat on his stomach with Mera sitting on his back. As he pushed up, Mera reached down and put an arm under his throat, grabbed the bicep of her opposite arm, and started to squeeze. Melatar kicked violently. Unphased, Mera locked her legs around his thighs and rolled over onto her back. She held him solidly in a rear naked choke from which he had no way out. He continued to resist, arms flailing, until they finally fell limp as he passed out.

"Please make her stop," asked Ternia wide-eyed with desperation.

"Mera!" said Hanna. "That's enough! You won. Don't kill him."

Mera let go and stood up. She walked past a stunned, silent crowd to where Hanna sat. Ternia leapt from the stage and pushed past them to fall down beside Melatar. She helped him up to a seated position and shook him vigorously. He finally came to his senses, and Ternia ordered several pirates to take him to the infirmary.

Mera sat down in Ternia's seat and began to eat one of the roasted animals, enjoying her triumph.

"I knew you could do it," said Hanna smiling. "I'm glad you didn't kill him."

"It still counts," smiled Mera. "Thanks for believing in me, Hanna. It might have turned out differently otherwise."

"To the first female Bimber to defeat a male Bimber in combat," prided Stiggs, raising his glass.

"Hear, hear," said Hanna.

Ternia made her way back to her seat. Seeing that it was occupied by a large female Bimber, she decided to take an open seat next to Hanna.

"Thank you for sparing his life," she said humbly. "I can't say I would have done the same were our places reversed. But I am very grateful and in your debt." Ternia breathed deep and continued. "I rescued Melatar long ago from a horrible death, and he has been a loyal friend ever since. I don't know what I would do without him."

"You're welcome," said Hanna. "I never wanted him to die. I take it our deal is still in place and that you will use all your resources to help me find my parents?" she inquired.

"I will honor my part of the deal," said Ternia solemnly. "I also offer my protection anytime and anywhere. You can always contact me."

"Thank you."

"I believe we have some planning to do," said Stiggs. "Let us not waste any more time."

"As you wish," said Ternia. The four of them stood up, and Mera suddenly collapsed.

"One more for the infirmary, I guess," said Ternia. "She fought bravely, but now we need to tend to her wounds. Don't worry," she added. "Bimbers heal quickly."

"I'm fine," protested Mera, her voice catching.

"No, you're not," challenged Hanna. "Go and get patched up. And no more fighting with Melatar."

"Unless he asks for it," she laughed.

"Unless he asks for it," laughed Hanna.

Stiggs, Hanna, and Ternia moved off to a planning room while a few pirates led Mera down to the infirmary.

#

Ternia glided into a gilded chair with cushioned armrests made of a soft and opulent material. Hanna and Stiggs were already seated on less decorous stools. The room was otherwise sparse, with just a table and a few additional unoccupied chairs of various shapes and sizes.

"As I see it, Captain Ternia," began Stiggs, "we have two possible courses of action. We could send a small team on one of your transports, perhaps the same one Veemo and Bart used, or we could take a stealthier approach using the *Eloise*."

Ternia eyed Stiggs. "What qualifies you to lead this planning session?" she inquired.

"My apologies, Captain," muttered Stiggs.

"Forgiven," she waved. "There is an obvious choice here. One of our transports could get us in, but it could not get us out," Captain Ternia explained. "They aren't fast enough and don't have the fire power." Stiggs nodded and Captain Ternia continued. "I was looking over Haranda Su's work on your vessel. She managed to pack almost as much firepower into that ship as there is in my entire *Death Bringer*," the pirate captain boasted. "It's incredible."

"I am certain she would appreciate your compliment," interrupted Stiggs, standing up from his stool. "Please, if you would allow me to continue."

Ternia's hand sought out the hilt of a blade tucked into her belt, and she tenderly rubbed her palm against the blood red Haraxian crystal adorning the pommel. Stiggs opened his mouth but decided to remain silent and fell back into his chair.

"If we were to arrive undetected in the Earth ship," Ternia eventually continued, "we could take out any Dorian cruisers patrolling the area and destroy the landing platform before the Dorians reacted. We could assault the launch pad, enter the mines, and bring out any Earth people. Your Earth vessel is faster than anything the Dorians have. We'd make it back to a corridor engine and across the border before they could even send communications."

It was now Stiggs' turn to eye Captain Ternia. She had just described his entire plan.

Hanna switched her gaze back and forth between Stiggs and Ternia. Were there any flaws in this plan? Were there any signs of betrayal from the pirate captain? Stiggs was a hard frog to read, his face full of expressionless contemplation.

"I agree," Stiggs croaked.

"So do I," stated Hanna. "Stiggs, how many people do we need for this?" Hanna asked, but it was Ternia who answered.

"We need just enough people to have one team to go into the mines and one team to stay with the ship and provide cover," she replied. "I will join you. Melatar should be recovered by now and he can come along as well. I can't leave out Grull and Grall; they hate Dorians. That should be enough," Ternia concluded.

"What about Veemo and Bart? Don't they know the area?" asked Hanna.

"Those two are no good in a fight, and the Dorians don't know they work for me; I'd like to keep it that way," responded Ternia.

"Two Bimber, two Garellians," said Stiggs, "a pirate Captain, an Earth girl, and a Belafian," he concluded. "That should be adequate. Quite right."

"We don't really need a Belafian," mocked Ternia.

"Stiggs comes," Hanna insisted. "Go on, Stiggs."

"Hanna and Mera should be enough to guard the ship," explained Stiggs. Hanna knew that what he really meant was Mera could guard *her* and the ship. "I can lead the Garellians, you, and Melatar into the mines."

"You can lead?" taunted Ternia. "I'll lead us through the Dorians. We will be well shielded and will cut you a clear path. You just have to follow Melatar and I into the mines and get the transport discs to the prisoners. Grull and Grall can guard the mine entrance."

Ternia looked very satisfied with herself and Stiggs nodded in approval at her plan. The question of who was actually leading meant little to him in this particular skirmish. Stiggs had just one objective: to find the Earth people and return them to the Monarch.

Beep! Beep! Captain Ternia's radio indicated an incoming call.

"What is it?" she asked.

"We have more guests in the brig," responded the radio.

"Please join me," said Ternia to Hanna. Stiggs followed.

When they entered the brig, Hanna gasped. There stood Mung and Boother along with Vlad, Haranda Su, and Henry.

"Henry!" Hanna ran to the cell. "You're alive. Are my parents okay?"

"Hanna! Oh man!" Henry said. "We finally found you. We've been tracking you all over this galaxy. Your parents were okay the last I saw them. They helped me escape to try and find help."

"That sounds about right," laughed Hanna. "Haranda Su? Vlad? Boother? Mung? What are you all doing here?" she jolted, surprise and curiosity traversing her features. Boother's bumps were bright yellow with excitement.

"Like Henry said," answered Mung, "we've been looking for you."

"Hello, Vlad," greeted Ternia in a sultry voice, one of her hands caressing his cheek.

"Captain Ternia," he grinned. "I was not expecting to see you." He turned to Hanna. "Did you win fight? Captain Ternia has Bimber like you, only he is boy Bimber."

"Her Bimber won," said Ternia.

"Ha!" laughed Vlad. "I told you. Plan is simple."

"You and I have some unfinished business, Vlad," Ternia stated seriously.

Vlad gulped. "I suppose we do."

"Well, you found me," said Hanna to everyone. "I'm going to rescue my parents. I hope you're not here to stop me," she warned.

"Our orders from Command are to help you," said Mung.

"Mung is right," said Vlad. "We want help you. It is why we are all here."

"That's right," said Haranda Su, "we're here to help."

"We already have a plan in place," hooted Ternia, "and it doesn't include the lot of you."

"Now, hold on," said Mung. "We have been all over this galaxy looking for Hanna Storm, and now that we have found her, she is not leaving our sight," he insisted.

"There's room on the *Eloise*. If you want to help, I welcome it," said Hanna in defiance of Ternia. She summoned a menacing stare for the pirate captain. After all, Hanna's best had bested Ternia's best. Ternia met her gaze with a cool smirk and nodded her approval.

"As you command, Captain Storm," laughed Ternia.

"You," Hanna said, pointing to the large rhinoceros guard. "Let them out."

"Yes Captain Storm," he obeyed in his lowest, most grumbly voice. "My name is Grull, by the way," he complained. "Not that you care," he added under his breath while pushing the button on the panel to release the force field.

"I do care," apologized Hanna, "and I am thankful to you and Grall for joining us on this dangerous mission to save my parents and friends from the Dorians."

"Beg your pardon?" rumbled Grull. "Did you hear that, Grall? We might get to fight Dorians," he beamed. The two butted heads and left the room in high spirits.

CHAPTER 21

Rescued at Last

Hanna and Haranda Su stood on the bridge of the *Eloise* preparing for their mission. Haranda Su showed Hanna more specifics on how to work the weapons systems. There were automatic targeting systems for both the energy and projectile weapons. All Hanna had to do was select her target and the level of destruction desired, and the voice interface would do the rest.

Henry walked onto the bridge. "Hi Hanna," he said sheepishly. Hanna jumped in surprise. "I'm so sorry. I didn't mean to scare you," Henry apologized.

Hanna laughed. "I'm just nervous. I've never led a rescue mission before," Hanna admitted. That wasn't entirely true. There had been one occasion when one of her clients wandered off on a hike in the Andes of Ecuador and Mr. Storm had assigned her to lead the search. She had set up a pattern grid and had the other members of the hiking party methodically criss-cross the terrain until the woman was eventually found asleep under a tree. Hanna recalled this experience and it reassured her, giving her the courage she could lead again. "At least, not one in space," she pondered, "unless you count rescuing us from the zoo," she added, gaining more confidence. "But that was mostly Stiggs. And Mera."

"I get it," Henry laughed. "I'm coming too, right?" he petitioned. Hanna stood up and grabbed his hand.

"You don't have to Henry," she said.

"It was crazy there, for sure," exhaled Henry. "I pushed through it, though, and escaped. You guys need me."

"I guess I'm scared," she confided. "I'm afraid I'm going to fail, that I can't do it, but then I think of my parents, Donovan Watts, Marie, and I feel my courage grow," Hanna answered. "And you're right, Henry, we do need you."

"What do you need me to do?" asked Henry.

"Go check the cargo hold and figure out how many people we can fit down there," smiled Hanna.

"Aye! Aye! Captain Storm," cheered Henry, saluting. He turned and exited the bridge.

Hanna glimpsed Mera out of the cockpit window walking toward the *Eloise*. Was she with Melatar? She was with Melatar! Hanna watched the scene unfold, as Mera smiled and laughed at something Melatar said. Then she spoke, and Melatar, arm in a sling, erupted in laughter at whatever quip Mera volleyed back. Hanna stood at the top of the ramp and gawked at her Bimber friend as the two approached.

"You're looking pretty healthy," said Hanna, hands on her hips.

"Yeah, yeah," said Mera dismissively. "I was just catching up with Melatar here. We're actually from the same city back on Bimber Prime."

"And we were both denied death by headstrong women who had to rescue us and claim our lives," grumped Melatar, a wry smile escaping lips.

"That was the best thing ever to happen to you, you Aporian hell beast," gibed Captain Ternia, who had just walked up behind the two Bimbers. Vlad stood obediently by her side, her arm threaded through his elbow. He glowed.

Grull and Grall trailed behind them. They were armored from head to toe in shiny, metallic armor imbued with a faint bluish glow. Each gripped a massive hand cannon with ease, as though it were a toy.

"We're ready to go too," said Mung and Boother, entering the already overcrowded bridge. They donned their full Corridor Police battle gear, including energy batons and standard issue hand cannons. Boother also had a belt of non-standard issue grenades draped across his chest, or belly, or whatever part of him constituted the front.

"Letzzz do thizzz," bellowed Boother, his bumps a determined bright blue color that Hanna had not yet observed.

"All right, then," agreed Hanna. She took her seat with Ternia to her left in the copilot seat and Stiggs at navigation. "Everybody on board?"

Henry wondered at the look of excitement on his fellow rescuers' faces.

"What an adventure!" exclaimed Haranda Su.

"That's one way to look at it," squeaked Henry, a slight tremor in his voice.

"I can't wait to smash Dorians," laughed Grull in his deep, throaty voice. Grall echoed his sentiment.

"Won't they be monitoring the corridors? They will know as soon as one is activated," said Mung nervously.

"We give them a strong incentive to look the other way," answered Ternia. "They won't think twice about a corridor trip to the Kamal-Etet system. We use it all the time," said Ternia dismissively. It wasn't lost on Hanna that the Corridor Police and pirates didn't usually play on the same team.

"That is good to know," said Mung. "We would never tolerate such a thing in the Galactic Treaty corridors."

"Of course not!" said Ternia with a hint of sarcasm.

"It's time," Hanna commanded. "Watch yourself, Saldo," she said to herself, though the others could hear. "There's a Storm coming for you."

"Woohoo!" shouted Mera.

"Hello, *Eloise*," voiced Hanna.

"Welcome, Hanna Storm," replied the ship's computer voice interface.

Haranda Su leaped up on the console and punched in a few commands. "Let me fix that for you, Hanna," she explained.

"Welcome, Hanna Storm, Captain," corrected the voice interface. Hanna smiled and shook her head at Haranda Su. Mera whooped, and the others cheered. The title was catching on.

"Okay. Stations everyone," ordered Hanna Storm, Captain.

Ternia and Stiggs both went for the copilot seat next to Hanna, but Ternia glided in first. Stiggs took Haruka's chair as navigator. Mera leaped for the weapons station, though controls also lay on the captain's console.

Hanna manipulated the throttle, and the *Eloise* took flight as the others made their way to the main cabin and buckled in. She steered it deftly out of the hangar and into open space. The thrill of it put a smile on her face.

"Stiggs! Get us across the border and lay in coordinates for the nearest Dorian corridor engine," ordered Hanna.

"Yes Captain Storm," said Stiggs.

Hanna hit the sublight-modified Wolverine rocket and the *Eloise* soared into the stars.

#

The battle outside the mines raged on. The humans were pinned down inside the building, but they managed to keep any Dorian guards from entering. More ships arrived with more Dorian soldiers until the entire platform was covered with armed lizards.

"We can defend, but I don't see how we make it to a transport," said Captain Jack to Captain Bask and Haruka. "We'd have to cut our way through wave after wave of soldiers. Any ideas?"

"Zora!" called Captain Bask. Zora came running over. "Do we have any defensive weapons, like shields?"

"No," said Zora plainly.

"Any ideas on how we can make it to a transport?" asked Captain Jack.

"You must defeat the Dorians that stand in your way," Zora said, as though the answer were obvious.

"Thank you. You've been very helpful," Captain Jack said sarcastically. "Sebastian!"

Mr. Storm had assumed a position in which he could pick off any enemy forces attempting to enter the building. Several had tried to do so at their leaders' command, but the bodies were starting to pile up near the entrance.

"No breaches so far, Captain Jack," he responded.

The air suddenly filled with a strange, yet familiar, buzzing noise. Mrs. Storm's eyes grew wide. A series of pops filled the room. She clobbered a Dorian who materialized next to her, and he slumped to the ground. Dorian fighters appeared and slapped discs onto any human within reach. A particularly large alien with huge scars and an eyepatch did not slap discs on anyone. He materialized in an instant, lifted Captain Jack in a giant bear hug, and began to squeeze. Captain Jack turned purple.

Mr. Storm switched his focus from the entryway to the uninvited guests. Whenever they would send off a human, Mr. Storm would take aim and shoot the Dorian before he could move on to another person. Seeing Captain Jack in trouble, he moved in swiftly, only to have the large Dorian with the eyepatch release one of his arms from the bear hug and place a hand cannon against Captain Jack's temple.

"You should drop your weapon, unless you want his brain matter splattered all over the walls," said Boran.

"Don't do it," choked Captain Jack. "Keep fighting!" He struggled to breathe. Mr. Storm looked around the room. He could not see his wife or Haruka, or anyone. It was just the three of them.

"Drop your weapon, or he loses his head," threatened Boran. "I won't ask again." Mr. Storm, having weighed his options, lowered his hand cannon to the floor and kicked it away. The huge Dorian smiled. He pulled out a single disc and slapped it onto Captain Jack, who disappeared with the usual buzz and a pop.

"It appears to be just you and I," said Boran, dropping his hand cannon.

"I'll take those odds," said Mr. Storm, charging his opponent. The two collided and clenched each other around the neck. The Dorian threw quick uppercuts that caught Mr. Storm by surprise, but he retaliated with severe blows to the alien's middle. They were almost evenly matched for strength. The Dorian threw a huge right cross, which Mr. Storm parried while leaping forward with a huge blow to the lizard's rib cage. Boran doubled over, and Mr. Storm drove a knee into his face, knocking him to his back. He dove in to finish the Dorian off but was caught by a surprise slap to his shoulder. Mr. Storm slammed into a wall. As he shook off the shock of the sudden scenery change, he found himself in a holding cell with the other humans. His wife found him and gave him a big hug, relieved that he was okay.

"I guess we're back to where we started," said Captain Jack. "This won't end well."

"Maybe we can keep the focus on you and me," said Mr. Storm, "and they will spare the others."

"Don't talk like that," said Mrs. Storm. "I've never known you to give up so easily."

"It's not giving up, love," said Mr. Storm, kissing her gently on the forehead. "It's strategic and will give you and the others another chance."

"He's right," said Captain Jack. "Before, they were only planning to execute one. They may pick two or three of us now, but if we make it clear that the two of us were responsible, they might not look for a third."

"No," said Mrs. Storm. "They have already set their sights on me. Sebastian and I will take responsibility. We haven't been apart for more than a week in over fifteen years; I'm not about to start living alone now."

"Sara," said Mr. Storm tenderly. "Please don't."

"You've made up your mind, and I love you for it," Mrs. Storm said passionately. "It's brave and it's the right thing for you to do. I'm brave too and it's the right thing for me to do. We're together until the end and then beyond, forever. Remember?" Mr. Storm remembered a pledge they had made to one another, long ago. He knew that he had as much say in her decision as she had in his. He loved his wife, and he had always supported her. He supposed there was no good reason for him to stop now.

"Okay," he cried, "Okay. We'll do it together." Mr. Storm turned to Captain Jack. "We wouldn't be able to talk her out of it anyway," he explained, defeated.

Master Slythe approached the holding cell and smiled villainously, a bleeding Boran at his side with Saldo and Administrator Serno a step behind. Mr. and Mrs. Storm stepped forward. Boran instinctively took a step back. Mr. Storm smiled and Boran shook with anger. None of this was lost on Master Slythe.

"The family Storm," said Master Slythe in a sinister tone. "I think we can make a fine example out of you both. We'll skip the fanfare on this one though. Guards! Bring these two to the execution pad. The rest of them go back to work in the mines, double shifts." The guards opened the cage and yanked out Mr. and Mrs. Storm. Boran again took an instinctive step backward, as did Administrator Serno.

"Oh, come on, Boran," berated Slythe. "Did he beat you that badly? I should just have you two fight it out." Boran looked concerned. "I'm only joking, Boran. Relax." Slythe turned to address the group and stared directly at Captain Jack. "We'll hang their bodies on the wall of your cell as a reminder of what happens to those who try to escape." Master Slythe led the guards and his two victims out of the holding cells.

"I hope it was worth it," said Genevieve to Captain Jack. "Now we have to work double shifts."

"You are lucky to be alive," exploded the usually cheery Marie, "and you have the audacity, the *audacity*," she emphasized, "to complain about double shifts while Sebastian and Sara go to their execution?"

Genevieve gave no response. She turned to her husband Rory for support and found him with his head down and hands in his pockets.

"Shame on you," said Marie.

"You might not be alive if it wasn't for the Storms," agreed Mr. Watts. "Learn from their courage."

"What do we do now?" asked Valentina.

"Nothing," replied Captain Jack. "There is nothing we can do right now for them but stay alive ourselves." For the first time any of the passengers or crew could remember, hope was absent from Captain Jack's eyes as he stared after the departing couple.

"We have to help them!" cried Valentina. "We cannot quit now!"

"Valentina," calmed Captain Bask, "we can't do anything right now. We'll get out of here somehow. I believe that. Honestly. I don't think we can save the Storms. Mr. Watts is right. The best we can do is learn from their courage."

"Courage then," attempted Valentina. "Courage for the Storms." She burst into tears and trudged to the back of the cell.

#

Mr. and Mrs. Storm were led to the same platform where they had witnessed their daughter's execution. Two Dorians were replacing the chain moorings Mr. Storm had broken. There was now a third pole that already had an occupant.

"Zora!" yelled Mrs. Storm. "You can't," she commanded Slythe. "She was under duress. We forced her to cooperate," she cried with mounting indignation.

"Now, now, Sara, is it?" mused Slythe. "Zora is getting exactly what she deserves," he sneered.

"It is alright, mother Sara," said Zora. "I will no longer hide. I will proudly stand with you against Slythe's tyranny. You are my example. I saw your daughter die for my cause; how can I do less?"

"I'm so sorry, Zora," said Mrs. Storm through tears as the guards shackled her next to the female Dorian.

"I am, as well," said Zora, "for everything."

"This isn't the way I was planning to go out," said Mr. Storm, "but if I had to choose, being executed as a freedom fighter on a hostile alien planet isn't the worst way to go." Mrs. Storm laughed.

"No, it is not," she said. "The company isn't bad either," she winked.

"I'm going to miss you," he said softly.

"Until we meet again," she replied.

A sudden explosion high in the atmosphere arrested everyone's attention. Out of nowhere, a battleship blasted through the transports on the launch pad.

Master Slythe had never seen such significant firepower from so small a ship. There was something familiar to him about it. It couldn't be! It was the Earth vessel they encountered on their previous mission.

"It's the *Eloise*!" shouted Mr. Storm. "At least, I think it is."

Master Slythe, Boran, Saldo, and Administrator Serno ran for cover along with the rest of the Dorian guard force. The *Eloise* landed not far from the prisoners' position. Mr. and Mrs. Storm saw two enormous gray aliens with rhinoceros-like horns on their snouts emerge with battle cries and rip through the fleeing crowd of Dorian guards.

#

"We're arriving at the Kamal-Etet system," reported Stiggs. "I see one battle cruiser in low orbit over the primary mine."

"*Eloise*," said Hanna.

"Yes Hanna Storm, Captain," replied the computerized voice.

"Target that battle cruiser's engines and weapons system and fire on my mark."

"Yes Hanna Storm, Captain." The *Eloise* burst into a turn and positioned itself at the stern of the Dorian battlecruiser. The whirring of machinery and the noise of charging energy rang inside the cockpit as the *Eloise* prepared its weapons.

"Fire!" commanded Hanna.

The lasers lit their marks, and a single projectile missile hurled toward the enemy craft. They never saw what hit them.

"I'm going to take us down," Hanna continued, without missing a beat. "Hold on, everybody! *Eloise*!"

"Yes Hanna Storm, Captain?"

"Target any transport vessels on the launch pad and take them out," she ordered.

"Hold, *Eloise*," croaked Stiggs. "Minimize casualties and abort if any species other than Dorian is detected."

"Yes, Stiggs," answered the *Eloise*. "Hanna Storm, Captain, please confirm."

"Confirmed! Thanks, Stiggs," smiled Hanna. The ship's forward gun went into a flurry as they flew low across the landing pad.

"Look at all those Dorians," said Mera, her eyes widening.

"The plan stays the same," shouted Ternia. "I'll take Grull, Grall, Stiggs, and Melatar to the mines. The rest of you and Hanna will secure the platform and the *Eloise*," instructed Ternia.

With the platform cleared of transports, the *Eloise* began her approach to an undamaged landing platform. Ternia arose from her chair and exited the bridge with a nod to Hanna. She gathered her contingent for the salvo on the mines and was checking weapons when Vlad approached.

"I go with you, Ternia," said Vlad smiling. "I worry for you. Is good idea."

Ternia returned the smile and threw a hand cannon to Vlad, which he fumbled before finally steadying it into a holster.

Haranda Su handed out packs of transport discs to everyone. "These are coded to the main cabin of the *Eloise*. Just attach them to any Earth person you find."

In the back of the cabin, Grull and Grall were arguing.

"I'm going first," asserted Grull.

"You mean, second," opposed Grall.

"You can go at the same time! For the love of King Kariloo's Treasure!" shouted Ternia. "Time to go!"

"Do you want the front or the flanks?" Melatar asked his captain, his arm still in a sling.

"I promised Grull and Grall the front. Vlad and I will flank. You take care of the leftovers," smiled Ternia, "and babysit the Belafian."

"Inefficient," stated Melatar.

"Ha, ha," came his captain's sarcastic reply.

The *Eloise* touched down and the ramp deployed. Grull and Grall charged out, followed by Ternia, Vlad, Melatar, and Stiggs. They made their way over to the mine entrance, Grull and Grall laying waste to any Dorian that crossed their path. Ternia and Vlad had nothing to flank, and Melatar had nothing to clean up. Grall and Grull also received the brunt of the enemy fire. A volley of shots hit their glowing blue armor and dissipated without slowing them down.

Ternia caught Melatar looking too long to the left and followed his gaze. There she saw a platform with two Earth people and a female Dorian chained to execution poles.

"On the way back," shouted Ternia to Melatar.

"Mines first," echoed Stiggs.

They maintained their forward pace as the condemned watched them go by. Grull and Grall reached the mine entrance and assumed defensive positions. The Dorians were recovering and regrouping from the initial surprise. They would come soon enough. Ternia, Melatar, Vlad and Stiggs rushed into the mines and began their search for the captive Earth people.

\#

Hanna stood at the top of the ramp and squinted to see two humans and a Dorian chained to metal poles. She couldn't tell for sure, but it looked like her mother and father.

"Boother, Mung, keep this ship secure. Henry can help. Mera, Haranda Su, you're with me."

"Wait!" shouted Haranda Su. She hit a button and a panel popped out of the wall. Inside were an assortment of grenades and hand cannons. "Take one of these." She tossed Hanna a hand cannon and took a few grenades for herself, hooking them onto her utility belt.

"You really did think of everything, didn't you?" said Hanna.

"What can I say? I take pride in my work," sassed Haranda Su.

They marched down the ramp. A few stray Dorians attacked on their way to regroup, but Mera made swift work of them. The energy blasts from their weapon didn't seem to affect the orange battle glow that enveloped her.

Mr. and Mrs. Storm watched the party approach the platform. Their eyes locked on Hanna, looking as though they had seen a ghost.

"Mom! Dad!" Hanna screamed.

"Hanna, is it really you?" asked Mr. Storm, confused. "But how?"

"Less talk and more rescue," said Mera. "They're regrouping."

"Haranda Su," said Hanna. "Can you get them out of there?"

"On it," she answered.

Haranda Su scurried up the pole and pulled a little device from her belt. She worked the locks on Mr. Storm's hands, and the latch on his chains popped open. Mr. Storm picked up his daughter and squeezed her tight.

"It really is you," he said, not believing his own words. Haranda Su had Mrs. Storm loose in a flash while Mera kept watch.

"What about the Dorian?" asked Haranda Su.

"Leave her," said Hanna, not without contempt.

"No!" said Mrs. Storm. "She comes with us."

"You can't trust them Mom!" Hanna shouted. She was still being held tight by her father. "Okay Dad, that's enough. You can put me down." Mr. Storm shook his head in defiance.

"Hanna, you have to trust me. She helped us and now she needs our help."

"No time to argue," said Mera. "It's now or never." The crowd of Dorians that stood between the platform and the *Eloise* thickened by the moment.

"She comes," said Mrs. Storm resolutely. Hanna knew better than to argue with her mother.

"Fine, cut her loose," said Hanna, "but keep an eye on her."

"Too late!" shouted Mera. She took out five transport discs and slapped them on Hanna, Haranda Su, and the three former prisoners. They disappeared with a buzz and a pop. Hanna and her parents reformed inside the main cabin of the *Eloise* along with Haranda Su and the female Dorian. Outside, the enemy fire intensified. Hanna ran to the bridge and watched through the window as Mera flew into motion. She was more bowling ball than ballerina as she tore through the Dorians, punching them, grabbing them, and throwing them. She worked her way to the ship, paused for a deep breath, and darted back into the fray. She moved in broad semicircles, keeping the enemy at bay. Boother and Mung kept the flanks tight by throwing grenades and opening fire from behind their standard issue Corridor Patrol force fields.

"Hanna," said her mother, "there is a lot to process here, but first things first: we saw you die."

Hanna's heart sank. Could it be true? Was Blue really gone? A wave of shock and pain washed over her. Tears formed in her eyes. She didn't respond, so her mother continued.

"You were to be executed on that very platform," she explained.

"We came up with a plan to save you, but it didn't work," said Mr. Storm. "I failed. You were shot dead by someone named Slythe. Your body is still in the office building, or, at least, I think it is."

"He's really gone," said Hanna, tears streaming down her face. "Oh, Mom!" she sobbed, embracing her mother. "He did it for me. He saved me."

"Who saved you?" said Mr. Storm, still very confused.

"He was from a planet called Makara," Hanna said between sobs. "They're shapeshifters. I called him Blue." Hanna wiped her eyes. "He told me not to trust this Dorian Saldo, but I did. I shouldn't have, but I did," she dissolved into fresh tears. "He changed his shape and Saldo thought he had kidnapped me, but it was really Blue."

"Oh Hanna," said her mother, "I'm so sorry! We tried to save him. We tried our very best." Compassionate tears trailed down Mrs. Storm's face.

"He made his choice," interjected Mera, entering the *Eloise* in a sweat. "He was very brave. Show me where the body is, and I'll go get it. He deserves the honor."

"Mom, Dad, this is Mera. She's a Bimber and the most amazing fighter I have ever met. Better than you, Dad."

"I don't doubt it," Mr. Storm replied, staring in awe at the incredible being before him. "The body is covered in a white sheet on the third floor of that building there." Mr. Storm pointed in the direction of the office building where they took cover.

"I need two more discs," Mera said to Haranda Su, who handed them over. They watched as Mera charged through a thick line of Dorians and made it to the building. In less than a minute, the body appeared with a buzz and a pop with Mera right behind. Hanna knelt down and tenderly kissed the image of herself that was Blue. Hanna wiped at her eyes as she thought of the kindness Blue had shown her.

"I'm so sorry, Blue," she said through tears. "Thank you. Thank you for saving me and my family. I will never forget you."

A surge of overwhelming emotion flooded Hanna. She had an urge to move. She walked to the ramp to survey the situation, attempting to divert her mind to the mission at hand. Mr. and Mrs. Storm steadfastly followed, neither wanting to lose sight of their daughter. Boother and Mung were being overrun by a fresh group of Dorian guards, but Hanna hardly noticed. She caught sight of Saldo making his way with a few others to a hangar on the far side of the landing area and felt something inside of her snap. Her rationality fled. She went back into the ship and opened the weapons panel. She took out another hand cannon and a belt of grenades that she slung over her shoulder.

"Hanna?" asked a concerned father. "Where are you going?"

"I have a wound that needs stitching," she said intensely, as she ran down the ramp. She fired at the line of Dorian foot soldiers and threw two grenades to open up a path between her and Saldo. Mera acted quickly.

"Haranda Su, get these Earth people some weapons. You have to help those two there hold the line and protect the ship. I'm going after Hanna." She leaped into action and was at Hanna's side in moments. Mr. Storm revealed his intent to follow by stepping in that direction, but Haranda Su shoved a huge hand cannon into his arms.

"We have to hold the line," she said. "Mera won't let anything happen to Hanna." Mr. Storm nodded and looked at his wife for direction.

"You take up position over there on the right flank. I'll take the left," she instructed.

"Got it," replied Mr. Storm and dutifully took his position next to a strange-looking alien with bumps on his head that were shifting colors from black to dark blue and back again. Mrs. Storm ended up next to a tall and dignified looking alien with a flat head and large eyes. There was a ferocity about his demeanor that she found inspiring.

"I want to help," said Henry to Haranda Su.

"I have just the thing." She went to the weapons closet and pulled out two long sniper-like hand cannons. "Let's have some fun," she said.

They lay down prone on their stomachs at the top of the ramp and aimed their scopes at the gaps in the defense being provided by the Storms and the Corridor Patrol.

#

Slythe heard shouting behind him and turned to see a Bimber and a familiar-looking Earth girl running toward them.

"Saldo!" the Earth girl yelled. "You traitor! I trusted you!"

"Master, the Bimber. Perhaps they'll be satisfied with just Saldo," suggested Boran to Slythe, not bothering to keep it quiet.

"No!" said Saldo. "That's a terrible idea." Slythe aimed his hand cannon at Saldo and shot him in the foot. He fell to the ground while Slythe, Boran, and Serno ran for the hangar.

"I trusted you, Saldo," Hanna reproached him angrily. Saldo grabbed his leg and breathed through his pain.

"So, I had the Makaran?" Saldo said. "How disappointing!" Hanna pointed the hand cannon and Saldo cowered with his hands up.

"Please, don't. I didn't kill him. It was Slythe." Saldo pointed in the direction of the hangar. A small ship burst out and was off into the atmosphere in seconds.

Hanna moved the gun closer to Saldo's face and prepared to pull the trigger. His hands were up defensively as he whimpered. She waited a moment to let the fear take hold.

"I'm not going to kill you," said Hanna. "I don't kill for revenge, but if you ever come near anyone I care about, I'll do what it takes to keep them safe. I don't ever want to see you again."

"What?" said Mera, suddenly lifting Saldo up by both his arms. "What do you mean you don't kill for revenge?" Saldo's eyes bulged. A strange liquid streamed off his feet to the dirt below. Mera casually continued. "Revenge is one of the best reasons to kill. Isn't that right, Saldo?" Mera pulled at his arms and Saldo screamed in pain.

"Mera, stop!" Hanna shouted. Mera relaxed her grip.

"Hanna, this is the proper way to avenge someone," insisted Mera. "Ripping their arms off is like a bare minimum."

"No. That is not okay, even for Saldo. Do not rip his arms off, that's final." Hanna asserted, like a mother reprimanding a child.

"Hmph, fine. He can keep his arms."

An aura of red gathered around Mera as she spun Saldo and released him into the air. Hanna watched in shock as Saldo's figure faded into the distant orange sky.

"Mera!" was all Hanna could muster.

"What? He still has his arms." Mera looked off into the distance, watching Saldo disappear. "Goodbye, Saldo," said Mera in satisfaction. She turned back to Hanna and gave her a look of reproach. "You and I are going to have to talk about this."

"We certainly are," said Hanna, aghast. "You can't just kill defenseless people."

"Excuse me? He kept his arms. I meant we have to talk about how to properly avenge someone!"

"We'll finish this conversation later," harrumphed Hanna.

The two made their way back to the ship and encountered very little resistance. With the leadership having fled, chaos reigned among the Dorian ranks, and they retreated. Haranda Su's and Henry's sniping had cleared a path from the *Eloise* all the way to the mine entrance where Grull and Grall stood guard.

#

In the mine tunnels, Stiggs veered off down a passageway while Ternia and Melatar continued onward. They were not aware that Stiggs was a professional caliber liberator of both people and things, but Vlad was; he followed Stiggs. Every guard that Stiggs encountered met with an unhappy end as this ninja-like alien pushed his way through until he reached where the humans were gathered. He whipped out a small black pouch and took out a sharp-looking instrument.

"Who are you?" asked Captain Jack. He noticed that the second liberator was a human, but not part of his passengers or crew.

"My name is Stiggs," he answered with a bow. "I am personal attendant to the Monarch." Ternia and Melatar came through another tunnel and into the room.

"Why didn't you tell us you knew where to go?" Ternia asked, out of breath. She gave Vlad the stink eye, and he smiled sheepishly.

Stiggs started toward the lock when Melatar gently pulled him back. "Allow me," said the Bimber. He placed his one good hand on the bars and opened it with the ease of popping the top off a soda can. Captain Jack motioned for everyone to get behind him.

"Who are you?" he asked again.

"I'm Ternia, Captain of the pirate ship *Death Bringer*," she declared with pride. "Who are you?"

Captain Jack hesitated. He wasn't sure that going from mining-alien prisoners to pirate-alien prisoners was a step up.

"I'm Captain Jack of the space cruiser *Eloise*," he said.

"Ha!" said Ternia. "Last I checked, Hanna Storm was captain of the *Eloise*." A murmur ran through the group of humans.

"Hanna is dead," said Captain Jack suspiciously. "I saw it myself."

"You'll have to tell her that when you're back on the *Eloise*. Melatar! The transport discs please."

"Hold on now, we aren't being trapped by those things again," said Captain Bask.

"You have no choice in the matter," explained Stiggs. "Please remember, this is a rescue." He grabbed the discs from Melatar and leaped through the human crowd, delicately placing discs on the astonished captives. Each disappeared in turn with a buzz and pop.

Back on the *Eloise*, Captain Jack appeared in the main cabin and saw that Mr. and Mrs. Storm provided cover fire from the rear of the ship with some other aliens. They appeared to be safe along with Zora. To his surprise, Henry lay prone not far away and occasionally pulled the trigger on a very large weapon. A series of buzzes and pops heralded the arrival of the remaining prisoners. Captain Jack pointed out Henry to Valentina.

"Henry!" she screamed.

Henry jerked in surprise and accidentally shot off a round that hit an unsuspecting Dorian soldier in the leg. "Auntie Val?" he asked, standing up. The two embraced.

Hanna and Mera approached the *Eloise*, and Mrs. Storm ran to hug her daughter.

"Thank you for keeping her safe," Mrs. Storm said to Mera. The fighting was winding down, and they all mounted the ramp, followed by Boother and Mung, to a ship full of bewildered fellow humans.

"No time to explain," Hanna said, holding up her hand to the surprised faces. "We need to get out of here and back into Galactic Treaty Planet space."

"I guess she really is Captain," said Carlie Bask to a stunned Jack De La Vega.

Hanna made her way to the bridge and sat down in the captain's chair. Stiggs and the others had also returned by transport disc. He took his chair at navigation while Ternia took her copilot seat.

Hanna spoke into a loudspeaker that Haranda Su had installed: "Grull! Grall! Time to go!" The two came running for the *Eloise*. As soon as they were up the ramp, Hanna lifted off. Captain Jack made his way from the main cabin to the bridge.

"Captain Storm," he said. "I see I'm out of a job."

Hanna half-smiled. "Good to see you Captain Jack," she said.

"Listen. I have intel," said Jack. Mung's ears perked up. "They are building some sort of device that will allow them to get to Earth. They plan to enslave the entire population and bring them back to the mines," Captain Jack explained. "We can't stop them entirely right now, but we can slow them down by blowing up that device. It's a large aperture, like a ring."

"Hanna," said Mung, "or Captain Storm, rather. This Dorian corridor device may be your only means of returning to Earth. Are you sure you want to destroy it?"

"We have no choice," Captain Jack answered for her. "I know it's a sacrifice, but we can't let them enslave Earth."

"If they had Earth's resources, including its labor, it could place them in a position to relaunch their conquest of Galaxy Prime," said Mung.

"If the Dorianzzz found a way to Earth without an engine, zzzo can you," said Boother.

"Stiggs?" asked Hanna.

"I have a location for a large ring-shaped construct not far from here. It is most likely the aperture. I can set the coordinates now."

"Do it." Hanna said.

The *Eloise* lurched forward and quickly decelerated as it neared a large, partially constructed ring.

"I've never seen a corridor engine that big," said Ternia.

"I don't think it's a corridor engine," corrected Haranda Su. "If there really were intergalactic corridors—naturally occurring, I mean—an aperture this size could conceivably keep them open and stable for short periods of time," postulated Haranda Su.

"*Eloise*," said Hanna.

"Yes Hanna Storm, Captain," came the computerized reply.

"Do we have enough firepower to destroy that corridor engine?"

"Yes."

"Destroy it on my mark," said Hanna.

"Fire!"

The gigantic construct burst into pieces.

"*Eloise*, shields," Hanna said. The Talrisian metal shields enveloped the *Eloise* as she maneuvered through the debris from the explosion.

"The *Eloise* can talk now," said Captain Jack matter-of-factly. "Not the strangest thing I've seen today."

"Stiggs, plot a course back to the *Death Bringer*. I have some catching up to do," Hanna resolved. Stiggs nodded and Hanna left her seat and went to the main cabin where everyone was discussing the current state of their affairs.

"What have you done to my *Eloise*?" asked Mr. Watts. Hanna hesitated to answer.

"Haranda Su and I," she motioned over to the small alien with four hands, "we uh, made some modifications." Hanna braced, waiting for a reprimand. She looked nervously at the floor.

"It's marvelous!" said Mr. Watts. "I saw the ramp, vertical takeoff and landing, shields, weapons, and who knows what else!"

"I know what else, geezer" smiled Haranda Su.

"Haranda Su! It's not nice to call someone a geezer," said Hanna.

"It's a term of endearment on Rinaria," defended Haranda Su. "It's not my fault the translator got it wrong."

"Geezer is just fine and fairly accurate," laughed Mr. Watts. "I would love to know more about your modifications. What did you think of our Wolverine rocket?" The two moved off to a corner of the main cabin and continued their conversation.

"Your mother told us about your friend Blue and how he saved you," comforted Captain Bask. "We're so sorry you lost a friend, but we are so glad to have you back," she said, giving Hanna a hug. A pang of sorrow hit Hanna, her grief for Blue still raw.

"How on Earth...?" started Mr. Storm, "I mean, how in the world? No that's not it. How in the *universe* did you find us?"

"When I saw the Dorian ship go into the corridor, I just pointed the *Eloise* in the right direction and fired the Wolverine rocket," she explained. "Boother and Mung from the Corridor Patrol found me and took me to the Sendori Sanitarium for Homeless, Lost, and Discarded Children. That's where I met Blue," she grieved.

"The Sendori Sanitarium for what?" asked Henry.

"Homeless, Lost, and Discarded Children. I was lost," answered Hanna. "Anyway, the freaking Headmistress Blurch and her henchman Mr. Gambrio sold us to the zoo. That's where I met Mera," she smiled, "and Saldo," she grimaced.

"We won't be seeing him again," Mera smiled back.

"Then, Stiggs helped us escape and took us to see the Monarch," grinned Hanna slyly. "You'll never guess who he is! Stiggs, tell us the Monarch's full title."

"He is the Monarch of Mineral and Rotation."

"The Monarch of Mineral and Rotation?" asked Haruka, tapping her foot. "No. It can't be!" she squealed. "How is he still alive?"

"It's true," said Henry. "When I escaped, that's where the smugglers took me. He's paying a bounty for anybody claiming to be from Earth. I think it was really him."

"It was the Monarch who sent us to Vlad, the first human in space," explained Hanna.

"I thought Yuri Gagarin was the first man in space," said Captain Bask.

"Bah!," blurted out Vlad. "Little Yuri Gagarin was first man in space?" he spat. "No! It was I, Vladyslav Evgenyevich Zelenko, cosmonaut supreme. The Soviet propaganda is too much!"

"Vlad helped us plan our rescue. He told us to challenge some pirates to a contest with our best fighter to gain their support," Hanna explained. "After Haranda Su made some modifications to the Eloise, that's what we did. Mera stepped up as our champion and won against their Bimber."

"Their male Bimber," corrected Mera. "I am the first female Bimber to ever best a male Bimber in single combat."

"She was amazing!" agreed Hanna.

"Hmmph!" griped Melatar. "She was using some sort of magical trickery, grabbing and hugging me all over." Mera laughed.

"Ternia, the pirate captain of the *Death Bringer*, helped us rescue you. That's pretty much it," said Hanna.

"What about the Dorians?" said Captain Jack. "I know we just destroyed their stable path to Earth, but they can rebuild it. Zora said the only way to permanently protect Earth was for the Galactic Treaty planets to take back the Kamal-Etet system and deny them access to the corridor that leads to Earth."

"Or Earth could join the Galactic Treaty, placing it under their protection," said Mung.

"They won't be able to enforce it, though," said Captain Bask, "as long as the Dorians hold the only entrance to Earth. Taking back the system is probably the only way."

"We will have to present this to the Galactic Senate," stated Mung. "We must convince them the Galactic Treaty planets are in danger from Dorian aggression if they continue to have access to Earth and the labor it supplies."

"We have to get to the Galactic Senate to make our case," said Hanna.

"The first stop is the Corridor Police Force Command," said Mung. "You will need their support to win the Senate."

"It sounds like we're on a mission to protect Earth," sighed Mr. Storm. "A worthy cause if ever there was one."

The *Eloise* slowed down and docked with the *Death Bringer*. Grull and Grall happily strolled onto their ship. Vlad gave Captain Ternia a kiss.

"I think we still have business," he said.

"We do," said Ternia. "Until next time, Vlad." She turned toward Hanna. "It has been my honor to fight with you, Captain Storm," her usual smirk replaced with a genuine look of respect. "According to the code, my debt to your victory over me is paid, but I will follow you into battle again when the time comes to take back Kamal-Etet.

Our galaxy depends on it, and I am indebted to you for sparing Melatar."

"Thank you Ternia," Hanna said, embracing her. "Thank you for believing in me."

"I knew from the moment you challenged me that you would succeed in your quest," admitted Ternia. "By the way, if we retake the Kamal-Etet system and establish a corridor to Earth, I want exclusive shipping rights on cocoa beans." Hanna reached into her pack and handed her last chocolate bar to Ternia.

"You earned it," Hanna said. Ternia smiled and exited with Melatar.

Boother and Mung returned to their police cruiser and started for the Galactic Police Force Command. Hanna had Stiggs ease the ship out of the docking bay and lay in a course to follow Boother and Mung. She returned to the main cabin, where everyone was still exchanging stories.

"I'm so glad to see you two," sobbed Hanna to her parents. She hugged them tightly.

"We're very thankful for the rescue," said Mrs. Storm.

"Yeah, thanks, Captain Storm," said Mr. Storm. "I'm so glad you take after your mother. Another flawless rescue." Mr. Storm smiled through his own teary eyes, then paused, noting the look on Hanna's face. "Bug, what's wrong? You look distressed under that mask of ease."

"Dad, I miss Blue so much! I know he chose it, but I still miss him. There is a hole in my heart. I feel so sad." Hanna sobbed anew and cried into her father's arms.

"Oh, my darling little girl. I'm so sorry! No one should have to work through something like this, let alone a youth your age. He was so brave and I am so grateful to him for protecting you. He was a blessing." Mr. Storm held Hanna as she cried.

"Hanna," Mrs. Storm spoke softly. "You are so strong. You are such a light to everyone around you. Your friend Blue saw that and he chose to honor and protect it so you could continue to shine your light for others. Cry as much as you need and we will help you honor his sacrifice. The best way to do that is to be yourself, helping and loving others like you always do."

Hanna let go of her parents and wiped her tears. "Mom, Blue was so funny, he purposely got out in dodgeball and didn't even try. He was so used to people being mean. He was also so kind. He let me be his friend even though he thought I was weird." Hanna's parents laughed at this and hugged her again.

Hanna released her parents, brushed herself off, and wandered over to Henry. She stared at him for a moment, then pulled him in for a hug that he gladly returned.

"I'm glad you escaped," said Henry.

"I'm glad you helped with the rescue," said Hanna. "I heard you were quite the sniper," she laughed.

"Haranda Su taught me pretty quick, so maybe there is some natural talent there. Not a career I want to pursue though," said Henry seriously.

"I get that," Hanna said. "It was easy for me to forget that these are actual beings, no matter how cruel they were. I'm still not comfortable with Zora, but I trust my mom."

"I know. I don't feel good about killing," admitted Henry, "but I don't know how else we would have gotten out of there. Anyway, I hope taking back the Kamal-Etet system is less bloody than it sounds."

Hanna grabbed his hand, glad to have a friend her own age. She felt the weight of the world on her shoulders. It was up to her to save Earth and the galaxy—both galaxies. Up to her and Henry. She looked around. It was up to her and Henry, Captain Jack and Captain Bask, Haruka, her parents, Mr. Watts, Chief Attendant.

Marie, Valentina, even Rory, Genevieve, and all the other human passengers. It was up to Vlad and the Monarch. It was even up to aliens like Mera, Haranda Su, Boother, and Mung. Even pirates would help when the time came. Hanna felt her confidence grow as she realized that she didn't have to shoulder this responsibility alone. If Earth needed saving, even if galaxies needed saving, the Storms and company would do it.

#

"Administrator Serno," said Slythe. "Explain to me again how this happened." Boran unleashed another blow to Serno's sternum.

"I'm sorry, Master Slythe. The Earth people are...are...are...tenacious. They value freedom above life, it seems." Boran let a vicious backhand whip across Serno's face.

"Perhaps," said Master Slythe. "Or perhaps you were just too soft on them." Slythe took out a hand phasor and blasted Serno in the chest. He slumped over, dead.

"I have word that the corridor ring was destroyed," said Slythe. Boran did not reply. "No matter," he said. "We can rebuild it, though it will take some time. I am more concerned about the summons I received from the Royal Court. If the Emperor has caught wind of our activities here, it could prove most disruptive to our plans."

"You know how to handle the elites, Master Slythe," said Boran. "I do not worry, but I can gather more men if a confrontation becomes inevitable. We have several lesser clans at our disposal."

"I think of Zora and her treachery," Slythe hissed. "I will not be subject to that again. Be sure your men are well-trained and disciplined." Slythe paused, then added, "and find a way to track that Earth ship." Irritation and impatience accompanied the order.

"As you command, Master Slythe," said Boran, rubbing his jaw. "The Earth people will pay with blood."

"Stop being so dramatic, Boran."
"Yes, Master Slythe."

END

ABOUT THE AUTHORS

C.J. Starbright and the Stargazers are a group of visionary writers who unite under starlit skies to craft stories woven from cosmic curiosity. With telescopes as their tools and imagination as their guide, they explore the mysteries of the universe, inspiring their tales of adventure. Their collaborative spirit and shared passion for the cosmos bring to life the thrilling adventures of Hanna Storm, igniting imaginations with the endless possibilities of space.

www.ingramcontent.com/pod-product-compliance
Lightning Source LLC
Chambersburg PA
CBHW051146130726
47988CB00005B/2012